PENGUIN BOOKS

# Horror Stories

E. Nesbit was born in Surrey in 1858. A world-famous children's author, her works include *The Railway Children* and *Five Children and It*. She also wrote several short stories for adults. With her husband, Hubert Bland, she was one of the founding members of the socialist Fabian Society; their household became a centre of the socialist and literary circles of the times. She died in 1924.

Naomi Alderman is the author of three novels: *Disobedience*, *The Lessons* and *The Liars' Gospel*. She has won the Orange Award for New Writers and the *Sunday Times* Young Writer of the Year Award, and each of her literary novels has been broadcast on BBC Radio 4's *Book at Bedtime*. She was selected for *Granta*'s once-a-decade list of Best of Young British Novelists, Waterstone's Writers for the Future, and was mentored by Margaret Atwood as part of the Rolex Mentor and Protégé Arts Initiative. She presents *Science Stories* on BBC Radio 4, is Professor of Creative Writing at Bath Spa University and she is the co-creator and lead writer of the bestselling smartphone audio adventure app *Zombies, Run!*. She lives in London.

# Horror Stories

### E. NESBIT

*With an introduction by*
*Naomi Alderman*

PENGUIN BOOKS

PENGUIN BOOKS

UK | USA | Canada | Ireland | Australia
India | New Zealand | South Africa

Penguin Books is part of the Penguin Random House group of companies
whose addresses can be found at global.penguinrandomhouse.com.

This collection published with a new introduction by Penguin Books 2016

002

Introduction copyright © Naomi Alderman, 2016

The moral right of the copyright holders has been asserted

Set in 11/13 pt Bembo Book MT Std
Typeset by Jouve (UK), Milton Keynes
Printed in Great Britain by Clays Ltd, St Ives plc

A CIP catalogue record for this book is available from the British Library

ISBN: 978-0-241-26177-4

www.greenpenguin.co.uk

MIX
Paper from
responsible sources
FSC® C018179

Penguin Random House is committed to a
sustainable future for our business, our readers
and our planet. This book is made from Forest
Stewardship Council® certified paper.

# Contents

# Introduction

## by Naomi Alderman

Those of us who grew up with E. Nesbit's wonderful novels for children – *The Railway Children*, *Five Children and It*, *The Phoenix and the Carpet* – may be surprised to learn that she wrote ghost stories for adults. And it might be even more surprising to encounter some of the grim underpinnings of these delicious fireside tales. Lurking in the background of some of these stories are dead children, thwarted love, jealousy, vengeance and the sense that even the best kind of love – the famous love that never falters, the love that pays the price – has something dark lurking within it.

'This is not an artistically rounded-off ghost story,' says the narrator of 'The Shadow', 'and nothing is explained in it, and there seems to be no reason why any of it should have happened.' Which of course begs the reader to ask themselves what the explanation for the story is, and why any of it should have happened. There is a young couple, very much in love, expecting their first baby. And there is Miss Eastwich, a woman so silent that the children she looks after later in life never think of treating her as 'other than a machine'. She tells her story of the 'shadow' that crept into the house of her two friends whom she had 'loved more than anything in the world' and who had married each other. The narrator understands, as does the reader, that Miss Eastwich had trusted her best friend Mabel – one half of that connubial bliss – not to take the man she loved, but Mabel had taken him anyway. And then what happens? Well, there's a 'shadow'. Is Miss Eastwich the shadow? Is she the one responsible for all that happens in the house? Take a look at the story and see what you think.

The darkness teems at the corners of these stories, like that gathering shadow – ordinary callousness turning into something more disturbing. 'There'll be more wedding tomorrow than ever you'll take the first part in,' snarls the narrator of 'John Charrington's Wedding' to his spinster sister – another man so consumed with jealousy that he sneaks around eavesdropping on the happy couple. What happens to them reads as a dark enactment of his deepest wishes. The nurse narrator of 'The Violet Car' – presented with a couple who each claim the other is the mad one in need of her care – mentions with cool appraisal 'that importance, that conscious competence, that one feels in the presence of other people's troubles'. The whole story is concerned with the complicated business of apportioning blame, guilt and justice. A lot of inconvenient people are got rid of in these stories, one way or another; and they're more disquieting than they seem at first read.

But of course, it was always so. Nesbit's stories for children are always prefigured by adult sadness – it's just that she never made the children look in that direction. Think of the father of the railway children, sent to prison after being falsely accused of spying. Think of the smug and awful young man that the Lamb turns into in *Five Children and It*. Nesbit had always known that adults could be rapacious, contemptuous, malicious and sadistic – her own biography includes an adulterous husband who got one of her dearest friends pregnant. She knew about anger, hatred and sexual jealousy. And in these very chilling grown-up stories she lets the knowledge out that she held back so carefully in her work for children.

# Hurst of Hurstcote

We were at Eton together, and afterwards at Christ Church, and I always got on very well with him; but somehow he was a man about whom none of the other men cared very much. There was always something strange and secret about him; even at Eton he liked grubbing among books and trying chemical experiments better than cricket or the boats. That sort of thing would make any boy unpopular. At Oxford, it wasn't merely his studious ways and his love of science that went against him; it was a certain habit he had of gazing at us through narrowing lids, as though he were looking at us more from the outside than any human being has a right to look at any other, and a bored air of belonging to another and a higher race, whenever we talked the ordinary chatter about athletics and the Schools.

A wild paper on 'Black Magic', which he read to the Essay Society, filled to overflowing the cup of his College's contempt for him. I suppose no man was ever so much disliked for so little cause.

When we went down I noticed – for I knew his people at home – that the sentiment of dislike which he excited in most men was curiously in contrast to the emotions which he inspired in women. They all liked him, listened to him with rapt attention, talked of him with undisguised enthusiasm. I watched their strange infatuation with calmness for several years, but the day came when he met Kate Danvers, and then I was not calm any more. She behaved like all the rest of the women, and to her, quite suddenly, Hurst threw the handkerchief. He was not Hurst of Hurstcote then, but his family was good, and his means not despicable, so he and she were conditionally engaged. People said it was a poor match for the beauty of the county; and her people, I know, hoped she would think better of it. As for me – well, this is not the story of my life, but of his. I need only say that I thought him a lucky man.

I went to town to complete the studies that were to make me MD; Hurst went abroad, to Paris or Leipzig or somewhere, to study hypnotism and prepare notes for his book on 'Black Magic'. This came out in the autumn, and had a strange and brilliant success. Hurst became famous, famous as men do become nowadays. His writings were asked for by all the big periodicals. His future seemed assured. In the spring they were married; I was not present at the wedding. The practice my father had bought for me in London claimed all my time, I said.

It was more than a year after their marriage that I had a letter from Hurst.

> Congratulate me, old man! Crowds of uncles and cousins have died, and I am Hurst of Hurstcote, which God wot I never thought to be. The place is all to pieces, but we can't live anywhere else. If you can get away about September, come down and see us. We shall be installed. I have everything now that I ever longed for – Hurstcote – cradle of our race – and all that, the only woman in the world for my wife, and – But that's enough for any man, surely.
>
> JOHN HURST OF HURSTCOTE

Of course I knew Hurstcote. Who does not? Hurstcote, which seventy years ago was one of the most perfect, as well as the finest, brick Tudor mansions in England. The Hurst who lived there seventy years ago noticed one day that his chimneys smoked, and called in a Hastings architect. 'Your chimneys,' said the local man, 'are beyond me, but with the timbers and lead of your castle I can build you a snug little house in the corner of your park, much more suitable for a residence than this old brick building.' So they gutted Hurstcote, and built the new house, and faced it with stucco. All of which things you will find written in the Guide to Sussex. Hurstcote, when I had seen it, had been the merest shell. How would Hurst make it habitable? Even if he had inherited much money with the castle, and intended to restore the building, that would be a work of years, not months. What would he do?

In September I went to see.

Hurst met me at Pevensey Station.

'Let's walk up,' he said; 'there's a cart to bring your traps. Eh, but it's good to see you again, Bernard!'

It was good to see him again. And to see him so changed. And so changed for good, too. He was much stouter, and no longer wore the untidy ill-fitting clothes of the old days. He was rather smartly got up in grey stockings and knee-breeches, and wore a velvet shooting-jacket. But the most noteworthy change was in his face; it bore no more the eager, inquiring, half-scornful, half-tolerant look that had won him such ill-will at Oxford. His face now was the face of a man completely at peace with himself and with the world.

'How well you look!' I said, as we walked along the level winding road through the still marshes.

'How much better, you mean!' he laughed. 'I know it. Bernard you'll hardly believe it, but I'm on the way to be a popular man!'

He had not lost his old knack of reading one's thoughts.

'Don't trouble yourself to find the polite answer to that,' he hastened to add. 'No-one knows as well as I how unpopular I was; and no-one knows so well why,' he added, in a very low voice. 'However,' he went on gaily, 'unpopularity is a thing of the past. The folk hereabout call on us, and condole with us on our hutch. A thing of the past, as I said – but what a past it was, eh! You're the only man who ever liked me. You don't know what that's been to me many a dark day and night. When the others were – you know – it was like a hand holding mine, to think of you. I've always thought I was sure of one soul in the world to stand by me.'

'Yes,' I said – 'yes.'

He flung his arm over my shoulder with a frank, boyish gesture of affection, quite foreign to his nature as I had known it.

'And I know why you didn't come to our wedding,' he went on; 'but that's all right now, isn't it?'

'Yes,' I said again, for indeed it was. There are brown eyes in the world, after all, as well as blue, and one pair of brown that meant heaven to me as the blue had never done.

'That's well,' Hurst answered, and we walked on in satisfied silence, till we passed across the furze-crowned ridge, and went down the hill to Hurstcote. It lies in the hollow, ringed round by its moat, its dark red walls showing the sky behind them. There was no welcoming sparkle of early litten candle, only the pale amber of the September evening shining through the gaunt unglazed windows.

Three planks and a rough handrail had replaced the old draw-bridge. We passed across the moat, and Hurst pulled a knotted rope that hung beside the great iron-bound door. A bell clanged loudly inside. In the moment we spent there, waiting, Hurst pushed back a briar that was trailing across the arch, and let it fall outside the handrail.

'Nature is too much with us here,' he said, laughing. 'The clematis spends its time tripping one up, or clawing at one's hair, and we are always expecting the ivy to force itself through the window and make an uninvited third at our dinner-table.'

Then the great door of Hurstcote Castle swung back, and there stood Kate, a thousand times sweeter and more beautiful than ever. I looked at her with momentary terror and dazzlement. She was indeed much more beautiful than any woman with brown eyes could be. My heart almost stopped beating.

With life or death in the balance: Right!

To be beautiful is not the same thing as to be dear, thank God. I went forward and took her hand with a free heart.

It was a pleasant fortnight I spent with them. They had had one tower completely repaired, and in its queer eight-sided rooms we lived, when we were not out among the marshes, or by the blue sea at Pevensey.

Mrs Hurst had made the rooms quaintly charming by a medley of Liberty stuffs and Wardour Street furniture. The grassy space within the castle walls, with its underground passages, its crumbling heaps of masonry, overgrown with lush creepers, was better than any garden. There we met the fresh morning; there we lounged through lazy noons; there the grey evenings found us.

I have never seen any two married people so utterly, so undisguisedly in love as these were. I, the third, had no embarrassment in so being – for their love had in it a completeness, a childish abandonment, to which the presence of a third – a friend – was no burden. A happiness, reflected from theirs, shone on me. The days went by, dreamlike, and brought the eve of my return to London, and to the commonplaces of life.

We were sitting in the courtyard; Hurst had gone to the village to post some letters. A big moon was just showing over the battlements, when Mrs Hurst shivered.

'It's late,' she said, 'and cold; the summer is gone. Let us go in.' So we went in to the little warm room, where a wood fire flickered on a brick hearth, and a shaded lamp was already glowing softly. Here we sat on the cushioned seat in the open window, and looked out through the lozenge panes at the gold moon, and ah! the light of her making ghosts in the white mist that rose thick and heavy from the moat.

'I am so sorry you are going,' she said presently; 'but you will come and skate on the moat with us at Christmas, won't you? We mean to have a medieval Christmas. You don't know what that is? Neither do I; but John does. He is very, very wise.'

'Yes,' I answered, 'he used to know many things that most men don't even dream of as possible to know.'

She was silent a minute, and then shivered again. I picked up the shawl she had thrown down when we came in, and put it round her.

'Thank you! I think – don't you? – that there are some things one is not meant to know, and someone is meant *not* to know. You see the distinction?'

'I suppose so – yes.'

'Did it never frighten you in the old days,' she went on, 'to see that John would never – was always –'

'But he has given all that up now?'

'Oh yes, ever since our honeymoon. Do you know, he used to mesmerise me. It was horrible. And that book of his –'

'I didn't know you believed in Black Magic.'

'Oh, I don't – not the least bit. I never was at all superstitious, you know. But those things always frighten me just as much as if I believed in them. And besides – I think they are wicked; but John – Ah, there he is! Let's go and meet him.'

His dark figure was outlined against the sky behind the hill. She wrapped the soft shawl more closely around her, and we went out in the moonlight to meet her husband.

The next morning when I entered the room I found that it lacked its chief ornament. The sparkling white and silver breakfast accessories were there, but for the deft white hands and kindly welcoming blue eyes of my hostess I looked in vain. At ten minutes past nine Hurst came in looking horribly worried, and more like his old self than I had ever expected to see him.

'I say, old man,' he said hurriedly, 'are you really set on going back to town today – because Kate's awfully queer? I can't think what's wrong. I want you to see her after breakfast.'

I reflected a minute. 'I can stay if I send a wire,' I said.

'I wish you would, then,' Hurst said, wringing my hand and turning away; 'she's been off her head most of the night, talking the most astounding nonsense. You must see her after breakfast. Will you pour out the coffee?'

'I'll see her now, if you like,' I said, and he led me up the winding stair to the room at the top of the tower.

I found her quite sensible, but very feverish. I wrote a prescription, and rode Hurst's mare over to Eastbourne to get it made up. When I got back she was worse. It seemed to be a sort of aggravated marsh fever. I reproached myself with having let her sit by the open window the night before. But I remembered with some satisfaction that I had told Hurst that the place was not quite healthy. I only wished I had insisted on it more strongly.

For the first day or two I thought it was merely a touch of marsh fever, that would pass off with no more worse consequence than a little weakness; but on the third day I perceived that she would die.

Hurst met me as I came from her bedside, stood aside on the narrow landing for me to pass, and followed me down into the little sitting-room, which, deprived for three days of her presence, already bore the air of a room long deserted. He came in after me and shut the door.

'You're wrong,' he said abruptly, reading my thoughts as usual; 'she won't die – she can't die.'

'She will,' I bluntly answered, for I am no believer in that worst refinement of torture known as 'breaking bad news gently'. 'Send for any other man you choose. I'll consult with the whole College of Physicians if you like. But nothing short of a miracle can save her.'

'And you don't believe in miracles,' he answered quietly. 'I do, you see.'

'My dear old fellow, don't buoy yourself up with false hopes. I know my trade; I wish I could believe I didn't! Go back to her now; you have not very long to be together.'

I wrung his hand; he returned the pressure, but said almost cheerfully – 'You know your trade, old man, but there are some things you don't know. Mine, for instance – I mean my wife's constitution. Now I know that thoroughly. And you mark my words – she won't die. You might as well say *I* was not long for this world.'

'*You*,' I said with a touch of annoyance; 'you're good for another thirty or forty years.'

'Exactly so,' he rejoined quickly, 'and so is she. Her life's as good as mine, you'll see – she won't die.'

At dusk on the next day she died. He was with her; he had not left her since he had told me that she would not die. He was sitting by her holding her hand. She had been unconscious for some time, when suddenly she dragged her hand from his, raised herself in bed, and cried out in a tone of acutest anguish – 'John! John! Let me go! For Heaven's sake let me go!'

Then she fell back dead.

He would not understand – would not believe; he still sat by her, holding her hand, and calling on her by every name that love could teach him. I began to fear for his brain. He would not leave her, so by-and-by I brought him a cup of coffee in which I had mixed a strong opiate. In about an hour I went back and found him fast asleep with his face on the pillow close by the face of his dead wife. The gardener and I carried him down to my bedroom, and I sent for a woman from the village. He slept for twelve hours. When he awoke his first words were – 'She is not dead! I must go to her!'

I hoped that the sight of her – pale, and beautiful, and still – with the white asters about her, and her cold hands crossed on her breast, would convince him; but no. He looked at her and said – 'Bernard, you're no fool; you know as well as I do that this is not death. Why treat it so? It is some form of catalepsy. If she should awake and find herself like this the shock might destroy her reason.'

And, to the horror of the woman from the village, he flung the asters on to the floor, covered the body with blankets, and sent for hot-water bottles.

I was now quite convinced that his brain was affected, and I saw plainly enough that he would never consent to take the necessary steps for the funeral.

I began to wonder whether I had not better send for another doctor, for I felt that I did not care to try the opiate again on my own responsibility, and something must be done about the funeral.

I spent a day in considering the matter – a day passed by John Hurst beside his wife's body. Then I made up my mind to try all my powers to bring him to reason, and to this end I went once more into the chamber of death. I found Hurst talking wildly, in low whispers. He seemed to be talking to someone who was not there. He did not know me, and suffered himself to be led away. He was, in fact, in the first stage of brain fever. I actually blessed his illness, because it opened a way out of the dilemma in which I found myself. I wired for a trained nurse from town, and for the local undertaker. In a week she was buried, and John Hurst still lay unconscious and unheeding; but I did not look forward to his first renewal of consciousness.

Yet his first conscious words were not the inquiry I dreaded. He only asked whether he had been ill long, and what had been the matter. When I had told him, he just nodded and went off to sleep again.

A few evenings later I found him excited and feverish, but quite himself, mentally. I said as much to him in answer to a question which he put to me – 'There's no brain disturbance now? I'm not mad or anything?'

'No, no, my dear fellow. Everything is as it should be.'

'Then,' he answered slowly, 'I must get up and go to her.'

My worst fears were realised.

In moments of intense mental strain the truth sometimes overpowers all one's better resolves. It sounds brutal, horrible. I don't know what I meant to say; what I said was – 'You can't; she's buried.'

He sprang up in bed, and I caught him by the shoulders.

'Then it's true!' he cried, 'and I'm not mad. Oh, great God in heaven, let me go to her; let me go! It's true! It's true!'

I held him fast, and spoke. 'I am strong – you know that. You are weak and ill; you are quite in my power – we're old friends, and there's nothing I wouldn't do to serve you. Tell me what you mean; I will do anything you wish.' This I said to soothe him.

'Let me go to her,' he said again.

'Tell me all about it,' I repeated. 'You are too ill to go to her. I will go, if you can collect yourself and tell me why. You could not walk five yards.'

He looked at me doubtfully.

'You'll help me? You won't say I'm mad, and have me shut up? You'll help me?'

'Yes, yes – I swear it!' All the time I was wondering what I should do to keep him from his mad purpose.

He lay back on his pillows, white and ghastly; his thin features and sunken eyes showed hawklike above the rough growth of his four weeks' beard. I took his hand. His pulse was rapid, and his lean fingers clenched themselves round mine.

'Look here,' he said, 'I don't know – There aren't any words to tell you how true it is. I am not mad, I am not wandering. I am as sane as you are. Now listen, and if you've a human heart in you, you'll help me. When I married her I gave up hypnotism and all the old studies; she hated the whole business. But before I gave it up I hypnotised her, and when she was completely under my control I forbade her soul to leave its body till my time came to die.'

I breathed more freely. Now I understood why he had said, 'She *cannot* die.'

'My dear old man,' I said gently, 'dismiss these fancies, and face your grief boldly. You can't control the great facts of life and death by hypnotism. She is dead; she is dead, and her body lies in its place. But her soul is with God who gave it.'

'No!' he cried, with such strength as the fever had left him. 'No! no! Ever since I have been ill I have seen her, every day, every night, and always wringing her hands and moaning, "Let me go, John – let me go".'

'Those were her last words, indeed,' I said; 'it is natural that they should haunt you. See, you bade her soul not leave her body. It has left it, for she is dead.'

His answer came almost in a whisper, borne on the wings of a long breathless pause.

'*She is dead, but her soul has not left her body.*'

I held his hand more closely, still debating what I should do.

'She comes to me,' he went on; 'she comes to me continually. She does not reproach, but she implores, "Let me go, John – let me go!" And I have no more power now; I cannot let her go, I cannot reach her. I can do nothing, nothing. Ah!' he cried, with a sudden sharp change of voice that thrilled through me to the ends of my fingers and feet: 'Ah, Kate, my life, I will come to you! No, no, you shan't be left alone among the dead. I am coming, my sweet.'

He reached his arms out towards the door with a look of longing and love, so really, so patently addressed to a sentient presence, that I turned sharply to see if, in truth, perhaps – nothing, of course – nothing.

'She is dead,' I repeated stupidly. 'I was obliged to bury her.'

A shudder ran through him.

'I must go and see for myself,' he said.

Then I knew – all in a minute – what to do.

'I will go,' I said. 'I will open her coffin, and if she is not – is not as other dead folk, I will bring her body back to this house.'

'Will you go now?' he asked, with set lips.

It was nigh on midnight. I looked into his eyes.

'Yes, now,' I said; 'but you must swear to lie still till I return.'

'I swear it.' I saw I could trust him, and I went to wake the nurse. He called weakly after me, 'There's a lantern in the tool-shed – and, Bernard –'

'Yes, my poor old chap.'

'There's a screwdriver in the sideboard drawer.'

I think until he said that I really meant to go. I am not accustomed to lie, even to mad people, and I think I meant it till then.

He leaned on his elbow, and looked at me with wide-open eyes.

'Think,' he said, 'what she must feel. Out of the body, and yet tied to it, all alone among the dead. Oh, make haste, make haste; for if I am not mad, and I have really fettered her soul, there is but one way!'

'And that is?'

'I must die too. Her soul can leave her body when I die.'

I called the nurse, and left him. I went out, and across the wold to the church, but I did not go in. I carried the screwdriver and the lantern, lest he should send the nurse to see if I had taken them. I leaned on the churchyard wall, and thought of her. I had loved the woman, and I remembered it in that hour.

As soon as I dared I went back to him – remember I believed him mad – and told the lie that I thought would give him most ease.

'Well?' he said eagerly, as I entered.

I signed to the nurse to leave us.

'There is no hope,' I said. 'You will not see your wife again till you meet her in heaven.'

I laid down the screwdriver and the lantern, and sat down by him.

'You have seen her?'

'Yes.'

'And there's no doubt?'

'There is no doubt.'

'Then I *am* mad; but you're a good fellow, Bernard, and I'll never forget it in this world or the next.'

He seemed calmer, and fell asleep with my hand on his. His last word was a 'Thank you', that cut me like a knife.

When I went into his room next morning he was gone. But on his pillow a letter lay, painfully scrawled in pencil, and addressed to me.

'You lied. Perhaps you meant kindly. You didn't understand. She is not dead. She has been with me again. Though her soul may not leave her body, thank God it can still speak to mine. That vault – it is worse than a mere churchyard grave. Goodbye.'

I ran all the way to the church, and entered by the open door. The air was chill and dank after the crisp October sunlight. The stone that closed the vault of the Hursts of Hurstcote had been raised, and was lying beside the dark gaping hole in the chancel floor. The nurse, who had followed me, came in before I could shake off the horror that held me moveless. We both went down into the vault. Weak, exhausted by illness and sorrow, John Hurst had yet found strength to follow his love to the grave. I tell you he had crossed that wold alone, in the grey of the chill dawn; alone he had raised the stone and had gone down to her. He had opened her coffin, and he lay on the floor of the vault with his wife's body in his arms.

He had been dead some hours.

The brown eyes filled with tears when I told my wife this story.

'You were quite right, he was mad,' she said. 'Poor things! Poor lovers!'

But sometimes when I wake in the grey morning, and, between waking and sleeping, think of all those things that I must shut out from my sleeping and my waking thoughts, I wonder was I right or was he? Was he mad, or was I idiotically incredulous? For – and it is this thing that haunts me – when I found them dead together in the vault, she had been buried five weeks. But the body that lay in John Hurst's arms, among the mouldering coffins of the Hursts of Hurstcote, was perfect and beautiful as when first he clasped her in his arms, a bride.

# The Ebony Frame

To be rich is a luxurious sensation – the more so when you have plumbed the depths of hard-up-ness as a Fleet Street hack, a picker-up of unconsidered pars, a reporter, an unappreciated journalist – all callings utterly inconsistent with one's family feeling and one's direct descent from the Dukes of Picardy.

When my Aunt Dorcas died and left me seven hundred a year and a furnished house in Chelsea, I felt that life had nothing left to offer except immediate possession of the legacy. Even Mildred Mayhew, whom I had hitherto regarded as my life's light, became less luminous. I was not engaged to Mildred, but I lodged with her mother, and I sang duets with Mildred, and gave her gloves when it would run to it, which was seldom. She was a dear good girl, and I meant to marry her some day. It is very nice to feel that a good little woman is thinking of you – it helps you in your work – and it is pleasant to know she will say 'Yes' when you say 'Will you?'

But, as I say, my legacy almost put Mildred out of my head, especially as she was staying with friends in the country just then.

Before the first gloss was off my new mourning I was seated in my aunt's own armchair in front of the fire in the dining-room of my own house. My own house! It was grand, but rather lonely. I *did* think of Mildred just then.

The room was comfortably furnished with oak and leather. On the walls hung a few fairly good oil-paintings, but the space above the mantelpiece was disfigured by an exceedingly bad print, 'The Trial of Lord William Russell', framed in a dark frame. I got up to look at it. I had visited my aunt with dutiful regularity, but I never remembered seeing this frame before. It was not intended for a print, but for an oil-painting. It was of fine ebony, beautifully and curiously carved.

I looked at it with growing interest, and when my aunt's housemaid – I had retained her modest staff of servants – came in with the lamp, I asked her how long the print had been there.

'Mistress only bought it two days afore she was took ill,' she said; 'but the frame – she didn't want to buy a new one – so she got this out of the attic. There's lots of curious old things there, sir.'

'Had my aunt had this frame long?'

'Oh yes, sir. It come long afore I did, and I've been here seven years come Christmas. There was a picture in it – that's upstairs too – but it's that black and ugly it might as well be a chimney-back.'

I felt a desire to see this picture. What if it were some priceless old master in which my aunt's eyes had only seen rubbish?

Directly after breakfast next morning I paid a visit to the lumber-room.

It was crammed with old furniture enough to stock a curiosity shop. All the house was furnished solidly in the early Victorian style, and in this room everything not in keeping with the 'drawing-room suite' ideal was stowed away. Tables of papier mâché and mother-of-pearl, straight-backed chairs with twisted feet and faded needlework cushions, firescreens of old-world design, oak bureaux with brass handles, a little work-table with its faded, moth-eaten silk flutings hanging in disconsolate shreds; on these and the dust that covered them blazed the full daylight as I drew up the blinds. I promised myself a good time in re-enshrining these household gods in my parlour, and promoting the Victorian suite to the attic. But at present my business was to find the picture as 'black as the chimney-back'; and presently, behind a heap of hideous still-life studies, I found it.

Jane the housemaid identified it at once. I took it downstairs carefully and examined it. No subject, no colour was distinguishable. There was a splodge of a darker tint in the middle, but whether it was figure or tree or house no man could have told. It seemed to be painted on a very thick panel bound with leather. I decided to send it to one of those persons who pour on rotting family portraits the water of eternal youth – mere soap and water Mr Besant tells us it is; but even as I did so the thought occurred to me to try my own restorative hand at a corner of it.

My bath-sponge, soap, and nailbrush vigorously applied for a few seconds showed me that there was no picture to clean! Bare oak presented itself to my persevering brush. I tried the other side, Jane watching me with indulgent interest. The same result. Then the truth dawned on me. Why was the panel so thick? I tore off the leather binding, and the panel divided and fell to the ground in a cloud of dust. There were two pictures – they had been nailed face to face. I leaned them against the wall, and the next moment I was leaning against it myself.

For one of the pictures was myself – a perfect portrait – no shade of expression or turn of feature wanting. Myself – in a cavalier dress, 'love-locks and all!' When had this been done? And how, without my knowledge? Was this some whim of my aunt's?

'Lor', sir!' the shrill surprise of Jane at my elbow; 'what a lovely photo it is! Was it a fancy ball, sir?'

'Yes,' I stammered. 'I – I don't think I want anything more now. You can go.'

She went; and I turned, still with my heart beating violently, to the other picture. This was a woman of the type of beauty beloved of Burne-Jones and Rossetti – straight nose, low brows, full lips, thin hands, large deep luminous eyes. She wore a black velvet gown. It was a full-length portrait. Her arms rested on a table beside her, and her head on her hands; but her face was turned full forward, and her eyes met those of the spectator bewilderingly. On the table by her were compasses and instruments whose uses I did not know, books, a goblet, and a miscellaneous heap of papers and pens. I saw all this afterwards. I believe it was a quarter of an hour before I could turn my eyes away from hers. I have never seen any other eyes like hers. They appealed, as a child's or a dog's do; they commanded, as might those of an empress.

'Shall I sweep up the dust, sir?' Curiosity had brought Jane back. I acceded. I turned from her my portrait. I kept between her and the woman in the black velvet. When I was alone again I tore down 'The Trial of Lord William Russell', and I put the picture of the woman in its strong ebony frame.

Then I wrote to a frame-maker for a frame for my portrait. It had so long lived face to face with this beautiful witch that I had not the heart to banish it from her presence; from which it will be perceived that I am by nature a somewhat sentimental person.

The new frame came home, and I hung it opposite the fireplace. An exhaustive search among my aunt's papers showed no explanation of the portrait of myself, no history of the portrait of the woman with the wonderful eyes. I only learned that all the old furniture together had come to my aunt at the death of my great-uncle, the head of the family; and I should have concluded that the resemblance was only a family one, if everyone who came in had not exclaimed at the 'speaking likeness'. I adopted Jane's 'fancy ball' explanation.

And there, one might suppose, the matter of the portraits ended. One might suppose it, that is, if there were not evidently a good deal more written here about it. However, to me, then, the matter seemed ended.

I went to see Mildred; I invited her and her mother to come and stay with me; I rather avoided glancing at the picture in the ebony frame: I could not forget, nor remember without singular emotion, the look in the eyes of that woman when mine first met them. I shrank from meeting that look again.

I reorganised the house somewhat, preparing for Mildred's visit. I turned the dining-room into a drawing-room. I brought down much of the old-fashioned furniture, and, after a long day of arranging and re-arranging, I sat down before the fire, and, lying back in a pleasant languor, I idly raised my eyes to the picture. I met her dark, deep, hazel eyes, and once more my gaze was held fixed as by a strong magic – the kind of fascination that keeps one sometimes staring for whole minutes into one's own eyes in the glass. I gazed into her eyes, and felt my own dilate, pricked with a smart like the smart of tears.

'I wish,' I said, 'oh, how I wish you were a woman and not a picture! Come down! Ah, come down!'

I laughed at myself as I spoke; but even as I laughed, I held out my arms.

I was not sleepy; I was not drunk. I was as wide awake and as sober as ever was a man in this world. And yet, as I held out my arms, I saw the eyes of the picture dilate, her lips tremble – if I were to be hanged for saying it, it is true. Her hands moved slightly; and a sort of flicker of a smile passed over her face.

I sprang to my feet. 'This won't do,' I said, still aloud. 'Firelight does play strange tricks. I'll have the lamp.'

I pulled myself together and made for the bell. My hand was on it, when I heard a sound behind me, and turned – the bell still unrung. The fire had burned low, and the corners of the room were deeply shadowed; but, surely, there – behind the tall worked chair – was something darker than a shadow.

'I must face this out,' I said, 'or I shall never be able to face myself again.' I left the bell, I seized the poker, and battered the dull coals to a blaze. Then I stepped back resolutely, and looked up at the picture. The ebony frame was empty! From the shadow of the worked chair came a silken rustle, and out of the shadow the woman of the picture was coming – coming towards me.

I hope I shall never again know a moment of terror so blank and absolute. I could not have moved or spoken to save my life. Either all the known laws of nature were nothing, or I was mad. I stood trembling, but, I am thankful to remember, I stood still, while the black velvet gown swept across the hearthrug towards me.

Next moment a hand touched me – a hand soft, warm, and human – and a low voice said, 'You called me. I am here.'

At that touch and that voice the world seemed to give a sort of bewildering half-turn. I hardly know how to express it, but at once it seemed not awful – not even unusual – for portraits to become flesh – only most natural, most right, most unspeakably fortunate.

I laid my hand on hers. I looked from her to my portrait. I could not see it in the firelight.

'We are not strangers,' I said.

'Oh no, not strangers.' Those luminous eyes were looking up into mine – those red lips were near me. With a passionate cry – a sense of having suddenly recovered life's one great good, that had seemed wholly lost – I clasped her in my arms. She was no ghost – she was a woman – the only woman in the world.

'How long,' I said, 'O love – how long since I lost you?'

She leaned back, hanging her full weight on the hands that were clasped behind my head.

'How can I tell how long? There is no time in hell,' she answered.

It was not a dream. Ah, no – there are no such dreams. I wish to God there could be. When in dreams do I see her eyes, hear her voice, feel her lips against my cheek, hold her hands to my lips, as I did that night – the supreme night of my life? At first we hardly spoke. It seemed enough –

> . . . after long grief and pain,
> To feel the arms of my true love
> Round me once again.

It is very difficult to tell this story. There are no words to express the sense of glad reunion, the complete realisation of every hope and dream of a life, that came upon me as I sat with my hand in hers and looked into her eyes.

How could it have been a dream, when I left her sitting in the straight-backed chair, and went down to the kitchen to tell the maids I should want nothing more – that I was busy, and did not wish to be disturbed; when I fetched wood for the fire with my own hands, and, bringing it in, found her still sitting there – saw the little brown head turn as I entered, saw the love in her dear eyes; when I threw myself at her feet and blessed the day I was born; since life had given me this?

Not a thought of Mildred: all other things in my life were a dream – this, its one splendid reality.

'I am wondering,' she said after a while, when we had made such cheer each of the other as true lovers may after long parting – 'I am wondering how much you remember of our past.'

'I remember nothing,' I said. 'Oh, my dear lady, my dear sweetheart – I remember nothing but that I love you – that I have loved you all my life.'

'You remember nothing – really nothing?'

'Only that I am yours; that we have both suffered; that – Tell me, my mistress dear, all that you remember. Explain it all to me. Make me understand. And yet – No, I don't want to understand. It is enough that we are together.'

If it was a dream, why have I never dreamed it again?

She leaned down towards me, her arm lay on my neck, and drew my head till it rested on her shoulder. 'I am a ghost, I suppose,' she said, laughing softly; and her laughter stirred memories which I just grasped at, and just missed. 'But you and I know better, don't we? I will tell you everything you have forgotten. We loved each other – ah! no, you have not forgotten that – and when you came back from the war we were to be married. Our pictures were painted before you went away. You know I was more learned than women of that day. Dear one, when you were gone they said I was a witch. They tried me. They said I should be burned. Just because I had looked at the stars and had gained more knowledge than they, they must needs bind me to a stake and let me be eaten by the fire. And you far away!'

Her whole body trembled and shrank. Oh love, what dream would have told me that my kisses would soothe even that memory?

'The night before,' she went on, 'the devil did come to me. I was innocent before – you know it, don't you? And even then my sin was for you – for you – because of the exceeding love I bore you. The devil came, and I sold my soul to eternal flame. But I got a good price. I got the right to come back, through my picture (if anyone looking at it wished for me), as long as my picture stayed in its ebony frame. That frame was not carved by man's hand. I got the right to come back to you. Oh, my heart's heart, and another thing I won, which you shall hear anon. They burned me for a witch, they made me suffer hell on earth. Those faces, all crowding round, the crackling wood and the smell of the smoke –'

'O love! no more – no more.'

'When my mother sat that night before my picture she wept, and cried, "Come back, my poor lost child!" And I went to her, with glad leaps of heart. Dear, she shrank from me, she fled, she shrieked and moaned of ghosts. She had our pictures covered from sight and put again in the ebony frame. She had promised me my picture should stay always there. Ah, through all these years your face was against mine.'

She paused.

'But the man you loved?'

'You came home. My picture was gone. They lied to you, and you married another woman; but some day I knew you would walk the world again and that I should find you.'

'The other gain?' I asked.

'The other gain,' she said slowly, 'I gave my soul for. It is this. If you also will give up your hopes of heaven I can remain a woman, I can move in your world – I can be your wife. Oh, my dear, after all these years, at last – at last.'

'If I sacrifice my soul,' I said slowly, with no thought of the imbecility of such talk in our 'so-called nineteenth century' – 'if I sacrifice my soul, I win you? Why, love, it's a contradiction in terms. You *are* my soul.'

Her eyes looked straight into mine. Whatever might happen, whatever did happen, whatever may happen, our two souls in that moment met, and became one.

'Then you choose – you deliberately choose – to give up your hopes of heaven for me, as I gave up mine for you?'

'I decline,' I said, 'to give up my hope of heaven on any terms. Tell me what I must do, that you and I may make our heaven here – as now, my dear love.'

'I will tell you tomorrow,' she said. 'Be alone here tomorrow

night – twelve is ghost's time, isn't it? – and then I will come out
of the picture and never go back to it. I shall live with you, and
die, and be buried, and there will be an end of me. But we shall
live first, my heart's heart.'

I laid my head on her knee. A strange drowsiness overcame me.
Holding her hand against my cheek, I lost consciousness. When I
awoke the grey November dawn was glimmering, ghost-like,
through the uncurtained window. My head was pillowed on my
arm which rested – I raised my head quickly – ah! not on my lady's
knee, but on the needle-worked cushion of the straight-backed
chair. I sprang to my feet. I was stiff with cold, and dazed with
dreams, but I turned my eyes on the picture. There she sat, my
lady grave, my dear love. I held out my arms, but the passionate
cry I would have uttered died on my lips. She had said twelve
o'clock. Her lightest word was my law. So I only stood in front of
the picture and gazed into those grey-green eyes till tears of passionate happiness filled my own.

'Oh, my dear, my dear, how shall I pass the hours till I hold you
again?'

No thought, then, of my whole life's completion and consum-
mation being a dream.

I staggered up to my room, fell across my bed, and slept heavily
and dreamlessly. When I awoke it was high noon. Mildred and her
mother were coming to lunch.

I remembered, at one shock, Mildred's coming and her existence.

Now, indeed, the dream began.

With a penetrating sense of the futility of any action apart from
*her*, I gave the necessary orders for the reception of my guests.
When Mildred and her mother came I received them with cordiality; but my genial phrases all seemed to be someone else's. My
voice sounded like an echo; my heart was other where.

Still, the situation was not intolerable until the hour when
afternoon tea was served in the drawing-room. Mildred and her
mother kept the conversational pot boiling with a profusion
of genteel commonplaces, and I bore it, as one can bear mild

purgatories when one is in sight of heaven. I looked up at my sweetheart in the ebony frame, and I felt that anything that might happen, any irresponsible imbecility, any bathos of boredom, was nothing, if, after all, *she* came to me again.

And yet, when Mildred, too, looked at the portrait, and said, 'What a fine lady! One of your flames, Mr Devigne?' I had a sickening sense of impotent irritation, which became absolute torture when Mildred – how could I ever have admired that chocolate-box barmaid style of prettiness? – threw herself into the high-backed chair, covering the needlework with her ridiculous flounces, and added, 'Silence gives consent! Who is it, Mr Devigne? Tell us all about her: I am sure she has a story.'

Poor little Mildred, sitting there smiling, serene in her confidence that her every word charmed me – sitting there with her rather pinched waist, her rather tight boots, her rather vulgar voice – sitting in the chair where my dear lady had sat when she told me her story! I could not bear it.

'Don't sit there,' I said; 'it's not comfortable!'

But the girl would not be warned. With a laugh that set every nerve in my body vibrating with annoyance, she said, 'Oh, dear! mustn't I even sit in the same chair as your black-velvet woman?'

I looked at the chair in the picture. It *was* the same; and in her chair Mildred was sitting. Then a horrible sense of the reality of Mildred came upon me. Was all this a reality after all? But for fortunate chance might Mildred have occupied, not only her chair, but her place in my life? I rose.

'I hope you won't think me very rude,' I said, 'but I am obliged to go out.'

I forget what appointment I alleged. The lie came readily enough.

I faced Mildred's pouts with the hope that she and her mother would not wait dinner for me. I fled. In another minute I was safe, alone, under the chill, cloudy autumn sky – free to think, think, think of my dear lady.

I walked for hours along streets and squares; I lived over again and again every look, word, and hand-touch – every kiss; I was completely, unspeakably happy.

Mildred was utterly forgotten; my lady of the ebony frame filled my heart and soul and spirit.

As I heard eleven boom through the fog, I turned, and went home.

When I got to my street, I found a crowd surging through it, a strong red light filling the air.

A house was on fire. Mine.

I elbowed my way through the crowd.

The picture of my lady – that, at least, I could save!

As I sprang up the steps, I saw, as in a dream – yes, all this was *really* dream-like – I saw Mildred leaning out of the first-floor window, wringing her hands.

'Come back, sir,' cried a fireman, 'we'll get the young lady out right enough.'

But *my* lady? I went on up the stairs, cracking, smoking, and as hot as hell, to the room where her picture was. Strange to say, I only felt that the picture was a thing we should like to look on through the long glad wedded life that was to be ours. I never thought of it as being one with her.

As I reached the first floor I felt arms about my neck. The smoke was too thick for me to distinguish features.

'Save me!' a voice whispered. I clasped a figure in my arms, and, with a strange unease, bore it down the shaking stairs and out into safety. It was Mildred. I knew *that* directly I clasped her.

'Stand back,' cried the crowd.

'Every one's safe,' cried a fireman.

The flames leaped from every window. The sky grew redder and redder. I sprang from the hands that would have held me. I leaped up the steps. I crawled up the stairs. Suddenly the whole horror of the situation came on me. '*As long as my picture remains in the ebony frame.*' What if picture and frame perished together?

I fought with the fire, and with my own choking inability to fight with it. I pushed on. I must save my picture. I reached the drawing-room.

As I sprang in I saw my lady – I swear it – through the smoke and the flames, hold out her arms to me – to me – who came too late to save her, and to save my own life's joy. I never saw her again.

Before I could reach her, or cry out to her, I felt the floor yield beneath my feet, and I fell into the flames below.

How did they save me? What does that matter? They saved me somehow – curse them. Every stick of my aunt's furniture was destroyed. My friends pointed out that, as the furniture was heavily insured, the carelessness of a nightly-studious housemaid had done me no harm.

No harm!

That was how I won and lost my only love.

I deny, with all my soul in the denial, that it was a dream. There are no such dreams. Dreams of longing and pain there are in plenty, but dreams of complete, of unspeakable happiness – ah, no – it is the rest of life that is the dream.

But if I think that, why have I married Mildred, and grown stout and dull and prosperous?

I tell you it is all *this* that is the dream; my dear lady only is the reality. And what does it matter what one does in a dream?

# Man-Size in Marble

Although every word of this tale is true, I do not expect people to believe it. Nowadays a 'rational explanation' is required before belief is possible. Let me, at once, offer the 'rational explanation' which finds most favour among those who have heard the tale of my life's tragedy. It is held that we were 'under a delusion', she and I, on that 31st of October; and that this supposition places the whole matter on a satisfactory and believable basis. The reader can judge, when he, too, has heard my story, how far this is an 'explanation', and in what sense it is 'rational'. There were three who took part in this; Laura and I and another man. The other man lives still, and can speak to the truth of the least credible part of my story.

I never knew in my life what it was to have as much money as would supply the most ordinary needs of life – good colours, canvases, brushes, books and cab-fares – and when we were married we knew quite well that we should only be able to live at all by 'strict punctuality and attention to business'. I used to paint in those days, and Laura used to write, and we felt sure we could keep the pot at least simmering. Living in London was out of the question, so we went to look for a cottage in the country, which should be at once sanitary and picturesque. So rarely do these two qualities meet in one cottage that our search was for some time quite fruitless. We tried advertisements, but most of the desirable rural residences which we did look at proved to be lacking in both essentials, and when a cottage chanced to have drains, it always had stucco as well and was shaped like a tea-caddy. And if we found a vine or a rose-covered porch, corruption invariably lurked within. Our minds got so befogged by the eloquence of house-agents, and the rival disadvantages of the fever-traps and outrages to beauty which we had seen and scorned, that I very much doubt whether either of us, on our wedding morning, knew the difference between a house and a haystack. But when we got away from friends and house-agents on our honeymoon, our wits grew clear again, and we knew a pretty cottage when at last we saw one. It was at Brenzett – a little village set on a hill, over against the southern marshes. We had gone there from the little fishing village, where we were staying, to see the church, and two fields from the church we found this cottage. It stood quite by itself about two miles from Brenzett village. It was a low building with rooms sticking out in unexpected places. There was a bit of stonework – ivy-covered and moss-grown, just two old rooms, all that was left of a big house that once stood there – and round this stonework the house had grown up. Stripped of its roses and jasmine, it would have been hideous. As it stood it was charming, and after a brief examination, enthusiasm usurped the place of discretion and we took it. It was absurdly cheap. The rest of our honeymoon we spent in grubbing about in second-hand shops in Ashford, picking up bits of old oak and Chippendale chairs for our furnishing. We wound up with a run up to town and a visit to Liberty's, and soon the low, oak-beamed, lattice-windowed rooms began to be home. There was a jolly old-fashioned garden, with grass paths and no end of hollyhocks, and sunflowers, and big lilies, and roses with thousands of small sweet flowers. From the window you could see the marsh-pastures, and beyond them the blue, thin line of the sea. We were as happy as the summer was glorious, and settled down into work sooner than we ourselves expected. I was never tired of sketching the view and the wonderful cloud effects from the open lattice, and Laura would sit at the table and write verses about them, in which I mostly played the part of foreground.

We got a tall, old, peasant woman to do for us. Her face and figure were good, though her cooking was of the homeliest; but she understood all about gardening, and told us all the old names of the coppices and cornfields, and the stories of the smugglers and the highwaymen, and, better still, of the 'things that walked', and of the 'sights' which met one in lonely lanes of a starlight night. She was a great comfort to us, because Laura hated housekeeping as much as I loved folk-lore, and we soon came to leave all the domestic business to Mrs Dorman, and to use her legends in little magazine stories which brought in guineas.

We had three months of married happiness. We did not have a single quarrel. And then it happened. One October evening I had been down to smoke a pipe with the doctor – our only neighbour – a pleasant young Irishman. Laura had stayed at home to finish a comic sketch of a village episode for the *Monthly Marplot*. I left her laughing over her own jokes, and came in to see her a crumpled heap of pale muslin, weeping on the window seat.

'Good heavens, my darling, what's the matter?' I cried, taking her in my arms. She leaned her head against my shoulder, and went on crying. I had never seen her cry before – we had always been so happy, you see – and I felt sure some frightful misfortune had happened.

'What *is* the matter? Do speak!'

'It's Mrs Dorman,' she sobbed.

'What has she done?' I inquired, immensely relieved.

'She says she must go before the end of the month, and she says her niece is ill; she's gone down to see her now, but I don't believe that's the reason, because her niece is always ill. I believe someone has been setting her against us. Her manner was so queer –'

'Never mind, Pussy,' I said. 'Whatever you do, don't cry, or I shall have to cry, too, to keep you in countenance, and then you'll never respect your man again.'

She dried her eyes obediently on my handkerchief, and even smiled faintly.

'But, you see,' she went on, 'it is really serious, because these village people are so sheepy; and if one won't do a thing, you may be sure none of the others will. And I shall have to cook the dinners and wash up all the hateful, greasy plates; and you'll have to carry cans of water about, and clean the boots and knives – and we shall never have any time for work, or earn any money or anything. We shall have to work all day, and only be able to rest when we are waiting for the kettle to boil!'

I represented to her that, even if we had to perform these duties, the day would still present some margin for other toils and recreations. But she refused to see the matter in any but the greyest light. She was very unreasonable, and I told her so, but in my heart . . . well, who wants a woman to be reasonable?

'I'll speak to Mrs Dorman when she comes back, and see if I can't come to terms with her,' I said. 'Perhaps she wants a rise in her screw. It will be all right. Let's walk up to the church.'

The church was a large and lonely one, and we loved to go there, especially upon bright nights. The path skirted a wood, cut through it once, and ran along the crest of the hill through two meadows and round the churchyard wall, over which the old yews loomed in black masses of shadow. This path, which was partly paved, was called the 'bier-balk', for it had long been the way by which the corpses had been carried to burial. The churchyard was richly treed, and was shaded by great elms, which stood just outside and stretched their kind arms out over the dead. A large, low porch let one into the building by a Norman doorway and a heavy oak door studded with iron. Inside, the arches rose into darkness, and between them shone the reticulated windows, which stood out white in the moonlight. In the chancel, the windows were of rich glass, which showed in faint light their noble colouring and made the black oak of the choir pews hardly more solid than the shadows. But on each side of the altar lay a grey marble figure of a knight in full armour, lying upon a low slab, with hands held up in everlasting prayer, and these figures, oddly enough, were always to be seen if there was any glimmer of light in the church. Their names were lost, but the peasants told of them that they had been fierce and wicked men, marauders by land and sea, who had been the scourge of their time, and had been guilty of deeds so foul that the house they had lived in – the big house, by the way, that had stood on the site of our cottage – had been stricken by lightning and the vengeance of Heaven. But for all that, the gold of their heirs had bought them a place in the church. Looking at the bad, hard faces reproduced in the marble, this story was easily believed.

The church looked at its best on that night, for the shadows of the yew trees fell through the windows upon the floor of the nave, and touched the pillars with tattered shadow. We sat down together without speaking, and watched the solemn beauty of the old church with some of that awe which inspired its early builders. We walked to the chancel and looked at the sleeping warriors. Then we rested on the stone seat in the porch, looking out over the stretch of quiet moonlit meadows, feeling in every fibre of our being the peace of the night and of our happy love; and came away at last with a sense that even scrubbing and black-leading were, at their worst, but small troubles.

Mrs Dorman had come back from the village, and I at once invited her to a tête-à-tête.

'Now, Mrs Dorman,' I said, when I had got her into my painting-room, 'what's all this about your not staying with us?'

'I should be glad to get away, sir, before the end of the month,' she answered, with her usual placid dignity.

'Have you any fault to find, Mrs Dorman?'

'None at all, sir; you and your lady have always been most kind, I'm sure –'

'Well, what is it? Are your wages not high enough?'

'No, sir, I gets quite enough.'

'Then why not stay?'

'I'd rather not,' with some hesitation. 'My niece is ill.'

'But your niece has been ill ever since we came.'

No answer. There was a long and awkward silence. I broke it.

'Can't you stay for another month?' I asked.

'No, sir. I'm bound to go on Thursday.'

And this was Monday.

'Well, I must say, I think you might have let us know before. There's no time now to get anyone else, and your mistress is not fit to do heavy housework. Can't you stay till next week?'

'I might be able to come back next week.'

I was now convinced that all she wanted was a brief holiday, which we should have been willing enough to let her have as soon as we could get a substitute.

'But why must you go this week?' I persisted. 'Come, out with it.'

Mrs Dorman drew the little shawl, which she always wore, tightly across her bosom, as though she were cold. Then she said, with a sort of effort: 'They say, sir, as this was a big house in Catholic times, and there was a many deeds done here.'

The nature of the 'deeds' might be vaguely inferred from the inflection of Mrs Dorman's voice, which was enough to make one's blood run cold. I was glad that Laura was not in the room. She was always nervous, as highly strung natures are, and I felt that these tales about our house, told by this old peasant woman with her impressive manner and contagious credulity, might have made our home less dear to my wife.

'Tell me all about it, Mrs Dorman,' I said. 'You needn't mind about telling me. I'm not like the young people, who make fun of such things.'

Which was partly true.

'Well, sir,' she sank her voice, 'you may have seen in the church, beside the altar, two shapes –'

'You mean the effigies of the knights in armour?' I said cheerfully.

'I mean them two bodies drawed out man-size in marble,' she returned; and I had to admit that her description was a thousand times more graphic than mine.

'They do say as on All Saints' Eve them two bodies sits up on their slabs and gets off of them, and then walks down the aisle *in their marble*' – (another good phrase, Mrs Dorman) – 'and as the church clock strikes eleven, they walks out of the church door, and over the graves, and along the bier-balk, and if it's a wet night there's the marks of their feet in the morning.'

'And where do they go?' I asked, rather fascinated.

'They comes back to their old home, sir, and if anyone meets them –'

'Well, what then?' I asked.

But no, not another word could I get from her, save that her niece was ill, and that she must go. After what I had heard I scorned to discuss the niece, and tried to get from Mrs Dorman more details of the legend. I could get nothing but warnings.

'Whatever you do, sir, lock the door early on All Saints' Eve, and make the blessed cross-sign over the doorstep and on the windows.'

'But has anyone ever seen these things?' I persisted.

'That's not for me to say. I know what I know.'

'Well, who was here last year?'

'No-one, sir. The lady as owned the house only stayed here in the summer, and she always went to London a full month afore *the* night. And I'm sorry to inconvenience you and your lady, but my niece is ill, and I must go on Thursday.'

I could have shaken her for her reiteration of that obvious fiction.

She was determined to go, nor could our united entreaties move her in the least.

I did not tell Laura the legend of the shapes that 'walked in their marble', partly because a legend concerning our house might trouble my wife, and partly, I think, for some more occult reason. This was not quite the same to me as any other story, and I did not want to talk about it till the day was over. I had very soon almost ceased to think of the legend, however. I was painting a portrait of Laura, against the lattice window, and I could not think of much else. I had got a splendid background of yellow and grey sunset, and was working away with enthusiasm at her face. On Thursday Mrs Dorman went. She relented, at parting, so far as to say: 'Don't you put yourselves about too much, ma'am, and if there's any little thing I can do next week, I'm sure I shan't mind.'

From which I inferred that she wished to come back to us after Hallowe'en. Up to the last she adhered to the fiction of the niece.

Thursday passed off pretty well. Laura showed marked ability in the matter of steak and potatoes, and I confess that my knives, and the plates, which I insisted upon washing, were better done than I had dared to expect. It was all so good, so simple, so pleasant. As I write of it, I almost forget what came after. But now I must remember, and tell.

Friday came. It is about what happened on that Friday that this is written. I wonder if I should have believed it if anyone had told it to me. I will write the story of it as quickly and plainly as I can. Everything that happened on that day is burnt into my brain. I shall not forget anything, nor leave anything out.

I got up early, I remember, and lighted the kitchen fire, and had just achieved a smoky success, when my wife came running down, as sunny and sweet as the clear October morning itself. We prepared breakfast together, and found it very good fun. The housework was soon done, and when brushes and brooms and pails were quiet again, the house was still indeed. It is wonderful what a difference *one* makes in a house. We really missed Mrs Dorman, quite apart from considerations of pots and pans. We spent the day in dusting our books and putting them straight, and dined gaily on cold steak and coffee. Laura was, if possible, brighter and gayer and sweeter than usual, and I began to think that a little domestic toil was really good for her. We had never been so merry since we were married, and the walk we had that afternoon was, I think, the happiest time of all my life. When we had watched the deep scarlet clouds slowly pale into leaden grey against a pale-green sky, and saw the white mists curl up along the hedgerows in the distant marsh, we came back to the house, silently, hand in hand.

'You are sad, Pussy,' I said half-jestingly, as we sat down together in our little parlour. I expected a disclaimer, for my own silence had been the silence of complete happiness. To my surprise, she said: 'Yes, I think I am sad, or rather I am uneasy. I hope I am not going to be ill. I have shivered three or four times since we came in, and it's not really cold, is it?'

'No,' I said, and hoped it was not a chill caught from the treacherous marsh mists that roll up from the marshes in the dying light. No, she said, she did not think so. Then, after a silence, she spoke suddenly: 'Do you ever have presentiments of evil?'

'No,' I said, smiling; 'and I shouldn't believe in them if I had.'

'I do,' she went on; 'the night my father died I knew it, though he was right away in the north of Scotland.' I did not answer in words.

She sat looking at the fire in silence for some time, gently stroking my hand. At last she sprang up, came behind me, and drawing my head back, kissed me.

'There, it's over now,' she said. 'What a baby I am. Come, light the candles, and we'll have some of these new Rubinstein duets.'

And we spent a happy hour or two at the piano.

At about half-past ten, I began to fill the good-night pipe, but Laura looked so white that I felt that it would be brutal of me to fill our sitting-room with the fumes of strong cavendish.

'I'll take my pipe outside,' I said.

'Let me come too.'

'No, sweetheart, not tonight; you're much too tired. I shan't be long. Get to bed, or I shall have an invalid to nurse tomorrow, as well as the boots to clean.'

I kissed her and was turning to go, when she flung her arms round my neck and held me very closely. I stroked her hair.

'Come, Pussy, you're over-tired. The housework has been too much for you.'

She loosened her clasp a little and drew a deep breath.

'No. We've been very happy today, Jack, haven't we? Don't stay out too long.'

'I won't, Puss cat,' I said.

I strolled out of the front door, leaving it unlatched. What a night it was! The jagged masses of heavy, dark cloud were rolling at intervals from horizon to horizon, and thin, white wreaths covered the stars. Through all the rush of the cloud river, the moon swam, breasting the waves and disappearing again in the darkness. When, now and again, her light reached the woodlands, they seemed to be slowly and noiselessly waving in time to the clouds above them. There was a strange, grey light over all the earth; the fields had that shadowy bloom over them which only comes from the marriage of dew and moonshine, or frost and starlight.

I walked up and down, drinking in the beauty of the quiet earth and changing sky. The night was absolutely silent. Nothing seemed to be abroad. There was no scurrying of rabbits, or twitter of half-asleep birds. And though the clouds went sailing across the sky, the wind that drove them never came low enough to rustle the dead leaves in the woodland paths. Across the meadow, I could see the church tower standing out black and grey against the sky. I walked there, thinking over our three months of happiness, and of my wife – her dear eyes, her pretty ways. Oh, my girl! my own little girl; what a vision came to me then of a long, glad life for you and me together!

I heard a bell-beat from the church. Eleven already! I turned to go in but the night held me. I could not go back into our little warm rooms yet. I would go right on up to the church. I felt vaguely that it would be good to carry my love and thankfulness to the sanctuary, whither so many loads of sorrow and gladness had been borne by men and women dead long since.

I looked in at the low window as I went by. Laura was half lying on her chair in front of the fire. I could not see her face, only her head showed dark against the pale blue wall. She was quite still. Asleep no doubt. My heart reached out to her, as I went on. There must be a God, I thought, and a God that was good. How otherwise could anything so sweet and dear as she ever have been imagined?

I walked slowly along the edge of the wood. A sound broke the stillness of the night. I stopped and listened. The sound stopped too. I went on, and now distinctly I heard another step than mine answer mine like an echo. It was a poacher or a wood-stealer, most likely, for these were not unknown in our Arcadia. But, whoever it was, he was a fool not to step more lightly. I turned into the wood, and now the footstep seemed to come from the path I had just left. It must be an echo, I thought. The wood lay lovely in the moonlight. The large, dying ferns and the brushwood showed where, through thinning foliage, the pale light came down. The tree trunks stood up like Gothic columns all around me. They reminded me of the church, and I turned into the bier-balk and passed through the corpse-gate between the graves to the low porch. I paused for a moment on the stone seat where Laura and I had last night watched the fading landscape. Then I noticed that the door of the church was open, and I blamed myself for having left it unlatched the other night. We were the only people who ever cared to come to the church except on Sundays, and I was vexed to think that through our carelessness the damp autumn airs had had a chance of getting in and injuring the old fabric. I went in. It will seem strange perhaps that I should have gone half-way up the aisle before I remembered – with a sudden chill, followed by as sudden a rush of self-contempt – that this was the very day and hour when, according to tradition, the shapes 'drawed out man-size in marble', began to walk.

Having thus remembered the legend, and remembered it with a shiver of which I was ashamed, I could not do otherwise than walk up towards the altar, just to look at the figures – as I said to myself; really what I wanted was to assure myself, first, that I did not believe the legend, and, secondly, that it was not true. I was rather glad that I had come. I thought that now I could tell Mrs Dorman how vain her fancies were, and how peacefully the marble figures slept on through the ghostly hour. With my hands in my pockets, I passed up the aisle. In the grey, dim light, the eastern end of the church looked larger than usual, and the arches above the tombs looked larger too. The moon came out and showed me the reason. I stopped short, my heart gave a great leap that nearly choked me, and then sank sickeningly.

The 'bodies drawed out man-size' *were gone*, and their marble slabs lay wide and bare in the vague moonlight that slanted through the west window.

Were they really gone? or was I mad? Clenching my nerves, I stooped and passed my hand over the smooth slabs and felt their flat unbroken surface. Had someone taken the things away? Was it some vile practical joke? I would make sure, anyway. In an instant I had made a torch of a newspaper which happened to be in my pocket, and lighting it held it high above my head. Its yellow glare illumined the dark arches and those slabs. The figures *were* gone. And I was alone in the church; or was I alone?

And then a horror seized me, a horror indefinable and indescribable – an overwhelming certainty of supreme and accomplished calamity. I flung down the torch and tore along the aisle and out through the door, biting my lips as I ran to keep myself from shrieking aloud. Was I mad – or what was this that possessed me? I leaped the churchyard wall and took the straight cut across the fields, led by the light from our windows. Just as I got over the first stile, a dark figure seemed to spring out of the ground. Mad still with the certainty of misfortune, I made for the thing that stood in my path, shouting 'Get out of the way, can't you?'

But my push met with a very vigorous resistance. My arms were caught just above the elbow and held as in a vice, and the raw-boned Irish doctor actually shook me.

'Would ye?' he cried in his own unmistakable accents – 'would ye, then?'

'Let me go, you fool,' I gasped. 'The marble figures have gone from the church; I tell you they've gone.'

He broke into a ringing laugh. 'I'll have to give ye a draught tomorrow, I see. Ye've been smoking too much and listening to old wives' tales.'

'I'll tell you I've seen the bare slabs.'

'Well, come back with me. I'm going up to old Palmer's – his daughter's ill – it's only hysteria, but it's as bad as it can be; we'll look in at the church and let *me* see the bare slabs.'

'You go if you like,' I said, a little less frantic for his laughter, 'I'm going home to my wife.'

'Rubbish, man,' said he; 'D'ye think I'll permit of that? Are ye to go saying all yer life that ye've seen solid marble endowed with vitality, and me to go all my life saying ye were a coward? No, sir – ye shan't do ut!'

The quiet night – a human voice – and I think also the physical contact with this six feet of solid common sense, brought me back a little to my ordinary self, and the word 'coward' was a shower-bath.

'Come on, then,' I said sullenly, 'perhaps you're right.'

He still held my arm tightly. We got over the stile and back to the church. All was still as death. The place smelt very damp and earthy. We walked up the aisle. I am not ashamed to confess I shut my eyes; I knew the figures would not be there, I heard Kelly strike a match.

'Here they are, ye see, right enough; ye've been dreaming or drinking, asking yer pardon for the imputation.'

I opened my eyes. By Kelly's expiring vesta I saw two shapes lying 'in their marble' on their slabs. I drew a deep breath and caught his hand.

'I'm awfully indebted to you,' I said. 'It must have been some trick of the light, or I have been working rather hard, perhaps that's it. Do you know, I was quite convinced they were gone.'

'I'm aware of that,' he answered rather grimly; 'ye'll have to be careful of that brain of yours, my friend, I assure you.'

He was leaning over and looking at the right-hand figure, whose stone face was the most villainous and deadly in expression. He struck another match.

'By Jove!' he said, 'something has been going on here – this hand is broken.'

And so it was. I was certain that it had been perfect the last time Laura and I had been there.

'Perhaps someone had *tried* to remove them,' said the young doctor.

'That won't account for my impression,' I objected.

'Too much painting and tobacco will account for what you call your impression,' he said.

'Come along,' I said, 'or my wife will be getting anxious. You'll come in and have a drop of whisky, and drink confusion to ghosts and better sense to me.'

'I ought to go up to Palmer's but it's so late now, I'd best leave it till the morning,' he replied. 'I was kept late at the Union, and I've had to see a lot of people since. All right, I'll come back with ye.'

I think he fancied I needed him more than did Palmer's girl, so, discussing how such an illusion could have been possible, and deducing from this experience large generalities concerning ghostly apparitions, we saw, as we walked up the garden path, that bright light streamed out of the front door, and presently saw that the parlour door was open too. Had she gone out?

'Come in,' I said, and Dr Kelly followed me into the parlour. It was all ablaze with candles, not only the wax ones, but at least a dozen guttering, glaring, tallow dips, stuck in vases and ornaments in unlikely places. Light, I knew, was Laura's remedy for nervousness. Poor child! Why had I left her? Brute that I was.

We glanced round the room, and at first we did not see her. The window was open and the draught set all the candles flaring one way. Her chair was empty, and her handkerchief and book lay on the floor. I turned to the window. There, in the recess of the window, I saw her. Oh, my child, my love, had she gone to that window to watch for me? To what had she turned with that look of frantic fear and horror? Had she thought that it was my step she heard and turned to meet – what?

She had fallen back against a table in the window, and her body lay half on it and half on the window-seat, and her head hung down over the table, the brown hair loosened and fallen to the carpet. Her lips were drawn back and her eyes wide, wide open. They saw nothing now. What had they last seen?

The doctor moved towards her. But I pushed him aside and sprang to her; caught her in my arms, and cried – 'It's all right, Laura! I've got you safe, dear!'

She fell into my arms in a heap. I clasped her and kissed her, and called her by all her pet names, but I think I knew all the time that she was dead. Her hands were tightly clenched. In one of them she held something fast. When I was quite sure that she was dead, and that nothing mattered at all any more, I let him open her hand to see what she held.

It was a grey marble finger.

# The Violet Car

Do you know the downs – the wide windy spaces, the rounded shoulders of the hills leaned against the sky, the hollows where farms and homesteads nestle sheltered, with trees round them pressed close and tight as a carnation in a button-hole? On long summer days it is good to lie on the downs, between short turf and pale, clear sky, to smell the wild thyme, and hear the tiny tinkle of the sheep-bells and the song of the skylark. But on winter evenings when the wind is waking up to its work, spitting rain in your eyes, beating the poor, naked trees and shaking the dusk across the hills like a grey pall, then it is better to be by a warm fireside, in one of the farms that lie lonely where shelter is, and oppose their windows glowing with candlelight and firelight to the deepening darkness, as faith holds up its love-lamp in the night of sin and sorrow that is life.

I am unaccustomed to literary effort – and I feel that I shall not say what I have to say, nor that it will convince you, unless I say it very plainly. I thought I could adorn mystery with pleasant words, prettily arranged. But as I pause to think of what really happened, I see that the plainest words will be the best. I do not know how to weave a plot, nor how to embroider it. It is best not to try. These things happened. I have no skill to add to what happened; nor is any adding of mine needed.

I am a nurse – and I was sent for to go to Charlestown – a mental case. It was November – and the fog was thick in London, so that my cab went at a foot's pace, so I missed the train by which I should have gone. I sent a telegram to Charlestown, and waited in the dismal waiting room at London Bridge. The time was passed for me by a little child. Its mother, a widow, seemed too crushed to be able to respond to its quick questionings. She answered briefly, and not, as it seemed, to the child's satisfaction. The child itself presently seemed to perceive that its mother was not, so to speak, available. It leaned back on the wide, dusty seat and yawned. I caught its eye, and smiled. It would not smile, but it looked. I took out of my bag a silk purse, bright with beads and steel tassels, and turned it over and over. Presently, the child slid along the seat and said, 'Let me' — After that all was easy. The mother sat with eyes closed. When I rose to go, she opened them and thanked me. The child, clinging, kissed me. Later, I saw them get into a first class carriage in my train. My ticket was a third class one.

I expected, of course, that there would be a conveyance of some sort to meet me at the station — but there was nothing. Nor was there a cab or a fly to be seen. It was by this time nearly dark, and the wind was driving the rain almost horizontally along the unfrequented road that lay beyond the door of the station. I looked out, forlorn and perplexed.

'Haven't you engaged a carriage?' It was the widow lady who spoke.

I explained.

'My motor will be here directly,' she said, 'you'll let me drive you? Where is it you are going?'

'Charlestown,' I said, and as I said it, I was aware of a very odd change in her face. A faint change, but quite unmistakable.

'Why do you look like that?' I asked her bluntly. And, of course, she said, 'Like what?'

'There's nothing wrong with the house?' I said, for that, I found, was what I had taken that faint change to signify; and I was very young, and one has heard tales. 'No reason why I shouldn't go there, I mean?'

'No — oh no —' she glanced out through the rain, and I knew as well as though she had told me that there was a reason why *she* should not wish to go there.

'Don't trouble,' I said, 'it's very kind of you — but it's probably out of your way and . . . '

'Oh – but I'll take you – of *course* I'll take you,' she said, and the child said 'Mother, here comes the car.'

And come it did, though neither of us heard it till the child had spoken. I know nothing of motor cars, and I don't know the names of any of the parts of them. This was like a brougham – only you got in at the back, as you do in a waggonette; the seats were in the corners, and when the door was shut there was a little seat that pulled up, and the child sat on it between us. And it moved like magic – or like a dream of a train.

We drove quickly through the dark – I could hear the wind screaming, and the wild dashing of the rain against the windows, even through the whirring of the machinery. One could see nothing of the country – only the black night, and the shafts of light from the lamps in front.

After, as it seemed, a very long time, the chauffeur got down and opened a gate. We went through it, and after that the road was very much rougher. We were quite silent in the car, and the child had fallen asleep.

We stopped, and the car stood pulsating, as though it were out of breath, while the chauffeur hauled down my box. It was so dark that I could not see the shape of the house, only the lights in the downstairs windows, and the low-walled front garden faintly revealed by their light and the light of the motor lamps. Yet I felt that it was a fair-sized house, that it was surrounded by big trees, and that there was a pond or river close by. In daylight next day I found that all this was so. I have never been able to tell how I knew it that first night, in the dark, but I did know it. Perhaps there was something in the way the rain fell on the trees and on the water. I don't know.

The chauffeur took my box up a stone path, whereon I got out, and said my goodbyes and thanks.

'Don't wait, please, don't,' I said. 'I'm all right now. Thank you a thousand times!'

The car, however, stood pulsating till I had reached the doorstep, then it caught its breath, as it were, throbbed more loudly, turned, and went.

And still the door had not opened. I felt for the knocker, and rapped smartly. Inside the door I was sure I heard whispering. The car light was fast diminishing to a little distant star, and its panting sounded now hardly at all. When it ceased to sound at all, the place was quiet as death. The lights glowed redly from curtained windows, but there was no other sign of life. I wished I had not been in such a hurry to part from my escort, from human companionship, and from the great, solid, competent presence of the motor car.

I knocked again, and this time I followed the knock by a shout. 'Hullo!' I cried. 'Let me in. I'm the nurse!'

There was a pause, such a pause as would allow time for whisperers to exchange glances on the other side of a door.

Then a bolt ground back, a key turned, and the doorway framed no longer cold, wet wood, but light and a welcoming warmth – and faces.

'Come in, oh, come in,' said a voice, a woman's voice, and the voice of a man said: 'We didn't know there was anyone there.'

And I had shaken the very door with my knockings!

I went in, blinking at the light, and the man called a servant, and between them they carried my box upstairs.

The woman took my arm and led me into a low, square room, pleasant, homely, and comfortable, with solid mid-Victorian comfort – the kind that expressed itself in rep and mahogany. In the lamplight I turned to look at her. She was small and thin, her hair, her face, and her hands were of the same tint of greyish yellow.

'Mrs Eldridge?' I asked.

'Yes,' said she, very softly. 'Oh! I am so glad you've come. I hope you won't be dull here. I hope you'll stay. I hope I shall be able to make you comfortable.'

She had a gentle, urgent way of speaking that was very winning.

'I'm sure I shall be very comfortable,' I said; 'but it's I that am to take care of you. Have you been ill long?'

'It's not me that's ill, really,' she said, 'it's him —'

Now, it was Mr Robert Eldridge who had written to engage me to attend on his wife, who was, he said, slightly deranged.

'I see,' said I. One must never contradict them, it only aggravates their disorder.

'The reason . . . ' she was beginning, when his foot sounded on the stairs, and she fluttered off to get candles and hot water.

He came in and shut the door. A fair bearded, elderly man, quite ordinary.

'You'll take care of her,' he said. 'I don't want her to get talking to people. She fancies things.'

'What form do the illusions take?' I asked, prosaically.

'She thinks I'm mad,' he said, with a short laugh.

'It's a very usual form. Is that all?'

'It's about enough. And she can't hear things that I can hear, see things that I can see, and she can't smell things. By the way, you didn't see or hear anything of a motor as you came up, did you?'

'I came up *in* a motor car,' I said shortly. 'You never sent to meet me, and a lady gave me a lift.' I was going to explain about my missing the earlier train, when I found that he was not listening to me. He was watching the door. When his wife came in, with a steaming jug in one hand and a flat candlestick in the other, he went towards her, and whispered eagerly. The only words I caught were: 'She came in a real motor.'

Apparently, to these simple people a motor was as great a novelty as to me. My telegram, by the way, was delivered next morning.

They were very kind to me; they treated me as an honoured guest. When the rain stopped, as it did late the next day, and I was able to go out, I found that Charlestown was a farm, a large farm, but even to my inexperienced eyes it seemed neglected and unprosperous. There was absolutely nothing for me to do but to follow Mrs Eldridge, helping her where I could in her household duties, and to sit with her while she sewed in the homely parlour. When I had been in the house a few days, I began to put together the little things that I had noticed singly, and the life at the farm seemed suddenly to come into focus, as strange surroundings do after a while.

I found that I had noticed that Mr and Mrs Eldridge were very fond of each other, and that it was a fondness, and their way of showing it was a way that told that they had known sorrow, and had borne it together. That she showed no sign of mental derangement, save in the persistent belief of hers that *he* was deranged. That the morning found them fairly cheerful; that after the early dinner they seemed to grow more and more depressed; that after the 'early cup of tea' – that is just as dusk was falling – they always went for a walk together. That they never asked me to join them in this walk, and that it always took the same direction – across the downs towards the sea. That they always returned from this walk pale and dejected; that she sometimes cried afterwards alone in their bedroom, while he was shut up in the little room they called the office, where he did his accounts, and paid his men's wages, and where his hunting-crops and guns were kept. After supper, which was early, they always made an effort to be cheerful. I knew that this effort was for my sake, and I knew that each of them thought it was good for the other to make it.

Just as I had known before they showed it to me that Charlestown was surrounded by big trees and had a great pond beside it, so I knew, and in as inexplicable a way, that with these two fear lived. It looked at me out of their eyes. And I knew, too, that this fear was not her fear. I had not been two days in the place before I found that I was beginning to be fond of them both. They were so kind, so gentle, so ordinary, so homely – the kind of people who ought not to have known the name of fear – the kind of people to whom all honest, simple joys should have come by right, and no sorrows but such as come to us all, the death of old friends, and the slow changes of advancing years.

They seemed to belong to the land – to the downs, and the copses, and the old pastures, and the lessening corn-fields. I found myself wishing that I, too, belonged to these, that I had been born a farmer's daughter. All the stress and struggle of cram and exam, of school, and college, and hospital, seemed so loud and futile, compared with these open secrets of the down life. And I felt this the more, as more and more I felt that I must leave it all – that there was, honestly, no work for me here such as for good or ill I had been trained to do.

'I ought not to stay,' I said to her one afternoon, as we stood at the open door. It was February now, and the snowdrops were thick in tufts beside the flagged path. 'You are quite well.'

'*I* am,' she said.

'You are quite well, both of you,' I said. 'I oughtn't to be taking your money and doing nothing for it.'

'You're doing everything,' she said; 'you don't know how much you're doing.'

'We had a daughter of our own once,' she added vaguely, and then, after a very long pause, she said very quietly and distinctly: 'He has never been the same since.'

'How not the same?' I asked, turning my face up to the thin February sunshine.

She tapped her wrinkled, yellow-grey forehead, as country people do. 'Not right here,' she said.

'How?' I asked. 'Dear Mrs Eldridge, tell me; perhaps I could help somehow.'

Her voice was so sane, so sweet. It had come to this with me, that I did not know which of those two was the one who needed my help.

'He sees things that no-one else sees, and hears things no-one else hears, and smells things that you can't smell if you're standing there beside him.'

I remembered with a sudden smile his words to me on the evening of my arrival: 'She can't see, or hear, or smell.'

And once more I wondered to which of the two I owed my service.

'Have you any idea why?' I asked. She caught at my arm.

'It was after our Bessie died,' she said – 'the very day she was buried. The motor that killed her – they said it was an accident – it was on the Brighton Road. It was a violet colour. They go into mourning for Queens with violet, don't they?' she added; 'and my Bessie, she was a Queen. So the motor was violet. That was all right, wasn't it?'

I told myself now that I saw that the woman was not normal, and I saw why. It was grief that had turned her brain. There must have been some change in my look, though I ought to have known better, for she said suddenly, 'No. I'll not tell you any more.'

And then he came out. He never left me alone with her for very long. Nor did she ever leave him for very long alone with me.

I did not intend to spy upon them, though I am not sure that my position as nurse to one mentally afflicted would not have justified such spying. But I did not spy. It was chance. I had been to the village to get some blue sewing silk for a blouse I was making, and there was a royal sunset which tempted me to prolong my walk. That was how I found myself on the high downs where they slope to the broken edge of England – the sheer, white cliffs against which the English Channel beats for ever. The furze was in flower, and the skylarks were singing, and my thoughts were with my own life, my own hopes and dreams. So I found that I had struck a road, without knowing when I had struck it. I followed it towards the sea, and quite soon it ceased to be a road, and merged in the pathless turf as a stream sometimes disappears in sand. There was nothing but turf and furze bushes, the song of the skylarks, and beyond the slope that ended at the cliff's edge, the booming of the sea. I turned back, following the road, which defined itself again a few yards back, and presently sank to a lane, deep-banked and bordered with brown hedge stuff. It was there that I came upon them in the dusk. And I heard their voices before I saw them, and before it was possible for them to see me. It was her voice that I heard first.

'No, no, no, no, no,' it said.

'I tell you yes,' that was his voice; 'there – can't you hear it, that panting sound – right away – away? It must be at the very edge of the cliff.'

'There's nothing, dearie,' she said, 'indeed there's nothing.'

'You're deaf – and blind – stand back I tell you, it's close upon us.'

I came round the corner of the lane then, and as I came, I saw him catch her arm and throw her against the hedge – violently, as though the danger he feared were indeed close upon them. I stopped behind the turn of the hedge and stepped back. They had not seen me. Her eyes were on his face, and they held a world of pity, love, agony – his face was set in a mask of terror, and his eyes moved quickly as though they followed down the lane the swift passage of Something – something that neither she nor I could see. Next moment he was cowering, pressing his body into the hedge – his face hidden in his hands, and his whole body trembling so that I could see it, even from where I was a dozen yards away, through the light screen of the over-grown hedge.

'And the smell of it!' – he said, 'do you mean to tell me you can't smell it?'

She had her arms round him.

'Come home, dearie,' she said. 'Come home! It's all your fancy – come home with your old wife that loves you.'

They went home.

Next day I asked her to come to my room to look at the new blue blouse. When I had shown it to her I told her what I had seen and heard yesterday in the lane.

'And now I know,' I said, 'which of you it is that wants care.'

To my amazement she said very eagerly, 'Which?'

'Why, he – of course' – I told her, 'there was nothing there.'

She sat down in the chintz-covered armchair by the window, and broke into wild weeping. I stood by her and soothed her as well as I could.

'It's a comfort to know,' she said at last, 'I haven't known what to believe. Many a time, lately, I've wondered whether after all it could be me that was mad, like he said. And there was nothing there? There always *was* nothing there – and it's on him the judgment, not on me. On him. Well, that's something to be thankful for.'

So her tears, I told myself, had been more of relief at her own escape. I looked at her with distaste, and forgot that I had been fond of her. So that her next words cut me like little knives.

'It's bad enough for him as it is,' she said – 'but it's nothing to what it would be for him, if I was really to go off my head and him left to think he'd brought it on me. You see, now I can look after him the same as I've always done. It's only once in the day it comes over him. He couldn't bear it, if it was all the time – like it'll be for me now. It's much better it should be him – I'm better able to bear it than he is.'

I kissed her then and put my arms round her, and said, 'Tell me what it is that frightens him so – and it's every day, you say?'

'Yes – ever since. I'll tell you. It's a sort of comfort to speak out. It was a violet-coloured car that killed our Bessie. You know our girl that I've told you about. And it's a violet-coloured car that he thinks he sees – every day up there in the lane. And he says he hears it, and that he smells the smell of the machinery – the stuff they put in it – you know.'

'Petrol?'

'Yes, and you can *see* he hears it, and you can *see* he sees it. It haunts him, as if it was a ghost. You see, it was he that picked her up after the violet car went over her. It was that that turned him. I only saw her as he carried her in, in his arms – and then he'd covered her face. But he saw her just as they'd left her, lying in the dust . . . you could see the place on the road where it happened for days and days.'

'Didn't they come back?'

'Oh yes . . . they came back. But Bessie didn't come back. But there was a judgment on them. The very night of the funeral, that violet car went over the cliff – dashed to pieces – every soul in it. That was the man's widow that drove you home the first night.'

'I wonder she uses a car after that,' I said – I wanted something commonplace to say.

'Oh,' said Mrs Eldridge, 'it's all what you're used to. We don't stop walking because our girl was killed on the road. Motoring comes as natural to them as walking to us. There's my old man calling – poor old dear. He wants me to go out with him.'

She went, all in a hurry, and in her hurry slipped on the stairs and twisted her ankle. It all happened in a minute and it was a bad sprain.

When I had bound it up, and she was on the sofa, she looked at him, standing as if he were undecided, staring out of the window, with his cap in his hand. And she looked at me.

'Mr Eldridge mustn't miss his walk,' she said. 'You go with him, my dear. A breath of air will do you good.'

So I went, understanding as well as though he had told me, that he did not want me with him, and that he was afraid to go alone, and that he yet had to go.

We went up the lane in silence. At that corner he stopped suddenly, caught my arm, and dragged me back. His eyes followed something that I could not see. Then he exhaled a held breath, and said, 'I thought I heard a motor coming.' He had found it hard to control his terror, and I saw beads of sweat on his forehead and temples. Then we went back to the house.

The sprain was a bad one. Mrs Eldridge had to rest, and again next day it was I who went with him to the corner of the lane.

This time he could not, or did not try to, conceal what he felt. 'There – listen!' he said. 'Surely you can hear it?'

I heard nothing.

'Stand back,' he cried shrilly, suddenly, and we stood back close against the hedge.

Again the eyes followed something invisible to me, and again the held breath exhaled.

'It will kill me one of these days,' he said, 'and I don't know that I care how soon – if it wasn't for her.'

'Tell me,' I said, full of that importance, that conscious competence, that one feels in the presence of other people's troubles. He looked at me.

'I will tell you, by God,' he said. 'I couldn't tell *her*. Young lady, I've gone so far as wishing myself a Roman, for the sake of a priest to tell it to. But I can tell *you*, without losing my soul more than it's lost already. Did you ever hear tell of a violet car that got smashed up — went over the cliff?'

'Yes,' I said. 'Yes.'

'The man that killed my girl was new to the place. And he hadn't any eyes — or ears — or he'd have known me, seeing we'd been face to face at the inquest. And you'd have thought he'd have stayed at home that one day, with the blinds drawn down. But not he. He was swirling and swivelling all about the country in his cursed violet car, the very time we were burying her. And at dusk — there was a mist coming up — he comes up behind me in this very lane, and I stood back, and he pulls up, and he calls out, with his damned lights full in my face: "Can you tell me the way to Hexham, my man?" says he.

'I'd have liked to show him the way to hell. And that was the way for me, not him. I don't know how I came to do it. I didn't mean to do it. I didn't think I was going to — and before I knew anything, I'd said it. "Straight ahead," I said; "keep straight ahead." Then the motor-thing panted, chuckled, and he was off. I ran after him to try to stop him — but what's the use of running after these motor-devils? And he kept straight on. And every day since then, every dear day, the car comes by, the violet car that nobody can see but me — and it keeps straight on.'

'You ought to go away,' I said, speaking as I had been trained to speak. 'You fancy these things. You probably fancied the whole thing. I don't suppose you ever *did* tell the violet car to go straight ahead. I expect it was all imagination, and the shock of your poor daughter's death. You ought to go right away.'

'I can't,' he said earnestly. 'If I did, someone else would see the car. You see, somebody *has* to see it every day as long as I live. If it wasn't me, it would be someone else. And I'm the only person who *deserves* to see it — I wouldn't like anyone else to see it — it's too horrible. *It's* much more horrible than you think,' he added slowly.

I asked him, walking beside him down the quiet lane, what it was that was so horrible about the violet car. I think I quite expected him to say that it was splashed with his daughter's blood . . . What he did say was, 'It's too horrible to tell you,' and he shuddered.

I was young then, and youth always thinks it can move mountains. I persuaded myself that I could cure him of his delusion by attacking – not the main fort – that is always, to begin with, impregnable, but one, so to speak, of the outworks. I set myself to persuade him not to go to that corner in the lane, at that hour in the afternoon.

'But if I don't, someone else will see it.'

'There'll be nobody there *to* see it,' I said briskly.

'Someone will be there. Mark my words, someone will be there – and then they'll know.'

'Then I'll be the someone,' I said. 'Come – you stay at home with your wife, and *I'll* go – and if I see it I'll promise to tell you, and if I don't – well, then I will be able to go away with a clear conscience.'

'A clear conscience,' he repeated.

I argued with him in every moment when it was possible to catch him alone. I put all my will and all my energy into my persuasions. Suddenly, like a door that you've been trying to open, and that has resisted every key till the last one, he gave way. Yes – I should go to the lane. And he would not go.

I went.

Being, as I said before, a novice in the writing of stories, I perhaps haven't made you understand that it was quite hard for me to go – that I felt myself at once a coward and a heroine. This business of an imaginary motor that only one poor old farmer could see, probably appears to you quite commonplace and ordinary. It was not so with me. You see, the idea of this thing had dominated my life for weeks and months, had dominated it even before I knew the nature of the domination. It was this that was the fear that I had known to walk with these two people, the fear that shared their bed and board, that lay down and rose up with them. The old man's fear of this and his fear of his fear. And the old man was terribly convincing. When one talked with him, it was quite difficult to believe that he was mad, and that there wasn't, and couldn't be, a mysteriously horrible motor that was visible to him, and invisible to other people. And when he said that, if he were not in the lane, someone else would see it – it was easy to say 'Nonsense,' but to think 'Nonsense' was not so easy, and to *feel* 'Nonsense' quite oddly difficult.

I walked up and down the lane in the dusk, wishing not to wonder what might be the hidden horror in the violet car. I would not let blood into my thoughts. I was not going to be fooled by thought transference, or any of those transcendental follies. I was not going to be hypnotised into seeing things.

I walked up the lane – I had promised him to stand near that corner for five minutes, and I stood there in the deepening dusk, looking up towards the downs and the sea. There were pale stars. Everything was very still. Five minutes is a long time. I held my watch in my hand. Four – four and a half – four and a quarter. Five. I turned instantly. And then I saw that *he* had followed me – he was standing a dozen yards away – and his face was turned from me. It was turned towards a motor car that shot up the lane – It came very swiftly, and before it came to where he was, I knew that it was very horrible. I crushed myself back into the crackling bare hedge, as I should have done to leave room for the passage of a real car – though I knew that this one was not real. It looked real – but I knew it was not.

As it neared him, he started back, then suddenly he cried out. I heard him. 'No, no, no, no – no more, no more,' was what he cried, with that he flung himself down on the road in front of the car, and its great tyres passed over him. Then the car shot past me and I saw what the full horror of it was. There was no blood – that was not the horror. The colour of it was, as she had said, violet.

I got to him and got his head up. He was dead. I was quite calm and collected now, and felt that to be so was extremely creditable to me. I went to a cottage where a labourer was having tea – he got some men and a hurdle.

When I had told his wife, the first intelligible thing she said was: 'It's better for him. Whatever he did he's paid for now –' So it looks as though she had known – or guessed – more than he thought.

I stayed with her till her death. She did not live long.

You think perhaps that the old man was knocked down and killed by a real motor, which happened to come that way of all ways, at that hour of all hours, and happened to be, of all colours, violet. Well, a real motor leaves its mark on you where it kills you, doesn't it. But when I lifted up that old man's head from the road, there was no mark on him, no blood – no broken bones – his hair was not disordered, nor his dress. I tell you there was not even a speck of mud on him, except where he had touched the road in falling. There were no tyre marks in the mud.

The motor car that killed him came and went like a shadow. As he threw himself down, it swerved a little so that both its wheels should go over him.

He died, the doctor said, of heart-failure. I am the only person to know that he was killed by a violet car, which, having killed him, went noiselessly away towards the sea. And that car was empty – there was no-one in it. It was just a violet car that moved along the lanes swiftly and silently, and was empty.

# John Charrington's Wedding

No-one ever thought that May Foster would marry John Charrington; but he thought differently, and things which John Charrington intended should happen had a way of happening. He asked her to marry him before he went up to Oxford. She laughed and refused him. He asked her again next time he came home. Again she laughed, tossed her blonde head, and again refused. A third time he asked her; she said it was becoming a confirmed habit, and laughed at him more than ever.

John was not the only man who wanted to marry her; she was the belle of our village, and we were all in love with her more or less; it was a sort of fashion, like heliotrope ties or Inverness capes. Therefore we were as much annoyed as surprised when John Charrington walked into our little local club – we held it in a loft over the saddler's, I remember – and invited us all to his wedding.

'Your wedding?'

'You don't mean it?'

'Who's the happy fair? When's it to be?'

John Charrington filled his pipe and lighted it before he replied. Then he said: 'I'm sorry to deprive you fellows of your only joke, but Miss Foster and I are to be married in September.'

'You don't mean it?'

'He's got the mitten again, and it's turned his head.'

'No,' I said, rising, 'I see it's true. Lend me a pistol someone, or a first-class fare to the other end of Nowhere. Charrington has bewitched the only pretty girl in our twenty-mile radius. Was it mesmerism, or a love-potion, Jack?'

'Neither, sir, but a gift you'll never have – perseverance – and the best luck a man ever had in this world.'

There was something in his voice that silenced me, and all chaff of the other fellows failed to draw him further.

The queer thing about it was that, when we congratulated Miss Foster, she blushed, and smiled, and dimpled, for all the world as though she were in love with him and had been in love with him all the time. Upon my word, I think she had. Women are strange creatures.

We were all asked to the wedding. In Brixham, everyone who was anybody knew everybody else who was anyone. My sisters were, I truly believe, more interested in the *trousseau* than the bride herself, and I was to be best man. The coming marriage was much canvassed at afternoon tea-tables, and at our little club over the saddler's; and the question was always asked: 'Does she care for him?'

I used to ask that question myself in the early days of their engagement, but after a certain evening in August I never asked it again. I was coming home from the Club through the churchyard. Our church is on a thyme-grown hill, and the turf about it is so thick and soft that one's footsteps are noiseless.

I made no sound as I vaulted the low wall and threaded my way between the tombstones. It was at the same instant that I heard John Charrington's voice and saw her. May was sitting on a low, flat gravestone, her face turned towards the full splendour of the setting sun. Its expression ended, at once and for ever, any question of love for him; it was transfigured to a beauty I should not have believed possible, even to that beautiful little face.

John lay at her feet, and it was his voice that broke the stillness of the golden August evening.

'My dear, I believe I should come back from the dead, if you wanted me!'

I coughed at once to indicate my presence, and passed on into the shadow fully enlightened.

The wedding was to be early in September. Two days before, I had to run up to town on business. The train was late, of course, for we were on the South-Eastern, and as I stood grumbling with my watch in my hand, whom should I see but John Charrington and May Foster. They were walking up and down the unfrequented end of the platform, arm-in-arm, looking into each other's eyes, careless of the sympathetic interest of the porters.

Of course I knew better than to hesitate a moment before burying myself in the booking-office, and it was not till the train drew up at the platform that I obtrusively passed the pair with my Gladstone, and took the corner in a first-class smoking-carriage. I did this with as good an air of not seeing them as I could assume. I pride myself on my discretion, but if John were travelling alone, I wanted his company. I had it.

'Hullo, old man,' came his cheery voice, as he swung his bag into my carriage, 'here's luck. I was expecting a dull journey.'

'Where are you off to?' I asked, discretion still bidding me turn my eyes away, though I saw, without looking, that hers were red-rimmed.

'To old Branbridge's,' he answered, shutting the door, and leaning out for a last word with his sweetheart.

'Oh, I wish you wouldn't go, John,' she was saying in a low, earnest voice. 'I feel certain something will happen.'

'Do you think I should let anything happen to keep me, and the day after tomorrow our wedding day?'

'Don't go,' she answered, with a pleading intensity that would have sent my Gladstone on to the platform, and me after it. But she wasn't speaking to me. John Charrington was made differently — he rarely changed his opinion, never his resolutions.

He just touched the ungloved hands that lay on the carriage door.

'I must, May. The old boy has been awfully good to me, and now he's dying I must go and see him, but I shall come home in time —' The rest of the parting was lost in a whisper and in the rattling lurch of the starting train.

'You're sure to come?' she spoke, as the train moved.

'Nothing shall keep me,' he answered, and we steamed out. After he had seen the last of the little figure on the platform, he leaned back in his corner and kept silence for a minute.

When he spoke it was to explain to me that his godfather, whose heir he was, lay dying at Peasemarsh Place, some fifty miles away, and he had sent for John, and John had felt bound to go.

'I shall be surely back tomorrow,' he said, 'or, if not, the day after, in heaps of time. Thank Heaven, one hasn't to get up in the middle of the night to get married nowadays.'

'And suppose Mr Branbridge dies?'

'Alive or dead, I mean to be married on Thursday!' John answered, lighting a cigar and unfolding the *Times*.

At Peasemarsh station we said 'goodbye', and he got out, and I saw him ride off. I went on to London, where I stayed the night.

When I got home the next afternoon, a very wet one, by the way, my sister greeted me with: 'Where's Mr Charrington?'

'Goodness knows,' I answered testily. Every man since Cain has resented that kind of question.

'I thought you might have heard from him,' she went on, 'as you give him away tomorrow.'

'Isn't he back?' I asked, for I had confidently expected to find him at home.

'No, Geoffrey' – my sister always had a way of jumping to conclusions, especially such conclusions as were least favourable to her fellow-creatures – 'he has not returned, and, what is more, you may depend upon it, he won't. You mark my words, there'll be no wedding tomorrow.'

My sister Fanny has a power of annoying me which no other human being possesses.

'You mark my words,' I retorted with asperity, 'you had better give up making such a thundering idiot of yourself. There'll be more wedding tomorrow than ever you'll take first part in.'

But though I could snarl confidently to my sister, I did not feel so comfortable when, late that night, I, standing on the doorstep of John's house, heard that he had not returned. I went home gloomily through the rain. Next morning brought a brilliant blue sky, gold sun, and all such softness of air and beauty of cloud as go to make up a perfect day. I woke with a vague feeling of having gone to bed anxious, and of being rather averse from facing that anxiety in the light of full wakefulness.

With my shaving-water came a letter from John which relieved my mind, and sent me up to the Fosters with a light heart.

May was in the garden. I saw her blue gown among the holly-hocks as the lodge gates swung to behind me. So I did not go up to the house, but turned aside down the turfed path.

'He's written to you too,' she said, without preliminary greeting, when I reached her side.

'Yes, I'm to meet him at the station at three, and come straight on to the church.'

Her face looked pale, but there was a brightness in her eyes and a softness about the mouth that spoke of renewed happiness.

'Mr Branbridge begged him so to stay another night that he had not the heart to refuse,' she went on. 'He is so kind, but . . . I wish he hadn't stayed.'

I was at the station at half-past two. I felt rather annoyed with John. It seemed a sort of slight to the beautiful girl who loved him, that he should come, as it were out of breath, and with the dust of travel upon him, to take her hand, which some of us would have given the best years of our lives to take.

But when the three o'clock train glided in and glided out again, having brought no passengers to our little station, I was more than annoyed. There was no other train for thirty-five minutes; I calculated that, with much hurry, we might just get to the church in time for the ceremony; but, oh, what a fool to miss that first train! What other man would have done it?

That thirty-five minutes seemed a year, as I wandered round the station reading the advertisements and the time-tables and the company's bye-laws, and getting more and more angry with John Charrington. This confidence in his own power of getting everything he wanted the minute he wanted it, was leading him too far.

I hate waiting. Everyone hates waiting, but I believe I hate it more than anyone else does. The three-thirty-five was late too, of course.

I ground my pipe between my teeth and stamped with impatience as I watched the signals. Click. The signal went down. Five minutes later I flung myself into the carriage that I had brought for John.

'Drive to the church!' I said, as someone shut the door. 'Mr Charrington hasn't come by this train.'

Anxiety now replaced anger. What had become of this man? Could he have been taken suddenly ill? I had never known him have a day's illness in his life. And even so he might have telegraphed. Some awful accident must have happened to him. The thought that he had played her false never, no, not for a moment, entered my head. Yes, something terrible had happened to him, and on me lay the task of telling his bride. I almost wished the carriage would upset and break my head, so that someone else might tell her.

It was five minutes to four as we drew up at the churchyard. A double row of eager onlookers lined the path from lych-gate to porch. I sprang from the carriage and passed up between them. Our gardener had a good front place near the door. I stopped.

'Are they still waiting, Byles?' I asked, simply to gain time, for of course I knew they were, by the waiting crowd's attentive attitude.

'Waiting, sir? No, no, sir; why it must be over by now.'

'Over! Then Mr Charrington's come?'

'To the minute, sir; must have missed you somehow, and I say, sir,' lowering his voice, 'I never see Mr John the least bit so afore, but my opinion is he's 'ad more than a drop; I wouldn't be going too far if I said he's been drinking pretty free. His clothes was all dusty and his face like a sheet. I tell you I didn't like the looks of him at all, and the folks inside are saying all sorts of things. You'll see, something's gone very wrong with Mr John, and he's tried liquor. He looked like a ghost, and he went in with his eyes straight before him, with never a look or a word for none of us; him that was always such a gentleman.'

I had never heard Byles make so long a speech. The crowd in the churchyard were talking in whispers, and getting ready rice and slippers to throw at the bride and bridegroom. The ringers were ready with their hands on the ropes, to ring out the merry peal as the bride and bridegroom should come out.

A murmur from the church announced them; out they came. Byles was right. John Charrington did not look himself. There was dust on his coat, his hair was disarranged. He seemed to have been in some row, for there was a black mark above his eyebrow. He was deathly pale. But his pallor was not greater than that of the bride, who might have been carved in ivory – dress, veil, orange-blossoms, face and all.

As they passed out, the ringers stooped – there were six of them – and then, on the ears expecting the gay wedding peal, came the slow tolling of the passing bell.

A thrill of horror at so foolish a jest from the ringers passed through us all. But the ringers themselves dropped the ropes and fled like rabbits out into the sunlight. The bride shuddered, and grey shadows came about her mouth, but the bridegroom led her on down the path where the people stood with handfuls of rice; but the handfuls were never thrown, and the wedding bells never rang. In vain the ringers were urged to remedy their mistake; they protested, with many whispered expletives, that they had not rung that bell; that they would see themselves further before they'd ring anything more that day.

In a hush, like the hush in a chamber of death, the bridal pair passed into their carriage and its door slammed behind them.

Then the tongues were loosed. A babel of anger, wonder, conjecture from the guests and the spectators.

'If I'd seen his condition, sir,' said old Foster to me as we drove off, 'I would have stretched him on the floor of the church, sir, by Heaven I would, before I'd have let him marry my daughter!'

Then he put his head out of the window.

'Drive like hell,' he cried to the coachman; 'don't spare the horses.'

We passed the bride's carriage. I forbore to look at it, and old Foster turned his head away and swore.

We stood in the hall doorway, in the blazing afternoon sun, and in about half a minute we heard wheels crunching the gravel. When the carriage stopped in front of the steps, old Foster and I ran down.

'Great Heaven, the carriage is empty! And yet –'

I had the door open in a minute, and this is what I saw –

No sign of John Charrington; and of May, his wife, only a huddled heap of white satin, lying half on the floor of the carriage and half on the seat.

'I drove straight here, sir,' said the coachman, as the bride's father lifted her out, 'and I'll swear no-one got out of the carriage.'

We carried her into the house in her bridal dress, and drew back her veil. I saw her face. Shall I ever forget it? White, white, and drawn with agony and horror, bearing such a look of terror as I have never seen since, except in dreams. And her hair, her radiant blonde hair, I tell you it was white like snow.

As we stood, her father and I, half mad with the horror and mystery of it, a boy came up the avenue – a telegraph boy. They brought the orange envelope to me. I tore it open.

John Charrington was thrown from the dog-cart on his way to the station at half-past one. Killed on the spot.

Branbridge, Peasemarsh Place

And he was married to May Foster in our Parish Church at *half past three*, in presence of half the parish!

'*I shall be married on Thursday dead or alive!*'

What had passed in that carriage on the homeward drive? No-one knows – no-one will ever know.

Before a week was over they laid her beside her husband in the churchyard where they had kept their love-trysts.

Thus is the story of John Charrington's wedding.

# The Shadow

This is not an artistically rounded off ghost story, and nothing is explained in it, and there seems to be no reason why any of it should have happened. But that is no reason why it should not be told. You must have noticed that all the real ghost stories you have ever come close to are like this in these respects – no explanation, no logical coherence. Here is the story.

There were three of us and another, but she had fainted suddenly at the second extra of the Christmas dance, and had been put to bed in the dressing-room next to the room which we three shared. It had been one of those jolly, old-fashioned dances where nearly everybody stays the night, and the big country house is stretched to its utmost containing – guests harbouring on sofas, couches, settles, and even mattresses on floors. Some of the young men actually, I believe, slept on the great dining-table. We had talked of our partners, as girls will, and then the stillness of the manor house, broken only by the whisper of the wind in the cedar branches, and the scraping of their harsh fingers against our window panes, had pricked us to such a luxurious confidence in our surroundings of bright chintz and candle-flame and firelight, that we had dared to talk of ghosts – in which, we all said, we did not believe one bit. We had told the story of the phantom coach, and the horribly strange bed, and the lady in the sacque, and the house in Berkeley Square.

We none of us believed in ghosts, but my heart, at least, seemed to leap to my throat and choke me there, when a tap came to our door – a tap faint, not to be mistaken.

'Who's there?' said the youngest of us, craning a lean neck towards the door. It opened slowly, and I give you my word the instant of suspense that followed is still reckoned among my life's least confident moments. Almost at once the door opened fully, and Miss Eastwich, my aunt's housekeeper, companion and general stand-by, looked in on us.

We all said 'Come in', but she stood there. She was, at all normal hours, the most silent woman I have ever known. She stood and looked at us, and shivered a little. So did we – for in those days corridors were not warmed by hot-water pipes, and the air from the door was keen.

'I saw your light,' she said at last, 'and I thought it was late for you to be up – after all this gaiety. I thought perhaps –' her glance turned towards the door of the dressing-room.

'No,' I said, 'she's fast asleep.' I should have added a good-night, but the youngest of us forestalled my speech. She did not know Miss Eastwich as we others did; did not know how her persistent silence had built a wall round her – a wall that no-one dared to break down with the commonplaces of talk, or the littlenesses of mere human relationship. Miss Eastwich's silence had taught us to treat her as a machine; and as other than a machine we never dreamed of treating her. But the youngest of us had seen Miss Eastwich for the first time that day. She was young, crude, ill-balanced, subject to blind, calf-like impulses. She was also the heiress of a rich tallow-chandler, but that has nothing to do with this part of the story. She jumped up from the hearth-rug, her unsuitably rich silk lace-trimmed dressing-gown falling back from her thin collar-bones, and ran to the door and put an arm round Miss Eastwich's prim, lisse-encircled neck. I gasped. I should as soon have dared to embrace Cleopatra's Needle. 'Come in,' said the youngest of us – 'come in and get warm. There's lots of cocoa left.' She drew Miss Eastwich in and shut the door.

The vivid light of pleasure in the housekeeper's pale eyes went through my heart like a knife. It would have been so easy to put an arm round her neck, if one had only thought she wanted an arm there. But it was not I who had thought that – and indeed, my arm might not have brought the light evoked by the thin arm of the youngest of us.

'Now,' the youngest went on eagerly, 'you shall have the very biggest, nicest chair, and the cocoa-pot's here on the hob as hot as hot – and we've all been telling ghost stories, only we don't believe in them a bit; and when you get warm you ought to tell one too.'

Miss Eastwich – that model of decorum and decently done duties, tell a ghost story!

'You're sure I'm not in your way,' Miss Eastwich said, stretching her hands to the blaze. I wondered whether housekeepers have fires in their rooms even at Christmas time. 'Not a bit' – I said it, and I hope I said it as warmly as I felt it. 'I – Miss Eastwich – I'd have asked you to come in other times – only I didn't think you'd care for girls' chatter.'

The third girl, who was really of no account, and that's why I have not said anything about her before, poured cocoa for our guest. I put my fleecy Madeira shawl round her shoulders. I could not think of anything else to do for her, and I found myself wishing desperately to do something. The smiles she gave us were quite pretty. People can smile prettily at forty or fifty, or even later, though girls don't realise this. It occurred to me, and this was another knife-thrust, that I had never seen Miss Eastwich smile – a real smile, before. The pale smiles of dutiful acquiescence were not of the same blood as this dimpling, happy, transfiguring look.

'This is very pleasant,' she said, and it seemed to me that I had never before heard her real voice. It did not please me to think that at the cost of cocoa, a fire, and my arm round her neck, I might have heard this new voice any time these six years.

'We've been telling ghost stories,' I said. 'The worst of it is, we don't believe in ghosts. No-one we know has ever seen one.'

'It's always what somebody told somebody, who told somebody you know,' said the youngest of us, 'and you can't believe that, can you?'

'What the soldier said, is not evidence,' said Miss Eastwich. Will it be believed that the little Dickens quotation pierced one more keenly than the new smile or the new voice?

'And all the ghost stories are so beautifully rounded off – a murder committed on the spot – or a hidden treasure, or a warning . . . I think that makes them harder to believe. The most horrid ghost-story I ever heard was one that was quite silly.'

'Tell it.'

'I can't – it doesn't sound anything to tell. Miss Eastwich ought to tell one.'

'Oh do,' said the youngest of us, and her salt cellars loomed dark, as she stretched her neck eagerly and laid an entreating arm on our guest's knee.

'The only thing that I ever knew of was – was hearsay,' she said slowly, 'till just the end.'

I knew she would tell her story, and I knew she had never before told it, and I knew she was only telling it now because she was proud, and this seemed the only way to pay for the fire and the cocoa, and the laying of that arm round her neck.

'Don't tell it,' I said suddenly. 'I know you'd rather not.'

'I daresay it would bore you,' she said meekly, and the youngest of us, who, after all, did not understand everything, glared resentfully at me.

'We should just *love* it,' she said. '*Do* tell us. Never mind if it isn't a real, proper, fixed up story. I'm certain anything *you* think ghostly would be quite too beautifully horrid for anything.'

Miss Eastwich finished her cocoa and reached up to set the cup on the mantelpiece.

'It can't do any harm,' she said half to herself, 'they don't believe in ghosts, and it wasn't exactly a ghost either. And they're all over twenty – they're not babies.'

There was a breathing time of hush and expectancy. The fire crackled and the gas suddenly glared higher because the billiard lights had been put out. We heard the steps and voices of the men going along the corridors.

'It is really hardly worth telling,' Miss Eastwich said doubtfully, shading her faded face from the fire with her thin hand.

We all said 'Go on – oh, go on – do!'

'Well,' she said, 'twenty years ago – and more than that – I had two friends, and I loved them more than anything in the world. And they married each other –'

She paused, and I knew just in what way she had loved each of them. The youngest of us said – 'How awfully nice for you. Do go on.'

She patted the youngest's shoulder, and I was glad that I had understood, and that the youngest of all hadn't. She went on.

'Well, after they were married, I did not see much of them for a year or two; and then he wrote and asked me to come and stay, because his wife was ill, and I should cheer her up, and cheer him up as well; for it was a gloomy house, and he himself was growing gloomy too.'

I knew, as she spoke, that she had every line of that letter by heart.

'Well, I went. The address was in Lee, near London; in those days there were streets and streets of new villa-houses growing up round old brick mansions standing in their own grounds, with red walls round, you know, and a sort of flavour of coaching days, and post-chaises, and Blackheath highwaymen about them. He had said the house was gloomy, and it was called "The Firs", and I imagined my cab going through a dark, winding shrubbery, and drawing up in front of one of these sedate, old, square houses. Instead, we drew up in front of a large, smart villa, with iron railings, gay encaustic tiles leading from the iron gate to the stained-glass-panelled door, and for shrubbery only a few stunted cypresses and aucubas in the tiny front garden. But inside it was all warm and welcoming. He met me at the door.'

She was gazing into the fire, and I knew she had forgotten us. But the youngest girl of all still thought it was to us she was telling her story.

'He met me at the door,' she said again, 'and thanked me for coming, and asked me to forgive the past.'

'What past?' said that high priestess of the *inàpropos*, the youngest of all.

'Oh – I suppose he meant because they hadn't invited me before, or something,' said Miss Eastwich worriedly, 'but it's a very dull story, I find, after all, and –'

'Do go on,' I said – then I kicked the youngest of us, and got up to rearrange Miss Eastwich's shawl, and said in blatant dumb show, over the shawled shoulder: 'Shut up, you little idiot –'

After another silence, the housekeeper's new voice went on.

'They were very glad to see me, and I was very glad to be there. You girls, now, have such troops of friends, but these two were all I had – all I had ever had. Mabel wasn't exactly ill, only weak and excitable. I thought he seemed more ill than she did. She went to bed early and before she went, she asked me to keep him company through his last pipe, so we went into the dining room and sat in the two armchairs on each side of the fireplace. They were covered with green leather, I remember. There were bronze groups of horses and a black marble clock on the mantelpiece – all wedding-presents. He poured out some whisky for himself, but he hardly touched it. He sat looking into the fire. At last I said: "What's wrong? Mabel looks as well as you could expect."

'He said, "Yes – but I don't know from one day to another that she won't begin to notice something wrong. That's why I wanted you to come. You were always so sensible and strong-minded, and Mabel's like a little bird on a flower."

'I said yes, of course, and waited for him to go on. I thought he must be in debt, or in trouble of some sort. So I just waited. Presently he said: "Margaret, this is a very peculiar house –" he always called me Margaret. You see we'd been such old friends. I told him I thought the house was very pretty, and fresh, and homelike – only a little too new – but that fault would mend with time. He said: "It *is* new: that's just it. We're the first people who've ever lived in it. If it were an old house, Margaret, I should think it was haunted."

'I asked if he had seen anything. "No," he said, "not yet."

' "Heard then?" said I.

' "No – not heard either," he said "but there's a sort of feeling: I can't describe it – I've seen nothing and I've heard nothing, but

I've been so near to seeing and hearing, just near, that's all. And something follows me about – only when I turn round, there's never anything, only my shadow. And I always feel that I *shall* see the thing next minute – but I never do – not quite – it's always just not visible."

'I thought he'd been working rather hard – and tried to cheer him up by making light of all this. It was just nerves, I said. Then he said he had thought I could help him, and did I think anyone he had wronged could have laid a curse on him and did I believe in curses. I said I didn't – and the only person anyone could have said he had wronged forgave him freely, I knew, if there was anything to forgive. So I told him this too.'

It was I, not the youngest of us, who knew the name of that person, wronged and forgiving.

'So then I said he ought to take Mabel away from the house and have a complete change. But he said No; Mabel had got everything in order, and he could never manage to get her away just now without explaining everything – "and, above all," he said, "she mustn't guess there's anything wrong. I daresay I shan't feel quite such a lunatic now you're here."

'So we said goodnight.'

'Is that all the story!' said the third girl, striving to convey that even as it stood it was a good story.

'That's only the beginning,' said Miss Eastwich. 'Whenever I was alone with him he used to tell me the same thing over and over again, and at first when I began to notice things, I tried to think that it was his talk that had upset my nerves. The odd thing was that it wasn't only at night – but in broad daylight – and particularly on the stairs and passages. On the staircase the feeling used to be so awful that I have had to bite my lips till they bled to keep myself from running upstairs at full speed. Only I knew if I did I should go mad at the top. There was always something behind me – exactly as he had said – something that one could just not see. And a sound that one could just not hear. There was a long corridor at the top of the house. I have sometimes almost seen something – you know how one sees things without looking – but if I turned round, it seemed as if the thing drooped and melted into my shadow. There was a little window at the end of the corridor.

'Downstairs there was another corridor, something like it, with a cupboard at one end and the kitchen at the other. One night I went down into the kitchen to heat some milk for Mabel. The servants had gone to bed. As I stood by the fire, waiting for the milk to boil, I glanced through the open door and along the passage. I never could keep my eyes on what I was doing in that house. The cupboard door was partly open; they used to keep empty boxes and things in it. And, as I looked, I knew that now it was not going to be "almost" any more. Yet I said, "Mabel?" not because I thought it could be Mabel who was crouching down there, half in and half out of the cupboard. The thing was grey at first, and then it was black. And when I whispered, "Mabel", it seemed to sink down till it lay like a pool of ink on the floor, and then its edges drew in, and it seemed to flow, like ink when you tilt up the paper you have spilt it on, and it flowed into the cupboard till it was all gathered into the shadow there. I saw it go quite plainly. The gas was full on in the kitchen. I screamed aloud, but even then, I'm thankful to say, I had enough sense to upset the boiling milk, so that when he came downstairs three steps at a time, I had the excuse for my scream of a scalded hand. The explanation satisfied Mabel, but next night he said: – "Why didn't you tell me? It was that cupboard. All the horror of the house comes out of that. Tell me – have you seen anything yet? Or is it only the nearly seeing and nearly hearing still?"

'I said, "You must tell me first what you've seen." He told me, and his eyes wandered, as he spoke, to the shadows by the curtains, and I turned up all three gas lights, and lit the candles on the mantelpiece. Then we looked at each other and said we were both mad, and thanked God that Mabel at least was sane. For what he had seen was what I had seen.

'After that I hated to be alone with a shadow, because at any moment I might see something that would crouch, and sink, and lie like a black pool, and then slowly draw itself into the shadow that was nearest. Often that shadow was my own. The thing came first at night, but afterwards there was no hour safe from it. I saw it at dawn and at noon, in the dusk and in the firelight, and always it crouched and sank, and was a pool that flowed into some shadow and became part of it. And always I saw it with a straining of the eyes – a pricking and aching. It seemed as though I could only just see it, as if my sight, to see it, had to be strained to the uttermost. And still the sound was in the house – the sound that I could just not hear. At last, one morning early, I did hear it. It was close behind me, and it was only a sigh. It was worse than the thing that crept into the shadows.

'I don't know how I bore it. I couldn't have borne it, if I hadn't been so fond of them both. But I knew in my heart that, if he had no-one to whom he could speak openly, he would go mad, or tell Mabel. His was not a very strong character; very sweet, and kind, and gentle, but not strong. He was always easily led. So I stayed on and bore up, and we were very cheerful, and made little jokes, and tried to be amusing when Mabel was with us. But when we were alone, we did not try to be amusing. And sometimes a day or two would go by without our seeing or hearing anything, and we should perhaps have fancied that we had fancied what we had seen and heard – only there was always the feeling of there being something about the house, that one could just not hear and not see. Sometimes we used to try not to talk about it, but generally we talked of nothing else at all. And the weeks went by, and Mabel's baby was born. The nurse and the doctor said that both mother and child were doing well. He and I sat late in the dining-room that night. We had neither of us seen or heard anything for three days; our anxiety about Mabel was lessened. We talked of the future – it seemed then so much brighter than the past. We arranged that, the moment she was fit to be moved, he should take her away to the sea, and I should superintend the moving of their furniture into the new house he had already chosen. He was gayer than I had seen him since his marriage – almost like his old self. When I said goodnight to him, he said a lot of things about my having been a comfort to them both. I hadn't done anything much, of course, but still I am glad he said them.

'Then I went upstairs, almost for the first time without that feeling of something following me. I listened at Mabel's door. Everything was quiet. I went on towards my own room, and in an instant I felt that there *was* something behind me. I turned. It was crouching there; it sank, and the black fluidness of it seemed to be sucked under the door of Mabel's room.

'I went back. I opened the door a listening inch. All was still. And then I heard a sigh close behind me. I opened the door and went in. The nurse and the baby were asleep. Mabel was asleep too – she looked so pretty – like a tired child – the baby was cuddled up into one of her arms with its tiny head against her side. I prayed then that Mabel might never know the terrors that he and I had known. That those little ears might never hear any but pretty sounds, those clear eyes never see any but pretty sights. I did not dare to pray for a long time after that. Because my prayer was answered. She never saw, never heard anything more in this world. And now I could do nothing more for him or for her.

'When they had put her in her coffin, I lighted wax candles round her, and laid the horrible white flowers that people will send near her and then I saw he had followed me. I took his hand to lead him away.

'At the door we both turned. It seemed to us that we heard a sigh. He would have sprung to her side, in I don't know what mad, glad hope. But at that instant we both saw it. Between us and the coffin, first grey, then black, it crouched an instant, then sank and liquefied – and was gathered together and drawn till it ran into the nearest shadow. And the nearest shadow was the shadow of Mabel's coffin. I left the next day. His mother came. She had never liked me.'

Miss Eastwich paused. I think she had quite forgotten us.

'Didn't you see him again?' asked the youngest of us all.

'Only once,' Miss Eastwich answered, 'and something black crouched then between him and me. But it was only his second wife, crying beside his coffin. It's not a cheerful story is it? And it doesn't lead anywhere. I've never told anyone else. I think it was seeing his daughter that brought it all back.'

She looked towards the dressing-room door.

'Mabel's baby?'

'Yes – and exactly like Mabel, only with his eyes.'

The youngest of all had Miss Eastwich's hands, and was petting them.

Suddenly the woman wrenched her hands away, and stood at her gaunt height, her hands clenched, eyes straining. She was looking at something that we could not see, and I know what the man in the Bible meant when he said: 'The hair of my flesh stood up.'

What she saw seemed not quite to reach the height of the dressing-room door handle. Her eyes followed it down, down – widening and widening. Mine followed them – all the nerves of them seemed strained to the uttermost – and I almost saw – or did I quite see? I can't be certain. But we all heard the long-drawn, quivering sigh. And to each of us it seemed to be breathed just behind us.

It was I who caught up the candle – it dripped all over my trembling hand – and was dragged by Miss Eastwich to the girl who had fainted during the second extra. But it was the youngest of all whose lean arms were round the housekeeper when we turned away, and that have been round her many a time since, in the new home where she keeps house for the youngest of us.

The doctor who came in the morning said that Mabel's daughter had died of heart disease – which she had inherited from her mother. It was that that had made her faint during the second extra. But I have sometimes wondered whether she may not have inherited something from her father. I have never been able to forget the look on her dead face.

# The Five Senses

Professor Boyd Thompson's services to the cause of science are usually spoken of as inestimable, and so indeed they probably are, since in science, as in the rest of life, one thing leads to another, and you never know where anything is going to stop. At any rate, inestimable or not, they are world-renowned, and he with them. The discoveries which he gave to his time are a matter of common knowledge among biological experts, and the sudden ending of his experimental activities caused a few days' wonder in even lay circles. Quite unintelligent people told each other that it seemed a pity, and persons on omnibuses exchanged commonplaces starred with his name.

But the real meaning and cause of that ending have been studiously hidden, as well as the events which immediately preceded it. A veil has been drawn over all the things that people would have liked to know, and it is only now that circumstances so arrange themselves as to make it possible to tell the whole story. I propose to avail myself of this possibility.

It will serve no purpose for me to explain how the necessary knowledge came into my possession; but I will say that the story was only in part pieced together by me. Another hand is responsible for much of the detail, and for a certain occasional emotionalism which is, I believe, wholly foreign to my own style. In my original statement of the following facts I dealt fully, as I am, I may say without immodesty, qualified to do, with all the scientific points of the narrative. But these details were judged, unwisely as I think, to be needless to the expert, and unintelligible to the ordinary reader, and have therefore been struck out; the merest hints have been left as necessary links in the story. This appears to me to destroy most of its interest, but I admit that the elisions are perhaps justified. I have no desire to assist or encourage callow students in such experiments as those by which Professor Boyd Thompson brought his scientific career to an end.

Incredible as it may appear, Professor Boyd Thompson was once a little boy who wore white embroidered frocks and blue sashes; in that state he caught flies and pulled off their wings to find out how they flew. He did not find out, and Lucilla, his little girl-cousin, also in white frocks, cried over the dead, dismembered flies, and buried them in little paper coffins. Later, he wore a holland blouse with a belt of leather, and watched the development of tadpoles in a tin bath in the stable yard. A microscope was, on his eighth birthday, presented to him by an affluent uncle. The uncle showed him how to surprise the secrets of a drop of pond water, which, limpid to the eye, confessed under the microscope to a whole cosmogony of strenuous and undesirable careers. At the age of ten, Arthur Boyd Thompson was sent to a private school, its Head-master an acolyte of Science, who esteemed himself to be a high priest of Huxley and Tyndall, a devotee of Darwin. Thence to the choice of medicine as a profession was, when the choice was insisted on by the elder Boyd Thompson, a short, plain step. Inorganic chemistry failed to charm, and under the cloak of Medicine and Surgery the growing fever of scientific curiosity could be sated on bodies other than the cloak-wearer's. He became a medical student and an enthusiast for vivisection.

The bow of Apollo was not always bent. In a rest-interval, the summer vacation, to be exact, he met again the cousin – second, once removed – Lucilla, and loved her. They were betrothed. It was a long, bright summer full of sunshine, garden-parties, picnics, archery – a decaying amusement – and croquet, then coming to its own. He exulted in the distinction already crescent in his career, but some half-formed wholly-unconscious desire to shine with increased lustre in the eyes of the beloved, caused him to invite, for the holidays' ultimate week, a fellow student, one who knew and could testify to the quality of the laurels already encircling the head of a young scientist. The friend came, testified, and in a vibrating interview under the lime-trees of Lucilla's people's garden, Mr Boyd Thompson learned that Lucilla never could, never would love or marry a vivisectionist.

The moon hung low and yellow in the spacious calm of the sky; the hour was propitious, the lovers fond. Mr Boyd Thompson vowed that his scientific research should henceforth deal wholly with departments into which the emotions of the non-scientific cannot enter. He went back to London, and within the week bought four dozen frogs, twelve guinea-pigs, five cats, and a spaniel. His scientific aspirations met his love-longings, and did not fight them. You cannot fight beings of another world. He took part in a debate on 'Blood Pressure', which created some little stir in medical circles, spoke eloquently, and distinction surrounded him with a halo.

He wrote to Lucilla three times a week, took his degree, and published that celebrated paper of his which set the whole scientific world by the ears, 'The Action of Choline on the Nervous System', I think its name was.

Lucilla surreptitiously subscribed to a press-cutting agency for all snippets of print relating to her lover. Three weeks after the publication of that paper, which really was the beginning of Professor Boyd Thompson's fame, she wrote to him from her home in Kent.

ARTHUR – you have been doing it again. You know how I love you, and I believe you love me; but you must choose between loving me and torturing dumb animals. If you don't choose right, then it's goodbye, and God forgive you.

Your Poor Lucilla, who loved you very dearly.

He read the letter, and the human heart in him winced and whined. Yet not so deeply now, nor so loudly, but that he bethought himself to seek out a friend and pupil, who would watch certain experiments, attend to the cutting of certain sections, before he started for Tenterden, where she lived. There was no station at Tenterden in those days, but a twelve-mile walk did not dismay him.

Lucilla's home was one of those houses of brave proportions and an inalienable bourgeois stateliness, which stand back a little from the noble High Street of that most beautiful of Kentish towns. He came there pleasantly exercised, his boots dusty, and his throat dry, and stood on the snowy doorstep, beneath the Jacobean lintel. He looked down the wide, beautiful street, raised eyebrows and shrugged uneasy shoulders within his professional frock-coat.

'It's all so difficult,' he said to himself.

Lucilla received him in a drawing-room scented with last year's rose leaves, and fresh with chintz that had been washed a dozen times. She stood, very pale and frail; her blonde hair was not teased into fluffiness, and rounded over the chignon of the period, but banded Madonna-wise, crowning her with heavy burnished plaits. Her gown was of white muslin, and round her neck black velvet passed, supporting a gold locket. He knew whose picture it held. The loose bell sleeves fell away from the slender arms with little black velvet bracelets, and she leaned one hand on a chiffonier of carved rosewood, on whose marble top stood, under a glass case, a Chinese pagoda, carved in ivory, and two Bohemian glass vases with medallions representing young women nursing pigeons. There were white curtains of darned net, in the fireplace white ravelled muslin spread a cascade brightened with threads of tinsel. A canary sang in a green cage, wainscoted with yellow tarlatan, and two red rosebuds stood in lank specimen glasses on the mantel-piece.

Every article of furniture in the room spoke eloquently of the sheltered life, the iron obstinacy of the well-brought-up.

It was a scene that invaded his mental vision many a time, in the laboratory, in the lecture-room. It symbolised many things, all dear, and all impossible.

They talked awkwardly, miserably. And always it came round to this same thing.

'But you don't mean it,' he said, and at last came close to her.

'I do mean it,' she said, very white, very trembling, very determined.

'But it's my life,' he pleaded, 'it's the life of thousands. You don't understand.'

'I understand that dogs are tortured. I can't bear it.'

He caught at her hand.

'Don't,' she said. 'When I think what that hand does!'

'Dearest,' he said very earnestly, 'which is the more important, a dog or a human being?'

'They're all God's creatures,' she flashed, unorthodoxly orthodox. 'They're all God's creatures,' with much more that he heard, and pitied, and smiled at miserably in his heart.

'You don't understand,' he kept saying, stemming the flood of her rhetorical pleadings. 'Spencer Wells alone has found out wonderful things, just with experiments on rabbits.'

'Don't tell me,' she said, 'I don't want to hear.'

The conventions of their day forbade that he should tell her anything plainly. He took refuge in generalities. 'Spencer Wells, that operation he perfected, it's restored thousands of women to their husbands – saved thousands of women for their children.'

'I don't care what he's done – it's wrong if it's done in that way.'

It was on that day that they parted, after more than an hour and more than two, of mutual misunderstood reiteration. He, she said, was brutal. And besides it was plain that he did not love her. To him, she seemed unreasonable, narrow, prejudiced, blind to the high ideals of the new science.

'Then it's goodbye,' he said at last. 'If I gave way, you'd only despise me. Because I should despise myself. It's no good. Goodbye, dear.'

'Goodbye,' she said. 'I know I'm right. You'll know I am, some day.'

'Never,' he answered, more moved and in a more diffused sense than he had ever believed he could be. 'I can't set my pleasure in you against the good of the whole world.'

'If that's all you think of me,' she said, and her silk and her muslin whirled from the room.

He walked back to Staplehurst, thrilled with the conflict. The thrill died down, went out, and left as ashes a cold resolve.

That was the end of Mr Boyd Thompson's engagement.

It was quite by accident that he made his greatest discovery. There are those who hold that all great discoveries are accident – or Providence. The terms are in this connection, interchangeable. He plunged into work to wash away the traces of his soul's wounds, as a man plunges into water to wash off red blood. And he swam there, perhaps, a little blindly. The injection with which he treated that white rabbit was not compounded of the drugs he had intended to use. He could not lay his hand on the thing he wanted, and in that sort of frenzy of experiment, to which no scientific investigator is wholly a stranger, he cast about for a new idea. The thing that came to his hand was a drug that he had never in his normal mind intended to use – an unaccredited, wild, magic, medicine obtained by a missionary from some savage South Sea tribe and brought home as an example of the ignorance of the heathen.

And it worked a miracle.

He had been fighting his way through the unbending opposition of known facts, he had been struggling in the shadows, and this discovery was like the blinding light that meets a man's eyes when his pickaxe knocks a hole in a dark cave, and he finds himself face to face with the sun. The effect was undoubted. Now it behoved him to make sure of the cause, to eliminate all those other factors to which that effect might have been due. He experimented cautiously, slowly. These things take years, and the years he did not grudge. He was never tired, never impatient; the slightest variations, the least indications, were eagerly observed, faithfully recorded.

His whole soul was in his work, Lucilla was the one beautiful memory of his life. But she was a memory. The reality was this discovery, the accident, the Providence.

Day followed day, all alike, and yet each taking, almost unperceived, one little step forward; or stumbling into sudden sloughs, those losses and lapses that take days and weeks to retrieve. He was Professor, and his hair was grey at the temples before his achievement rose before him, beautiful, inevitable, austere in its completed splendour, as before the triumphant artist rises the finished work of his art.

He had found out one of the secrets with which Nature has crammed her dark hiding-places. He had discovered the hidden possibilities of sensation. In plain English, his researches had led him thus far; he had found – by accident or by Providence – the way to intensify sensation. Vaguely, incredulously, he had perceived his discovery; the rabbits and guinea-pigs had demonstrated it plainly enough. Then there was a night when he became aware that those results must be checked by something else. He must work out in marble the form he had worked out in clay. He knew that by this drug, which had, so to speak, thrust itself upon him, he could intensify the five senses of any of the inferior animals. Could he intensify those senses in man? If so, worlds beyond the grasp of his tired mind opened themselves before him. If so, he would have achieved a discovery, made a contribution to the science he had loved so well and followed at such a cost, a discovery equal to any that any man had ever made.

Ferrier, and Leo, and Horsley; those he would outshine. Galileo, Newton, Harvey; he would rank with these.

Could he find a human rabbit to submit to the test?

The soul of the man Lucilla had loved, turned and revolted. No: he had experimented on guinea-pigs and rabbits, but when it came to experimenting on men, there was only one man on whom he chose to use his new-found powers. Himself.

At least she would not have it to say that he was a coward, or unfair, when it came to the point of what a man could do and dare, could suffer and endure.

His big laboratory was silent and deserted. His assistants were gone, his private pupils dispersed. He was alone with the tools of his trade. Shelf on shelf of smooth stoppered bottles, drugs and stains, the long bench gleaming with beakers, test tubes, and the glass mansions of costly apparatus. In the shadows at the far end of the room, where the last going assistant had turned off the electric lights, strange shapes lurked, wicker-covered carboys, kinographs, galvano-meters, the faintly threatening aspect of delicate complex machines all wires and coils and springs, the gaunt form of the pendulum myograph, and certain well-worn tables and copper troughs, for which the moment had no use.

He knew that this drug with others, diversely compounded and applied, produced in animals an abnormal intensification of the senses; that it increased — nay, as it were magnified a thousandfold, the hearing, the sight, the touch — and he was almost sure, the senses of taste and smell. But of the extent of the increase he could form no exact estimate.

Should he tonight put himself in the position of one able to speak on these points with authority? Or should he go to the Royal Society's meeting, and hear that ass Netherby maunder yet once again about the Secretion of Lymph?

He pulled out his notebook and laid it open on the bench. He went to the locked cupboard, unfastened it with the bright key that hung instead of seal or charm at his watch-chain. He unfolded a paper and laid it on the bench where no-one coming in could fail to see it. Then he took out little bottles, three, four, five, polished a graduated glass and dropped into it slow, heavy drops. A larger bottle yielded a medium in which all mingled. He hardly hesitated at all before turning up his sleeve and slipping the tiny needle into his arm. He pressed the end of the syringe. The injection was made.

Its effect, though not immediate, was sudden. He had to close his eyes, staggered indeed and was glad of the stool near him; for the drug coursed through him as a hunt in full cry might sweep over untrodden plains. Then suddenly everything seemed to settle; he was no longer the helpless scene of incredible meetings, but

Professor Boyd Thompson who had injected a mixture of certain drugs, and was experiencing their effect.

His fingers, still holding the glass syringe, sent swift messages to his brain. When he looked down at his fingers, he saw that what they grasped was the smooth, slender tube of clear glass. What he felt that they held was a tremendous cylinder, rough to the touch. He wondered, even at the moment, why, if his sense of touch were indeed magnified to this degree, everything did not appear enormous – his ring, his collar. He examined the new phenomenon with cold care. It seemed that only that was enlarged on which his attention, his mind, was fixed. He kept his hand on the glass syringe, and thought of his ring, got his mind away from the tube, back again in time to feel it small between his fingers, grow, increase, and become big once more.

'So *that's* a success,' he said, and saw himself lay the thing down. It lay just in front of the rack of test tubes, to the eye just that little glass cylinder. To touch it was like a water-pipe on a house side, and the test tubes, when he touched them, like the pipes of a great organ.

'Success,' he said again, and mixed the antidote. For he had found the antidote in one of those flashes of intuition, imagination, genius, that light the ways of science as stars light the way of a ship in dark waters. The action of the antidote was enough for one night. He locked the cupboard, and, after all, was glad to listen to the maunderings of Netherby. It had been lonely there, in the atmosphere of complete success.

One by one, day by day, he tested the action of his drugs on his other senses. Without being technical, I had perhaps better explain that the compelling drug was, in each case, one and the same. Its action was directed to this set of nerves or that by means of the other drugs mixed with it. I trust this is clear?

The sense of smell was tested, and its laboratory, with its mingled odours, became abominable to him. Hardly could he stay himself from rushing forth into the outer air, to wash his nostrils in the clear coolness of Hampstead Heath. The sense of taste gave him, magnified a thousand times, the flavour of his after-dinner coffee, and other tastes, distasteful almost beyond the bearing point.

But 'Success,' he said, rinsing his mouth at the laboratory sink after the drinking of the antidote, 'all along the line, success.'

Then he tested the action of his discovery on the sense of hearing. And the sound of London came like the roar of a giant, yet when he fixed his attention on the movements of a fly, all other sounds ceased, and he heard the sound of the fly's feet on the shelf when it walked. Thus, in turn, he heard the creak of boards expanding in the heat, the movement of the glass stoppers that kept imprisoned in their proper bottles the giants of acid and alkali.

'Success!' he cried aloud, and his voice sounded in his ears like the shout of a monster overcoming primeval forces. 'Success! success!'

Remained only the eyes, and here, strangely enough, the Professor hesitated, faint with a sudden heartsickness. Following all intensification there must be reaction. What if the reaction exceeded that from which it reacted, what if the wave of tremendous sight, stemmed by the antidote ebbing, left him blind? But the spirit of the explorer in science is the spirit that explores African rivers, and sails amid white bergs to seek the undiscovered Pole.

He held the syringe with a firm hand, made the required puncture, and braced himself for the result. His eyes seemed to swell to great globes, to dwindle to microscopic globules, to swim in a flood of fire, to shrivel high and dry on a beach of hot sand. Then he saw, and the glass fell from his hand. For the whole of the stable earth seemed to be suddenly set in movement, even the air grew thick with vast overlapping shapeless shapes. He opined later that these were the microbes and bacilli that cover and fill all things, in this world that looks so clean and bright.

Concentrating his vision, he saw in the one day's little dust on the bottles myriads of creatures, crawling and writhing, alive. The proportions of the laboratory seemed but little altered. Its large lines and forms remained practically unchanged. It was the little things that were no longer little, the invisible things that were now invisible no longer. And he felt grateful for the first time in his life, for the limits set by Nature to the powers of the human body. He had increased those powers. If he let his eyes stray idly about, as one does in the waltz for example, all was much as it used to be. But the moment he looked steadily at any one thing, it became enormous.

He closed his eyes. Success here had gone beyond his wildest dreams. Indeed he could not but feel that success, taking the bit between its teeth, had perhaps gone just the least little bit too far.

And on the next day he decided to examine the drug in all its aspects, to court the intensification of all his senses which should set him in the position of supreme power over men and things, transform him from a Professor into a demigod.

The great question was, of course, how the five preparations of his drug would act on or against each other. Would it be intensification, or would they neutralise each other? Like all imaginative scientists, he was working with stuff perilously like the spells of magic, and certain things were not possible to be foretold. Besides, this drug came from a land of mystery and the knowledge of secrets which we call magic. He did not anticipate any increase in the danger of the experiment. Nevertheless he spent some hours in arranging and destroying papers, among others certain pages of the yellow note-book. After dinner he detained his man as, laden with the last tray, he was leaving the room.

'I may as well tell you, Parker,' the Professor said, moved by some impulse he had not expected, 'that you will benefit to some extent by my will. On conditions. If any accident should cut short my life, you will at once communicate with my solicitor, whose name you will now write down.'

The model man, trained by fifteen years of close personal

service, drew forth a notebook neat as the Professor's own, wrote in it neatly the address the Professor gave.

'Anything more, sir?' he asked, looking up, pencil in hand.

'No,' said the Professor, 'nothing more. Good-night, Parker.'

'Good-night, sir,' said the model man.

The next words the model man opened his lips to speak were breathed into the night tube of the nearest doctor.

'My master, Professor Boyd Thompson; could you come round at once, sir. I'm afraid it's very serious.'

It was half past six when the nearest doctor – Jones was his unimportant name – stooped over the lifeless body of the Professor.

He shook his head as he stood up and looked round the private laboratory on whose floor the body lay.

'His researches are over,' he said. 'Yes, he's dead. Been dead some hours. When did you find him?'

'I went to call my master as usual,' said Parker; 'he rises at six, summer and winter, sir. He was not in his room, and the bed had not been slept in. So I came in here, sir. It is not unusual for my master to work all night when he has been very interested in his experiments, and then he likes his coffee at six.'

'I see,' said Dr Jones. 'Well, you'd better rouse the house and fetch his own doctor. It's heart failure, of course, but I daresay he'd like to sign the certificate himself.'

'Can nothing be done?' said Parker, much affected.

'Nothing,' said Dr Jones. 'It's the common lot. You'll have to look out for another situation.'

'Yes, sir,' said Parker; 'he told me only last night what I was to do in case of anything happening to him. I wonder if he had any idea?'

'Some premonition, perhaps,' the doctor corrected.

The funeral was a very quiet one. So the late Professor Boyd Thompson had decreed in his will. He had arranged all details. The body was to be clothed in flannel, placed in an open coffin covered only with a linen sheet, and laid in the family mausoleum, a moss-grown building in the midst of a little park which surrounded Boyd Grange, the birthplace of the Boyd Thompsons. A little property in Sussex it was. The Professor sometimes went there for week-ends. He had left this property to Lucilla, with a last love-letter, in which he begged her to give his body the hospitality of the death-house, now hers with the rest of the estate. To Parker he left an annuity of two hundred pounds, on the condition that he should visit and enter the mausoleum once in every twenty-four hours for fourteen days after the funeral.

To this end the late Professor's solicitor decided that Parker had better reside at Boyd Grange for the said fortnight, and Parker, whose nerves seemed to be shaken, petitioned for company. This made easy the arrangement which the solicitor desired to make – of a witness to the carrying out by Parker of the provisions of the dead man's will. The solicitor's clerk was quite good company, and arm-in-arm with him Parker paid his first visit to the mausoleum. The little building stands in a glade of evergreen oaks. The trees are old and thick, and the narrow door is deep in shadow even on the sunniest day. Parker went to the mausoleum, peered through its square grating, but he did not go in. Instead, he listened, and his ears were full of silence.

'He's dead, right enough,' he said, with a doubtful glance at his companion.

'You ought to go in, oughtn't you?' said the solicitor's clerk.

'Go in yourself, if you like, Mr Pollack,' said Parker, suddenly angry; 'anyone who likes can go in, but it won't be me. If he was alive, it 'ud be different. I'd have done anything for *him*. But I ain't going in among all them dead and mouldering Thompsons. See? If we both say I did, it'll be just the same as me doing it.'

'So it will,' said the solicitor's clerk; 'but where do I come in?'

Parker explained to him where he came in, to their mutual content.

'Right you are,' said the clerk; 'on those terms I'm fly. And if we both say you did it, we needn't come to the beastly place again,' he added, shivering and glancing over his shoulder at the door with the grating.

'No more we need,' said Parker.

Behind the bars of the narrow door lay deeper shadows than those of the ilexes outside. And in the blackest of the shadow lay a man whose every sense was intensified as though by a magic potion. For when the Professor swallowed the five variants of his great discovery, each acted as he had expected it to act. But the union of the five vehicles conveying the drug to the nerves, which served his five senses, had paralysed every muscle. His hearing, taste, touch, scent and sight were intensified a thousandfold – as they had been in the individual experiments – but the man who felt all this exaggerated increase of sensation was powerless as a cat under kurali. He could not raise a finger, stir an eyelash. More, he could not breathe, nor did his body advise him of any need of breathing. And he had lain thus immobile and felt his body slowly grow cold; had heard in thunder the voices of Parker and the doctor; had felt the enormous hands of those who made his death-toilet; had smelt intolerably the camphor and lavender that they laid round him in the narrow, black bed; had tasted the mingled flavours of the drug and its five mediums; and, in an ecstasy of magnified sensation, had made the lonely train journey which coffins make, and known himself carried into the mausoleum and left there alone. And every sense was intensified, even his sense of time, so that it seemed to him that he had lain there for many years. And the effect of the drugs showed no sign of any diminution or reaction. Why had he not left directions for the injection of the antidote? It was one of those slips which wreck campaigns, cause the discovery of hidden crimes. It was a slip, and he had made it. He had thought of death, but in all the results he had anticipated, death's semblance had found no place. Well, he had made his bed, and he must lie on it. This narrow bed, whose scent of clean oak and French polish was distinct among the musty, intolerable odours of the charnel house.

It was perhaps twenty hours that he had lain there, powerless, immobile, listening to the sounds of unexplained movements about him, when he felt with a joy, almost like delirium, a faint quivering in the eyelids.

They had closed his eyes, and till now, they had remained closed. Now, with an effort as of one who lifts a grave-stone, he raised his eyelids. They closed again quickly, for the roof of the vault, at which he gazed earnestly, was alive with monsters; spiders, earwigs, crawling beetles and flies, far too small to have been perceived by normal eyes, spread giant forms over him. He closed his eyes and shuddered. It felt like a shudder, but no-one who had stood beside him could have noted any movement.

It was then that Parker came – and went.

Professor Boyd Thompson heard Parker's words, and lay listening to the thunder of Parker's retreating feet. He tried to move – to call out. But he could not. He lay there helpless, and somehow he thought of the dark end of the laboratory, where the assistant before leaving had turned out the electric lights.

He had nothing but his thoughts. He thought how he would lie there, and die there. The place was sequestered; no-one passed that way. Parker had failed him, and the end was not hard to picture. He might recover all his faculties, might be able to get up, able to scream, to shout, to tear at the bars. The bars were strong, and Parker would not come again. Well, he would try to face with a decent bravery whatever had to be faced.

Time, measureless, spread round. It seemed as though someone had stopped all the clocks in the world, as though he were not in time but in eternity. Only by the waxing and waning light he knew of the night and the day.

His brain was weary with the effort to move, to speak, to cry out. He lay, informed with something like despair – or fortitude. And then Parker came again. And this time a key grated in the lock. The Professor noted with rapture that it sounded no louder than a key should sound, turned in a lock that was rusty. Nor was the voice other than he had been used to hear it, when he was man alive and Parker's master. And –

'You can go in, of course, if you wish it, Miss,' said Parker disapprovingly; 'but it's not what I should advise myself. For me it's different,' he added on a sudden instinct of self-preservation; 'I've got to go in. Every day for a fortnight,' he added, pitying himself.

'I will go in, thank you,' said a voice. 'Yes, give me the candle, please. And you need not wait. I will lock the door when I come out.' Thus the voice spoke. And the voice was Lucilla's.

In all his life the Professor had never feared death or its trappings. Neither its physical repulsiveness, nor the supernatural terrors which cling about it, had he either understood or tolerated. But now, in one little instant, he did understand.

He heard Lucilla come in. A light held near him shone warm and red through his closed eyelids. And he knew that he had only to unclose those eyelids to see her face bending over him. And he could unclose them. Yet he would not. He lay there, still and straight in his coffin, and life swept through him in waves of returning power. Yet he lay like death. For he said, or something in him said: 'She believes me dead. If I open my eyes it will be like a dead man looking at her. If I move it will be a dead man moving under her eyes. People have gone mad for less. Lie still, lie still,' he told himself; 'take any risks yourself. There must be none for her.'

She had taken the candle away, set it down somewhere at a distance, and now she was kneeling beside him and her hand was under his head. He knew he could raise his arm and clasp her – and Parker would come back perhaps, when she did not return to the house, come back to find a man in grave-clothes, clasping a mad woman. He lay still. Then her kisses and tears fell on his face, and she murmured broken words of love and longing. But he lay still. At any cost he must lie still. Even at the cost of his own sanity, his own life. And the warmth of her hand under his head, her face against his, her kisses, her tears, set his blood flowing evenly and strongly. Her other arm lay on his breast, softly pressing over his heart. He would not move. He would be strong. If he were to be saved, it must be by some other way, not this.

Suddenly tears and kisses ceased; her every breath seemed to have stopped with these. She had drawn away from him. She spoke. Her voice came from above him. She was standing up.

'Arthur!' she said, 'Arthur!' Then he opened his eyes, the narrowest chink. But he could not see her. Only he knew she was moving towards the door. There had been a new quality in her tone, a thrill of fear, or hope was it? or at least of uncertainty? Should he move; should he speak? He dared not. He knew too well the fear that the normal human being has of death and the grave, the fear transcending love, transcending reason. Her voice was further away now. She was by the door. She was leaving him. If he let her go, it was an end of hope for him. If he did not let her go, an end, perhaps, of reason, for her. No.

'Arthur,' she said, 'I don't believe . . . I believe you can hear me. I'm going to get a doctor. If you *can* speak, speak to me.'

Her speaking ended, cut off short as a cord is cut by a knife. He did not speak. He lay in a conscious, forced rigidity.

'Speak if you can,' she implored, 'just one word!'

Then he said, very faintly, very distinctly, in a voice that seemed to come from a great way off, 'Lucilla!'

And at the word she screamed aloud pitifully, and leapt for the entrance; and he heard the rustle of her crape in the narrow door. Then he opened his eyes wide, and raised himself on his elbow. Very weak he was, and trembling exceedingly. To his ears her scream held the note of madness. Vainly he had refrained. Selfishly he had yielded. The cold hand of a mortal faintness clutched at his heart.

'I don't want to live now,' he told himself, and fell back in the straight bed.

Her arms were round him.

'I'm going to get help,' she said, her lips to his ear; 'brandy and things. Only I came back. I didn't want you to think I was frightened. Oh, my dear! thank God, thank God!' He felt her kisses even through the swooning mist that swirled about him. Had she really fled in terror? He never knew. He knew that she had come back to him.

That is the real, true, and authentic narrative of the events which caused Professor Boyd Thompson to abandon a brilliant career, to promise anything that Lucilla might demand, and to devote himself entirely to a gentlemanly and unprofitable farming, and to his wife. From the point of view of the scientific world it is a sad ending to much promise, but at any rate there are two happy people hand in hand at the story's ending.

There is no doubt that for several years Professor Boyd Thompson had had enough of science, and, by a natural revulsion, flung himself into the full tide of commonplace sentiment. But genius, like youth, cannot be denied. And I, for one, am doubtful whether the Professor's renunciation of research will be a lasting one. Already I have heard whispers of a laboratory which is being built on to the house, beyond the billiard-room.

But I am inclined to believe the rumours which assert that, for the future, his research will take the form of extending paths already well trodden; that he will refrain from experiments with unknown drugs, and those dreadful researches which tend to merge the chemist and biologist in the alchemist and the magician. And he certainly does not intend to experiment further on the nerves of any living thing, even his own. The Professor had already done enough work to make the reputation of half-a-dozen ordinary scientists. He may be pardoned if he rests on his laurels, entwining them, to some extent, with roses.

The bottle containing the drug from the South Seas was knocked down on the day of his death and swept up in bits by the laboratory boy. It is a curious fact that the Professor has wholly forgotten the formulae of his great discovery, the notes of which he destroyed just before his experiment which so nearly was his last. This is a great satisfaction to his wife, and possibly to the Professor. But of this I cannot be sure; the scientific spirit survives much.

To the unscientific reader the strangest part of this story will perhaps be the fact that Parker is still with his old master, a wonderful example of the perfect butler. Professor Boyd Thompson was able to forgive Parker because he understood him. And he learned to understand Parker in those moments of agony, when his keen intellect and his awakened heart taught him, through his love for Lucilla, the depth of that gulf of fear which lies between the quick and the dead.

# The Head

*1*

When your personal appearance is best described by the enumeration of your clothes, your character by the trade mark on the gilt waistband of your cigar, and your profession 'just anything that comes along, don't you know', you are not exactly the right man in the right place, when you find yourself up to your knees in mud, your carriage with a wheel off lying prone in a ditch several fields off, and your chance of getting to the house, where a music hall star has given you an inconvenient rendezvous, less than the least crumb of the biscuit you wish you had put in your pocket before starting.

Morris Diehl cursed his luck in the grey of a winter's dusk. His driver had left the carriage and gone back with the horses to the inn where he had lunched. His boots were full of water, his high hat seamed and scratched by the skeleton-fingered trees that leaned here and there over the stone walls. His cigar, long since cold, its end wet and flattened and gnawed, lay foul between his lips. He threw it away. He was lost, beyond a doubt lost, on these confounded Derbyshire hills, where every field is just the same as every other field, and the stone walls have no more of individual distinction than the faint blue-grey lines of a copy book.

If he had only had the sense to stay where the coachman had left him or, better still, at the inn, the inn down in the valley, where the Station was – where there were lights, and voices and things to drink. Tottie de Vere, the star on whom hung all the hopes of his newest venture – a company for promoting *cafés chantants* in Manchester, Liverpool, and Bolton – Tottie de Vere had declined to give any appointment save this: he might call on her between six and seven at Sir Alexander Brisbane's, the grey house with acres of glass, ten miles from anywhere. And he had tried to keep the appointment, tried with unreasonable determination, and there he was.

Lights and voices – and things to drink. To eat, also. For Mr Diehl was not only thirsty. He was hungry as well, and cold and lonely. He thought of the Strand and the lights of the Strand, lights from restaurants and theatres, where one smelt French cooking, and the patchouli, and the Regalias. These were to him what, to some of us, the home pastures and the scent of stocks and wood smoke are. He had waited by the carriage till he had grown certain that all men were alike and that his driver would, warmed and comforted in the ale-house, not be such a fool as to keep his promise and come back 'with a trap'. He had walked up and down the road for a while, the bleak wind nuzzling in between his neck and the fur collar of his big coat; and then he had started to reach Sir Alexander's on foot, seen a light, and been beguiled by it to what he esteemed a short-cut. Even if it were not Sir Alexander's light yet any light meant a possible fire – shelter, at any rate, from that too intimate North-Easter.

He was going now, difficultly towards the light. Across the fields and over the eternal sameness of grey walls – black, they seemed, in that sombre twilight of cold stars. Beyond the last wall was a little hill brook. He was in it almost knee-deep before he guessed at anything worse than the cold muddy pastures. The next wall had a gate; he saw the blacker blank and made for it. His fur-lined coat caught on its hasp and ripped, loudly. And his hat was struck by some silly arch or other above the gate, and fell, rolling hollowly on the flags.

'Damn,' said Mr Diehl. 'Oh, damn and blast.' He groped for the hat in the dark dampness, found it; and then he was at the door of the cottage whose windows, all alight, had beckoned him from afar.

'There must be a wedding or a wake,' said he. 'Copy, either way.' He was, casually, a journalist when financial enterprises were cold to him.

He knocked. He had not been conscious of any movement in

the house, but now he was conscious of a cessation of movement, and of a silence, as though something inside the house were holding its breath.

'Who's there?' The voice came from behind the door – low down, as though the speaker had been trying to look out into the dark through the keyhole.

'I've lost my way,' said Mr Diehl.

'You'll find it – some way or other,' said the voice.

'I'm very wet – and tired. I should be very grateful for a night's lodging, Sir.'

He added the Sir because the note of the voice was distinctly feminine, and he saw that the door would open more readily to one whose honesty of purpose was so clear and fine, that it could persist even in the face of the conviction that there was 'a man in the house'. Mr Diehl's mind – it was not the mind of a fool – pictured a faded woman, her terror at this late visit soothed and charmed by the solid compliments it was part of his trade to sow broadcast, with both hands, on any soil. The harvest, he knew, rarely failed.

'Ah, have pity,' he said, all the pathos of a hundred melodramas reinforcing the earnest pleading of gross physical discomfort. 'I am lost on these wild moors – I shall die if you do not assist me. Have pity on me and God will reward you.'

'You can go back the way you came,' said the voice.

'I shall die,' he said, piteously, but very distinctly, as his elocution master had taught him in the days when he meant to be an actor. 'I shall die if you turn me away. My death will be at your door – Ah, save me, for the love of God.'

'For the love of God?' the voice repeated slowly. 'For the love . . .'

The rest was lost in the rusty withdrawal of bolts. The door creaked open a brilliant inch.

'No-one's crossed this door this ten years past,' said the voice – 'but I can't let a human creature perish by fire or by cold. For the love of God, come in.' The door was flung back. Within was a little square hall or lobby – narrow stairs led up in front of Mr Diehl. To the right, a closed door; to the left, the outer door held open.

'Go and stand on the stairs,' said the thin treble voice, ' 'til I get the door shut.'

From the stairs Morris watched to see the door closed by that spare, fluttering woman's form. But it was a man who shut the door and barred it, and then turned to the visitor the cold, calm face of one wholly self-possessed.

'Come in,' he said. 'Since you *are* here, I'll do what I can for you. Get off your wet things. I'll go and fetch you a change.'

Diehl, alone in a firelit kitchen, threw off the wet fur coat across a brown wood settle, loosened his squelching patent leather boots, and heard above him the muffled sound of footsteps on old worm-eaten boards, the creak of old beams, the opening and shutting of drawers and presses.

He had got to bare feet and a costume like that of a Corsican brother in reduced and muddy circumstances when his host returned, an armful of clothing over his arm.

'Here,' he said in his thin treble, 'get into these. It'll be easy. I was a bigger man than ever you'll be.'

He was, now, a smaller man – smaller by the stooping shoulders, the narrow chest, the yellow leanness of wrists and neck, by, in a word, age. He was an old man, white-haired and pale. Nothing was young in face and figure, save only the eyes – and they would not have shone amiss in the face of an adventurer of twenty.

Hot gin and water, the generous half of a plate-pie, one's feet in borrowed large shoes among the grey ashes, to whose centre fire had been forced to life by big bellows . . .

Morris Diehl expanded – and, when expanded, he looked better than in his fur coat. He was resolved to stay the night. He pledged his host again and again in the hot sugary drink, adding strength to the other's glass from the brown demijohn, whenever the old man left the fire for more wood, or to fill the kettle, or to bring out his tobacco jar from the disused oven where he stored it – 'to keep moist,' he said. He grew more cordial, and Diehl, who was by nature an actor anywhere but on the boards, which paralysed him, set so gay a tune of good fellowship that the other's mind soon danced to it.

'I'm glad I let you in. Yes, by God, I'm glad I broke my vow. You're a good fellow, sir, pardoning the liberty, and this night's the whitest I've known for ten years. How old would you take me to be, now?'

The question was awkward. As a woman of thirty is said to subtract passionately to make a total of twenty-seven, so men who are far gone in their seventies will add to their years, and claim your amazed admiration as gaffers of eighty-six.

Diehl looked hard at the old man. He would have liked to rest his decision on the spinning of a coin.

'Not much past sixty,' struck him as a tactful compromise.

The old man laughed, well pleased, as it seemed.

'I'm forty-three, come Lady Day, and seven days beyond,' he said. 'I was born on All Fools' Day, three-and-forty years ago, and christened April by the same token, like the fool I am. April Vane's my name. "Vane by name and vain by nature," they used to say when I was a young man – though you wouldn't think it to look at me now.'

'I beg your pardon.' Diehl had no other counter ready.

'Not at all, sir, not at all,' the old man rejoined. 'It 'ud be a wonder if you could guess my age. Why, my hair went white like you see it – in three days.'

'You had some shock, I suppose,' said Morris, and he sipped the hot gin, 'it's a sad world, God help us.'

'I don't tell my story to strangers,' said the other, with shrill, sudden dignity.

'I trust,' said Diehl in his best manner, 'that I can sympathise with another man's sorrows without seeking to thrust myself into his confidence.'

Even as he spoke, he saw how well the old man, the remote

house, the air of mystery, would serve him in an article for the *Daily Bellower* – could he but learn the secret of this hermit's grief. He saw the headlines:

AN ENGLISH HERMIT
TRAGIC STORY
A BROKEN LIFE

'No,' said the other; 'no – of course not. You're a gentleman. Anyone could see that. Let alone your fur coat.'

'I've known trouble myself,' said the guest, and told a tale. A long tale full of pathetic incidents, a tale whose dénouement may have been suggested by the prostrate stump of his cigar against the leg of the table – by that, or by something more subtle.

'I saw my angel girl,' he ended, 'at the window of that burning house. How could I save her? I rushed forward. "Darling," I cried, "I am coming to rescue you!" I plunged among the burning *débris*, and knew no more, 'til I woke in hospital with a broken heart – and this.'

He pulled up his sleeve and showed a scar, got in a drunken fight with a Jew in Johannesburg – the weapons, whisky bottles.

'They cured my face burns,' he added, smoothing his heavy moustache, 'these hardly show, even by daylight, but that scar I shall carry to my grave.'

There was a silence. Then, 'Why did you go on living?' asked the other man, his voice tense as the string of a violin.

'I . . . oh . . . my poor old mother,' said Diehl, whose mother had died in giving birth to him, her only child; 'for her sake, don't you know, and my little sister.'

'*I* went on living,' said the other man, and now his voice was no longer like stretched wire, but like the sharp, unyielding blade of a steel poignard. 'I went on living because . . . '

There was a silence. Diehl could almost hear his heart beat, so sure he was that there was here material for headlines – so keen was he to secure it.

He sighed elaborately. 'Ah,' he said, 'it is a relief to tell your troubles to someone who understands.'

He was quite right to say it. He really sometimes had a wonderful flair for the things to be said and not to say.

'Does it *really*?' asked the man with the young eyes – 'relief, I mean? I've lived here ten years, and never a word except when I bought the things I needed. *Does* talking help? Are you sure? Doesn't it open the old wounds wide till the blood squirts out of them? Don't you wish afterwards that you'd held your silly tongue? Aren't you ashamed, and afraid, and sick with yourself for every word that's passed your lips about *her*?'

'No,' said Diehl slowly, stretching his feet towards the ashes' red centre, 'no; but then I've never told my story before to anyone but you. There's something about you – I don't know what it is – that makes me feel I can trust you. So I'm glad I've told you my story. If it's not bored you?'

The last five words were a false lead, but the other man did not notice it.

'I don't know,' he said, 'you may be right; and perhaps if I told someone I could trust, my brain and heart would leave off feeling as though they were going to burst, and make my clean floor all in a mess. You don't think I'm mad, do you?'

It was just what he was thinking, so, suddenly very anxious to be alone, with a locked door between him and his host, he said hastily: 'Not at all. But I see I've awakened painful memories with my talk. Will you let me sleep here – on the settle – on the floor – anywhere – I don't want a bed. I won't give an ounce of trouble. May I?'

'May you what?'

'Spend the night,' said Diehl and, laboriously explaining, added, 'sleep here, you know.'

'In this house?'

'Of course.'

'Yes.' The answer was very strong, very definite. 'You shall sleep here in this house – if you can. But first I should like to show you the reason why I never sleep in this house. I sleep in the croft when it's warm, and, when it's winter, in the barn. But I keep the lights burning all night in every room.'

'I don't half like this,' Morris Diehl told himself, and perceived that attractive headlines may be bought too dearly. Aloud he said: 'I'm so tired, I could sleep anywhere. I believe I'm almost asleep now. Won't you show me whatever it is tomorrow?'

'Tomorrow may never come,' said the host cheerfully. 'I'll go first – just to turn the lights full up and that. Then you shall see.'

He went out, quite quietly and soberly, and Mr Diehl shivered. Now that he was warm and gin-filled, the bleak, windy hillside, in the chessboard of those confounded stone walls, seemed a safety lightly thrown away.

'Alone with a lunatic,' he mused, 'in a house a hundred miles from anywhere.' He fingered a short broad knife, whose sheath fitted closely against his hip.

'If the worst comes to the worst – in self-defence,' he assured himself. 'But all the same, I jolly well wish I was jolly well out of it. Silly lunatic!'

'Come, *now*!' said the voice of the silly lunatic, and said it so trustfully, yet so compellingly, that Mr Diehl rose and followed it, half reassured, half curious, and wholly overmastered.

'It's in the cellar,' said the voice; 'people do pry so.'

Mr Diehl drew back; he could not help it.

'You're not afraid of a *cellar*,' said the voice; 'besides, it's what we call a basement in London.'

Morris Diehl felt his knife's comforting weight and followed the voice.

The stairs were of stone, broad and shallow – there were many of them. The wavering, yellow light of the lamp the other man carried showed the stairs neatly yellowed, as the Mid Country lovingly yellows the stones which make the floors to its homes.

The stairs ended in a flagged passage, with doors. Outside the right-hand door the lamp-bearer paused.

'You told me your story with words,' said he. 'I never heard so many words all different in all my born days. I haven't got no power of jaw like that there. You told me your story; and it's the same as my story. That's why I'm a-going to show you my story. ''Cause I can't use my tongue worth tuppence — but my hands I can. Now, don't you be frightened; it ain't real.'

Mr Diehl reassured himself with a laugh.

'I'm not so easily frightened,' he said.

'Nor don't you laugh neither,' said the old man, with sudden, breathless intensity. 'I couldn't answer for myself what I should do, if you was to laugh in there. It's the work of my hands. And I love the work of my hands, same as Almighty God did. Don't you go to laugh in there, sir, or it'll be the worse for both of us. But you wouldn't,' his voice grew suddenly tender, 'ain't you showed me your 'art — put it into my 'and to look at? Don't I know you?'

The dramatic instinct told Mr Diehl to hold out his hand, in the dim lamplight, and press the other man's, with a fine show of manly emotion.

'I was a stone-mason by trade,' said the host, 'apprenticed in the King's Road, Chelsea, I was; that's how I got the hang of it.'

Mr Diehl had a sudden, swift vision of an elaborate monument erected in the cellar, over the body of the victim of homicidal mania.

'Now,' said the other, and flung open the door.

Mr Diehl was prepared for a shock of some sort, but he was not prepared for the shock he got.

The opened door disclosed a village street, lit warm and red, a village street at night. It was the village where the inn was that he wished he had stayed at — where the lights were, and the voices, and the drinks. There, by the same token was the Inn, its sign emblazoned with the arms of the local landowner, lit redly by the flames of conflagration. There was the square church tower, flushed against a dark sky, the tombstones in the raised churchyard, gleaming rosy beneath the yew shadows. There was a crowd in the street — men with pails and cans of water. This side of the Inn, half the street was in flames; from the window of a burning house a girl leaned out; below, a man, holding a ladder, was in act to plant it against the window. At his feet lay a body – a dead man, as it seemed, but not dead by burning. Blood showed at mouth and nose. The whole thing was worked out, with wax and wood and paint and paper, and a dozen odd, yet adequate, materials, at much less than half life-size, but so perfect were the perspective and the proportion, that the scene would have appeared to a spectator half-way up the village street just as, and not otherwise than, it now appeared to the spectator at the cellar door. The peculiar and desperate terror – the mad, splendid heroism that fire engenders – these were here, visible to the onlooker.

'Splendid. Ripping. A1.' The words sprang to Mr Diehl's lips ... and stayed there. The other man was speaking, and in a low, thin, untroubled voice.

'That's me,' he said, 'with the ladder. And that Dog in the gutter – that's him she threw me over for. She was Mrs Dog, her that was to have been Mrs April Vane. But I loved her. That's her leanin' out of their bedroom window. And when the fire broke out, where was he? In heaven, where he'd got the right to be by the marriage lines? Not him! He was in the public silly drunk. When I come along, he was crying – crying there in front of the house where she was a-burning, crying, and shivering, and saying, "Oh, I shall be burnt, I know I shall." And she was screaming, "For God's sake save the child!"'

'What did you do?' Mr Diehl's voice was tactfully attuned.

'Knocked him down, of course. Thought I'd killed him. Wish I had. Then, when I'd got the ladder, and set it up against the window, I was three-quarters up it, when the window-frame went – burnt from underneath. I never see'd him again. He went to London, I've heard say. But I've made his face. You go in an' look, and you'll see the man I wish I'd swung for. If he'd been where he ought to a bin ... but he left her all alone, along of the kid that wasn't three days old.'

Again Morris wrung his hand. The vision of attractive headlines had faded, grown dim, vanished in the red glow of the
burning village.

He walked gingerly into the picture, and looked closely at
the wax puppets. Perfect in every detail, each little effigy was in
itself a finer work of art even than the tableau which included
them all.

'It's . . . it's beautiful,' said Morris Diehl. 'I never saw anything
like it.'

'It's taken me my life to make,' said its maker.

'But why did you make it so small – why not life-size? There'd
have been room – for part of it, anyway.'

'Money,' came sharply the reply. 'I've only got the house and the
croft, and thirty pound a year that come to me from an uncle – too
late for me to marry her.'

'The whole thing's a marvel. You ought to have been a sculptor,
with a proper studio and all that,' said the guest.

'I ought to have been a married man with kids of my own,' said
the host.

'Wouldn't you like to make all this show life-size?' Morris
Diehl asked gently.

'I'm putting by every week for that very thing.'

'I could advance you the money,' said the man who took his
living where he found it.

'No, I won't be beholden to nobody.' The tone was decisive.

'You needn't be beholden. Come to London. I'll find you a fine
big room, twice the size of this; you shall make the things
life-size – the best materials money can buy. We'll charge a shil-
ling a head to come in and see it. You'll pay me back in no time,
and make your fortune besides.'

'I don't want to make my fortune,' said the old man, staring
with his young eyes at the blazing village street. 'I want to get
alongside of *him*.'

'Well,' said Mr Diehl, 'you're much more likely to do that in
London than here, you know. Suppose he saw the outside of our

show, having been in a fire himself, it's a million to one he'd turn in to have a look – and then you could tell him what you thought of him.'

'Do you think he *would*? Do you?'

'Certain of it,' said Mr Diehl, who thought nothing less likely.

'Then I'll do it. All life-size – life-size.'

'You could have men to help you.'

'Not with the faces. The houses and that, I don't say. Not the faces.'

'Of course not the faces,' Mr Diehl assented cordially. 'Let's come back to the fire, and talk it over. And tomorrow we'll get the agreement signed – and Tottie de Vere can go to the deuce. This is a big thing we're in now.'

'Eh?' the other party to the agreement queried. He had not heard. All his senses were deep plunged in the joy of his masterpiece. He sighed at last, and spoke.

'There ought to be *noise*,' he said – 'that's the worst thing about a fire; when it's taking hold, it's as quiet as a mouse. When it's got hold, it roars like a lion, and screams – like a woman.'

'We'll make it scream and roar. This thing's got to go. And it will go,' said Morris Diehl.

### 2

It did go. The whole picture – graduated houses, the little figures of wood, and wax, and paper, the ingenious lanterns that lighted, the tinsel flames that gleamed – all was taken to London, and set up in a big attic in Fitzroy Street. Mr Diehl brought men to see it. Men with shiny hats and fur coats, and cigars like his own. And when they had seen, they went away and drank brandy and soda at marble-topped tables, while Morris Diehl talked. And they 'came into it' with him, as he had known they would. April Vane was shy and moody at first; would have no help; but when he saw the life-sized body, produced by a trained workman from one of his own little models, he drew a long breath. 'You may go ahead,' he said. 'I'll have more time for the faces.'

It cost the enterprising Mr Diehl a great deal of patience, and his enterprising friends a great deal of money. The big fight was over the subject of the tableau. Vane wanted to reproduce the village scene, exactly as it had been burnt on his mind. Diehl wanted the Great Fire of London, with old London Bridge, and the heads of the traitors above the gate. But though Vane had been the other man's slave, since the night he had thought he had seen the other man's heart, he was obstinate till Diehl said: 'More people will come to the Great Fire of London than just to a village fire; you've got more chance of seeing *him*.'

Then Vane yielded.

No expense was spared. The best scene-painters and carpenters that the Syndicate could buy for money were bought. An eminent archaeologist was fee'd to advise; an expert in acoustics solved the problem of the roar of fire triumphant. The thing was boomed a month in advance by all the venal press. A big place in the West End, that had failed as an Art Gallery, was hired for this that should not fail. Vane was often wearied, often disheartened.

'I like the other best,' he said; 'that was mine. This will be everybody's.'

'Wait till you see the real thing all put together,' Diehl urged continually. He was very gentle and patient. It was important to him to keep the old man's adoration alive. '*That* will be yours, and you'll never be able to leave it. You mark my words.'

The old man marked them, and they came true.

The thing caught on. 'Have you seen the Great Fire of London?' people asked each other between dances and during dinners, in the train and on the tops of omnibuses. 'Like Madame Tussaud's? Oh, *no*, not in the least. It's absolutely thrilling. Just for the moment, you can hardly believe it's not real. You *must* go!'

And everybody went. And it was not like Madame Tussaud's, nor like any waxwork show that ever was before. To the making of Madame Tussaud's goes, perhaps, talent. To the making of the

*Musée Grévin*, certainly, genius. But to the making of this went the heart and soul of a man.

And from the first moment, when he saw the completed picture perfect, from the life-size figures in the foreground to the little paper figures in the far distance, he gave himself up to it, as to his real life. The interludes, when he showed it to visitors mechanically warned not to pass its low barrier, explained it in a monologue learned by heart – these were dull dreams. The real moments were those when he was alone – could overstep the barriers, clap the hurrying soldier on the back, whisper encouragement to the old woman hastening away on her son's strong arm, calling shrilly by name these images of dead citizens, who had been alive and furious in flight under the horror of that great blaze. For to him they were not strangers out of the time of the Second Charles. Each wore the face of some man or woman in the Derbyshire village. But to his own effigy he never spoke – nor to the woman whose face looked out of the burning window, nor to the corpse that lay at the feet of the ladder-bearer. For now there was no room for doubt that it was the figure of a corpse. That change he had made without consulting Mr Diehl and the Syndicate. Its mouth was bloody, as had been the mouth of the little effigy in the Derbyshire cellar, and the mouth of the man whom he had struck down long ago under the eyes of the deserted wife. Only now the throat too was bloody.

'Oh, let him alone,' said Mr Diehl, when one of the Syndicate remarked that by Jove it was just a bit too ghastly; 'it pleases him, and you can't lay the horror on too thick for the B. P.'

April Vane slept at his lodgings, but he did nothing else there, and not that every night. Sometimes he slept in the gallery on one of the red velvet seats, and always he ate and drank there, talking to the figures whenever he was alone with them. 'They're company for me,' he said, when Diehl tried remonstrance. And Diehl noted curiously that the life-sized figures did not hold for their maker the horror that, in the first little figures, had driven him to sleep in barn or croft – anywhere but in the house that held them.

It was in August, when the crowd had worn thin, that Vane stayed away for one day. 'I've seen *him*,' he told Diehl, standing by his bedside very early, for he had told the hotel people that it was a matter of life and death. 'I must have a day off; I must try to find him.'

'But who's to run the show?' asked Diehl, in his blue silk pyjamas and blue jowl.

'I must have my day off,' said Vane. 'I don't want to worry you, but I must have one day off. Shut the show up, or run it yourself.'

The show was, that day, run by Mr Diehl. The takings were two bags of silver only that day – and that day the head was stolen. It was the head of the corpse, broken off sharp at the neck, where the blood began. It was stolen, and the careless, silk-hatted custodian knew no more than you or I who had done it.

Vane had not found the man he sought – but when he found out that theft he forgot the fruitless search. His grief was like that of a mother who loses her child, a woman who loses her lover.

'But it's all right,' Diehl told him again and again. 'Throw the corner of the mantle up – so – and it'll never show. Or leave it as it is – it's pretty average ghastly like that.'

It was. But – 'I want his face,' Vane said, again and again.

'Well, then, for God's sake *make* his face' – Diehl was losing patience a little at last. 'Make his face again, and have done with it!' he said, and lit one of his eternal cigars; 'you can do it at home in the evenings.'

'I can't do it,' said Vane, very low. 'I've been trying – I can't see his face.'

'You sleep on it,' said Mr Diehl cheerfully; 'it'll come back to you all right in the morning. Besides, you've got the little one.'

'I cut the face off that,' said Vane gently; 'I cut it off a little bit at a time, to see if it would bleed. I can't remember his face.'

'That head must have been stolen for a lark,' said Diehl. 'Look here! I'll advertise for it, and we'll get it back all right.'

'Yes –' said Vane, with trembling eagerness. 'Get it back. I must see his face.'

He saw it next day on the shoulders of a living man – a tall, thick-set man, with dirty hands and a ready-made suit, who knocked at the gallery door, just as it was being closed. The same face, but not the same expression.

'You were advertising for a head,' said the man.

'Yes,' said Vane. 'Come in,' and he shut the door on the two of them.

'Well, I ain't a-goin' to name no names, but a pal of mine come in here day before yesterday, and one of your blasted dolls had got my pal's face – so he pinched it.'

'Why?' Vane softly asked.

'Well, if a man ain't got a right to his own chump, what has he got a right to? But he'll let you have it back, but not for the fiver you offers. I take it if you offers five, you'll give twenty. Say the word, and put it down in writing to prevent mistakes, and I guarantee you shall have the head.'

'Yes,' said Vane. 'I shall have the head.'

He advanced on the other man, and now, for the first time, his own face showed plainly.

'Great God,' – the man repeated, his hands held out as if to keep off something; and now he looked like the head that he had stolen. 'My great God, it's April Vane.'

'Yes, you'd better call on your God. It's April Vane,' April Vane said, and came at him.

It must have been a couple of days later that Diehl strolled in at closing time with that member of the Syndicate who had felt so squeamish about the cut throat. The lights were low. There was no blaze to light up the picture, and the machine was silent that, in the day, roared and screamed in the very voice of fire.

'So you've got the head all right; you remember I told you you would,' said Mr Diehl, glancing at the corpse.

'Yes,' said April. 'I've got the head – I remembered.'

Mr Diehl went into the enclosure, and the cinders crunched under his boots.

'By Jove,' he said, 'you're an artist, Vane. I say, Montague, look at the corpse, the thing you didn't like – why, it's the best of the lot. You've improved it, Vane, old chap. It's just the old expression, but by George it's more lifelike than ever. What is it? something in the lie of the body, I suppose. It's just like life, isn't it now, Monty?'

'It is more like death,' said Montague. 'I don't like it, and it's stuffy in here and the place is as quiet as a churchyard. Come along out.'

'You're a schoolgirl, Montague, a silly schoolgirl! I believe you're frightened of the thing.' Mr Diehl kicked it contemptuously and without violence. 'Good night, Vane. Why don't you go to one of the Halls and have a gay evening. I'll stand treat.'

'You're always kind,' said Vane gratefully, 'but all the evenings will be gay now. I have got the head. I have remembered.'

The two members of the Great Fire Syndicate went out into the light of Regent Street.

'Ugh,' said Montague, 'that place gives me the horrors.'

'It's jolly well meant to,' said Diehl, taking out his cigar-case. 'That corpse . . . '

'It's not canny,' said Montague and he laughed, not quite easily. 'Why, it makes me fancy . . . I say, what's that on your boot? Good God, man, it's blood, as the chap says in the story.'

'Don't talk rot,' said Diehl. He did not see that his right foot had stained the pavement.

Montague stopped.

'But – it *is* blood,' he said.

# In the Dark

It may have been a form of madness. Or it may be that he really was what is called haunted. Or it may – though I don't pretend to understand how – have been the development, through intense suffering, of a sixth sense in a very nervous, highly-strung nature. Something certainly led him where They were. And to him They were all one.

He told me the first part of the story, and the last part of it I saw with my own eyes.

1

Haldane and I were friends even in our school-days. What first brought us together was our common hatred of Visger, who came from our part of the country. His people knew our people at home, so he was put on to us when he came. He was the most intolerable person, boy and man, that I have ever known. He would not tell a lie. And that was all right. But he didn't stop at that. If he were asked whether any other chap had done anything – been out of bounds, or up to any sort of lark – he would always say, 'I don't know, sir, but I believe so.' He never did know – we took care of that. But what he believed was always right. I remember Haldane twisting his arm to say how he knew about that cherry tree business, and he only said, 'I don't know – I just feel sure. And I was right, you see.' What can you do with a boy like that?

We grew up to be men. At least Haldane and I did. Visger grew up to be a prig. He was a vegetarian and a teetotaller, and an all-wooler and Christian Scientist, and all the things that prigs are – but he wasn't a common prig. He knew all sorts of things that he oughtn't to have known, that he *couldn't* have known in any ordinary decent way. It wasn't that he found things out. He just knew them. Once, when I was very unhappy, he came into my rooms – we were all in our last year at Oxford – and talked about things I hardly knew myself. That was really why I went to India that winter. It was bad enough to be unhappy, without having that beast knowing all about it.

I was away over a year. Coming back, I thought a lot about how jolly it would be to see old Haldane again. If I thought about Visger at all, I wished he was dead. But I didn't think about him much.

I did want to see Haldane. He was always such a jolly chap – gay, and kindly, and simple, honourable, upright, and full of practical sympathies. I longed to see him, to see the smile in his jolly blue eyes, looking out from the net of wrinkles that laughing had made round them, to hear his jolly laugh, and feel the good grip of his big hand. I went straight from the docks to his chambers in Grey's Inn, and I found him cold, pale, anaemic, with dull eyes and a limp hand, and pale lips that smiled without mirth, and uttered a welcome without gladness.

He was surrounded by a litter of disordered furniture and personal effects half packed. Some big boxes stood corded, and there were cases of books, filled and waiting for the enclosing boards to be nailed on.

'Yes, I'm moving,' he said. 'I can't stand these rooms. There's something rum about them – something devilish rum. I clear out tomorrow.'

The autumn dusk was filling the corners with shadows. 'You got the furs,' I said, just for something to say, for I saw the big case that held them lying corded among the others.

'Furs?' he said. 'Oh yes. Thanks awfully. Yes. I forgot about the furs.' He laughed, out of politeness, I suppose, for there was no joke about the furs. They were many and fine – the best I could get for money, and I had seen them packed and sent off when my heart was very sore. He stood looking at me, and saying nothing.

'Come out and have a bit of dinner,' I said as cheerfully as I could.

'Too busy,' he answered, after the slightest possible pause, and a glance round the room – 'look here – I'm awfully glad to see you – If you'd just slip over and order in dinner – I'd go myself – only – Well, you see how it is.'

I went. And when I came back, he had cleared a space near the fire, and moved his big gate-table into it. We dined there by candle light. I tried to be amusing. He, I am sure, tried to be amused. We did not succeed, either of us. And his haggard eyes watched me all the time, save in those fleeting moments when, without turning his head, he glanced back over his shoulder into the shadows that crowded round the little lighted place where we sat.

When we had dined and the man had come and taken away the dishes, I looked at Haldane very steadily, so that he stopped in a pointless anecdote, and looked interrogation at me.

'Well?' I said.

'You're not listening,' he said petulantly. 'What's the matter?'

'That's what you'd better tell me,' I said.

He was silent, gave one of those furtive glances at the shadows, and stooped to stir the fire to – I knew it – a blaze that must light every corner of the room.

'You're all to pieces,' I said cheerfully. 'What have you been up to? Wine? Cards? Speculation? A woman? If you won't tell me, you'll have to tell your doctor. Why, my dear chap, you're a wreck.'

'You're a comfortable friend to have about the place,' he said, and smiled a mechanical smile not at all pleasant to see.

'I'm the friend you want, I think,' said I. 'Do you suppose I'm blind? Something's gone wrong and you've taken to something. Morphia, perhaps? And you've brooded over the thing till you've lost all sense of proportion. Out with it, old chap. I bet you a dollar it's not so bad as you think it.'

'If I could tell you – or tell anyone,' he said slowly, 'it wouldn't be so bad as it is. If I could tell anyone, I'd tell you. And even as it is, I've told you more than I've told anyone else.'

I could get nothing more out of him. But he pressed me to stay — would have given me his bed and made himself a shake-down, he said. But I had engaged my room at the Victoria, and I was expecting letters. So I left him, quite late — and he stood on the stairs, holding a candle over the banisters to light me down.

When I went back next morning, he was gone. Men were moving his furniture into a big van with somebody's Pantechnicon painted on it in big letters.

He had left no address with the porter, and had driven off in a hansom with two portmanteaux — to Waterloo, the porter thought.

Well, a man has a right to the monopoly of his own troubles, if he chooses to have it. And I had troubles of my own that kept me busy.

### 2

It was more than a year later that I saw Haldane again. I had got rooms in the Albany by this time, and he turned up there one morning, very early indeed — before breakfast in fact. And if he looked ghastly before, he now looked almost ghostly. His face looked as though it had worn thin, like an oyster shell that has for years been cast up twice a day by the sea on a shore all pebbly. His hands were thin as bird's claws, and they trembled like caught butterflies.

I welcomed him with enthusiastic cordiality and pressed break-fast on him. This time, I decided, I would ask no questions. For I saw that none were needed. He would tell me. He intended to tell me. He had come here to tell me, and for nothing else.

I lit the spirit lamp — I made coffee and small talk for him, and I ate and drank, and waited for him to begin. And it was like this that he began: 'I am going,' he said, 'to kill myself — oh, don't be alarmed,' — I suppose I had said or looked something — 'I shan't do it here, or now. I shall do it when I have to — when I can't bear it any longer. And I want someone to know why. I don't want to feel that I'm the only living creature who does know. And I can trust you, can't I?'

I murmured something reassuring.

'I should like you, if you don't mind, to give me your word, that you won't tell a soul what I'm going to tell you, as long as I'm alive. Afterwards . . . you can tell whom you please.'

I gave him my word.

He sat silent looking at the fire. Then he shrugged his shoulders.

'It's extraordinary how difficult it is to say it,' he said, and smiled. 'The fact is – you know that beast, George Visger.'

'Yes,' I said. 'I haven't seen him since I came back. Someone told me he'd gone to some island or other to preach vegetarianism to cannibals. Anyhow, he's out of the way, bad luck to him.'

'Yes,' said Haldane, 'he's out of the way. But he's not preaching anything. In point of fact, he's dead.'

'Dead?' was all I could think of to say.

'Yes,' said he; 'it's not generally known, but he is.'

'What did he die of?' I asked, not that I cared. The bare fact was good enough for me.

'You know what an interfering chap he always was. Always knew everything. Heart to heart talks – and have everything open and above board. Well, he interfered between me and someone else – told her a pack of lies.'

'Lies?'

'Well, the *things* were true, but he made lies of them the way he told them – *you* know.' I did. I nodded. 'And she threw me over. And she died. And we weren't even friends. And I couldn't see her – before – I couldn't even . . . Oh, my God . . . But I went to the funeral. He was there. They'd asked *him*. And then I came back to my rooms. And I was sitting there, thinking. And he came up.'

'He would do. It's just what he would do. The beast! I hope you kicked him out.'

'No, I didn't. I listened to what he'd got to say. He came to say,

No doubt it was all for the best. And he hadn't known the things he told her. He'd only guessed. He'd guessed right, damn him. What right had he to guess right? And he said it was all for the best, because, besides that, there was madness in my family. He'd found that out too –'

'And is there?'

'If there is, I didn't know it. And that was why it was all for the best. So then I said, "There wasn't any madness in my family before, but there is now," and I got hold of his throat. I am not sure whether I meant to kill him; I ought to have meant to kill him. Anyhow, I did kill him. What did you say?'

I had said nothing. It is not easy to think at once of the tactful and suitable thing to say, when your oldest friend tells you that he is a murderer.

'When I could get my hands out of his throat – it was as difficult as it is to drop the handles of a galvanic battery – he fell in a lump on the hearth-rug. And I saw what I'd done. How is it that murderers ever get found out?'

'They're careless, I suppose,' I found myself saying, 'they lose their nerve.'

'I didn't,' he said. 'I never was calmer, I sat down in the big chair and looked at him, and thought it all out. He was just off to that island – I knew that. He'd said goodbye to everyone. He'd told me that. There was no blood to get rid of – or only a touch at the corner of his slack mouth. He wasn't going to travel in his own name because of interviewers. Mr Somebody Something's luggage would be unclaimed and his cabin empty. No-one would guess that Mr Somebody Something was Sir George Visger, FRS. It was all as plain as plain. There was nothing to get rid of, but the man. No weapon, no blood – and I got rid of him all right.'

'How?'

He smiled cunningly.

'No, no,' he said; 'that's where I draw the line. It's not that I doubt your word, but if you talked in your sleep, or had a fever or anything. No, no. As long as you don't know where the body is, don't you see, I'm all right. Even if you could prove that I've said all this – which you can't – it's only the wanderings of my poor unhinged brain. See?'

I saw. And I was sorry for him. And I did not believe that he had killed Visger. He was not the sort of man who kills people. So I said: 'Yes, old chap, I see. Now look here. Let's go away together, you and I – travel a bit and see the world, and forget all about that beastly chap.'

His eyes lighted up at that. 'Why,' he said, 'you understand. You don't hate me and shrink from me. I wish I'd told you before – you know – when you came and I was packing all my sticks. But it's too late now.'

'Too late? Not a bit of it,' I said. 'Come, we'll pack our traps and be off tonight – out into the unknown, don't you know.'

'That's where *I'm* going,' he said. 'You wait. When you've heard what's been happening to me, you won't be so keen to go travelling about with me.'

'But you've told me what's been happening to you,' I said, and the more I thought about what he had told me, the less I believed it.

'No,' he said, slowly, 'no – I've told you what happened to *him*. What happened to me is quite different. Did I tell you what his last words were? Just when I was coming at him. Before I'd got his throat, you know. He said, "Look out. You'll never be able to get rid of the body – Besides, anger's sinful." You know that way he had, like a tract on its hind legs. So afterwards I got thinking of that. But I didn't think of it for a year. Because I did get rid of his body all right. And then I was sitting in that comfortable chair, and I thought, "Hullo, it must be about a year now, since that –" and I pulled out my pocket-book and went to the window to look at a little almanack I carry about – it was getting dusk – and sure enough it was a year, to the day. And then I remembered what he'd said. And I said to myself, "Not much trouble about getting rid of *your* body, you brute." And then I looked at the hearth-rug and – Ah!' he screamed suddenly and very loud – 'I can't tell you – no, I can't.'

My man opened the door – he wore a smooth face over his wriggling curiosity. 'Did you call, sir?'

'Yes,' I lied. 'I want you to take a note to the bank, and wait for an answer.'

When he was got rid of, Haldane said: 'Where was I? –'

'You were just telling me what happened after you looked at the almanack. What was it?'

'Nothing much,' he said, laughing softly, 'oh, nothing much – only that I glanced at the hearth-rug – and there *he* was – the man I'd killed a year before. Don't try to explain, or I shall lose my temper. The door was shut. The windows were shut. He hadn't been there a minute before. And he was there then. That's all.'

Hallucination was one of the words I stumbled among.

'Exactly what I thought,' he said triumphantly, 'but – I touched it. It was quite real. Heavy, you know, and harder than live people are somehow, to the touch – more like a stone thing covered with kid the hands were, and the arms like a marble statue in a blue serge suit. Don't you hate men who wear blue serge suits?'

'There are hallucinations of touch too,' I found myself saying.

'Exactly what I thought,' said Haldane more triumphant than ever, 'but there are limits, you know – limits. So then I thought someone had got him out – the real him – and stuck him there to frighten me – while my back was turned, and I went to the place where I'd hidden him, and he was there – ah! – just as I'd left him. Only . . . it was a year ago. There are two of him there now.'

'My dear chap,' I said, 'this is simply comic.'

'Yes,' he said, 'it is amusing. I find it so myself. Especially in the night when I wake up and think of it. I hope I shan't die in the dark, Winston. That's one of the reasons why I think I shall have to kill myself. I could be sure then of not dying in the dark.'

'Is *that* all?' I asked, feeling sure that it must be.

'No,' said Haldane at once. 'That's *not* all. He's come back to me again. In a railway carriage it was. I'd been asleep. When I woke up, there he was lying on the seat opposite me. Looked just the same. I pitched him out on the line in Red Hill Tunnel. And if I see him again, I'm going out myself. I can't stand it. It's too much. I'd sooner go. Whatever the next world's like, there aren't things in it like that. We leave them here, in graves and boxes and ... You think I'm mad. But I'm not. You can't help me – no-one can help me. He *knew*, you see. He said I shouldn't be able to get rid of the body. And I can't get rid of it. I can't. I can't. He knew. He always did know things that he *couldn't* know. But I'll cut his game short. After all, I've got the ace of trumps, and I play it on his next trick. I give you my word of honour, Winston, that I'm not mad.'

'My dear old man,' I said, 'I don't think you're mad. But I do think your nerves are very much upset. Mine are a bit, too. Do you know why I went to India? It was because of you and her. I couldn't stay and see it, though I wished for your happiness and all that; you know I did. And when I came back, she ... and you ... Let's see it out together,' I said. 'You won't keep fancying things if you've got me to talk to. And I always said you weren't half a bad old duffer.'

'She liked you,' he said.

'Oh, yes,' I said, 'she liked me.'

### 3

That was how we came to go abroad together. I was full of hope for him. He'd always been such a splendid chap – so sane and strong. I couldn't believe that he was gone mad, gone for ever, I mean, so that he'd never come right again. Perhaps my own trouble made it easy for me to see things not quite straight. Anyway, I took him away to recover his mind's health, exactly as I should have taken him away to get strong after a fever. And the madness seemed to pass away, and in a month or two we were perfectly jolly, and I thought I had cured him. And I was very glad because of that old friendship of ours, and because she had loved him and liked me.

We never spoke of Visger. I thought he had forgotten all about him. I thought I understood how his mind, over-strained by sorrow and anger, had fixed on the man he hated, and woven a nightmare web of horror round that detestable personality. And I had got the whip hand of my own trouble. And we were as jolly as sandboys together all those months.

And we came to Bruges at last in our travels, and Bruges was very full, because of the Exhibition. We could only get one room and one bed. So we tossed for the bed, and the one who lost the toss was to make the best of the night in the armchair. And the bed-clothes we were to share equitably.

We spent the evening at a *café chantant* and finished at a beer hall, and it was late and sleepy when we got back to the Grande Vigne. I took our key from its nail in the concierge's room, and we went up. We talked awhile, I remember, of the town, and the belfry, and the Venetian aspect of the canals by moonlight, and then Haldane got into bed, and I made a chrysalis of myself with my share of the blankets and fitted the tight roll into the armchair. I was not at all comfortable, but I was compensatingly tired, and I was nearly asleep when Haldane roused me up to tell me about his will.

'I've left everything to you, old man,' he said. 'I know I can trust you to see to everything.'

'Quite so,' said I, 'and if you don't mind, we'll talk about it in the morning.'

He tried to go on about it, and about what a friend I'd been, and all that, but I shut him up and told him to go to sleep. But no. He wasn't comfortable, he said. And he'd got a thirst like a lime kiln. And he'd noticed that there was no water-bottle in the room. 'And the water in the jug's like pale soup,' he said.

'Oh, all right,' said I. 'Light your candle and go and get some water, then, in Heaven's name, and let me get to sleep.'

But he said, 'No – you light it. I don't want to get out of bed in the dark. I might – I might step on something, mightn't I – or walk into something that wasn't there when I got into bed.'

'Rot,' I said, 'walk into your grandmother.' But I lit the candle all the same. He sat up in bed and looked at me – very pale – with his hair all tumbled from the pillow, and his eyes blinking and shining.

'That's better,' he said. And then, 'I say – look here. Oh – yes – I see. It's all right. Queer how they mark the sheets here. Blest if I didn't think it was blood, just for the minute.'

The sheet was marked, not at the corner, as sheets are marked at home, but right in the middle where it turns down, with big, red, cross-stitching.

'Yes, I see,' I said, 'it is a queer place to mark it.'

'It's queer letters to have on it,' he said. 'G. V.'

'Grande Vigne,' I said. 'What letters do you expect them to mark things with? Hurry up.'

'You come too,' he said. 'Yes, it does stand for Grande Vigne, of course. I wish you'd come down too, Winston.'

'I'll *go* down,' I said and turned with the candle in my hand.

He was out of bed and close to me in a flash.

'No,' said he, 'I don't want to stay alone in the dark.'

He said it just as a frightened child might have done.

'All right then, come along,' I said. And we went. I tried to make some joke, I remember, about the length of his hair, and the cut of his pyjamas – but I was sick with disappointment. For it was almost quite plain to me, even then, that all my time and trouble had been thrown away, and that he wasn't cured after all. We went down as quietly as we could, and got a carafe of water from the long bare dining table in the *salle-à-manger*. He got hold of my arm at first, and then he got the candle away from me, and went very slowly, shading the light with his hand, and looking very carefully all about, as though he expected to see something that he wanted very desperately not to see. And of course, I knew what that something was. I didn't like the way he was going on. I can't at all express how deeply I didn't like it. And he looked over his shoulder every now and then, just as he did that first evening after I came back from India.

The thing got on my nerves so that I could hardly find the way back to our room. And when we got there, I give you my word, I more than half expected to see what *he* had expected to see – that, or something like that, on the hearth-rug. But of course there was nothing.

I blew out the light and tightened my blankets round me – I'd been trailing them after me in our expedition. And I was settled in my chair when Haldane spoke.

'You've got all the blankets,' he said.

'No, I haven't,' said I, 'only what I've always had.'

'I can't find mine then,' he said and I could hear his teeth chattering. 'And I'm cold. I'm . . . For God's sake, light the candle. Light it. Light it. Something horrible . . . '

And I couldn't find the matches.

'Light the candle, light the candle,' he said, and his voice broke, as a boy's does sometimes in chapel. 'If you don't he'll come to me. It is so easy to come at anyone in the dark. Oh Winston, light the candle, for the love of God! I can't die in the dark.'

'I am lighting it,' I said savagely, and I was feeling for the matches on the marble-topped chest of drawers, on the mantelpiece – everywhere but on the round centre table where I'd put them. 'You're not going to die. Don't be a fool,' I said. 'It's all right. I'll get a light in a second.'

He said, 'It's cold. It's cold. It's cold,' like that, three times. And then he screamed aloud, like a woman – like a child – like a hare when the dogs have got it. I had heard him scream like that once before.

'What is it?' I cried, hardly less loud. 'For God's sake, hold your noise. What is it?'

There was an empty silence. Then, very slowly: 'It's Visger,' he said. And he spoke thickly, as through some stifling veil.

'Nonsense. Where?' I asked, and my hand closed on the matches as he spoke.

'Here,' he screamed sharply, as though he had torn the veil away, 'here, beside me. In the bed.'

I got the candle alight. I got across to him.

He was crushed in a heap at the edge of the bed. Stretched on the bed beyond him was a dead man, white and very cold.

Haldane had died in the dark.

It was all so simple.

We had come to the wrong room. The man the room belonged to was there, on the bed he had engaged and paid for before he died of heart disease, earlier in the day. A French *commis-voyageur* representing soap and perfumery; his name, Felix Leblanc.

Later, in England, I made cautious enquiries. The body of a man had been found in the Red Hill tunnel – a haberdasher man named Simmons, who had drunk spirits of salts, owing to the depression of trade. The bottle was clutched in his dead hand.

For reasons that I had, I took care to have a police inspector with me when I opened the boxes that came to me by Haldane's will. One of them was the big box, metal lined, in which I had sent him the skins from India – for a wedding present, God help us all!

It was closely soldered.

Inside were the skins of beasts? No. The bodies of two men. One was identified, after some trouble, as that of a hawker of pens in city offices – subject to fits. He had died in one, it seemed. The other body was Visger's, right enough.

Explain it as you like. I offered you, if you remember, a choice of explanations before I began the story. I have not yet found the explanation that can satisfy me.

# From the Dead

*1*

'But true or not true, your brother is a scoundrel. No man – no decent man – tells such things.'

'He did not tell me. How dare you suppose it? I found the letter in his desk; and since she was my friend and your sweetheart, I never thought there could be any harm in my reading anything she might write to my brother. Give me back the letter. I was a fool to tell you.'

Ida Helmont held out her hand for the letter.

'Not yet,' I said, and I went to the window. The dull red of a London sunset burned on the paper, as I read in the pretty hand-writing I knew so well, and had kissed so often –

DEAR —— I do – I do love you; but it's impossible. I must marry Arthur. My honour is engaged. If he would only set me free – but he never will. He loves me foolishly. But as for me – it is you I love – body, soul and spirit. There is no-one in my heart but you. I think of you all day, and dream of you all night. And we must part. Goodbye – Yours, yours, yours,

ELVIRA

I had seen the handwriting, indeed, often enough. But the passion there was new to me. That I had not seen.

I turned from the window. My sitting-room looked strange to me. There were my books, my reading-lamp, my untasted dinner still on the table, as I had left it when I rose to dissemble my surprise at Ida Helmont's visit – Ida Helmont, who now sat looking at me quietly.

'Well – do you give me no thanks?'

'You put a knife in my heart, and then ask for thanks?'

'Pardon me,' she said, throwing up her chin. 'I have done nothing but show you the truth. For that one should expect no gratitude – may I ask, out of pure curiosity, what you intend to do?'

'Your brother will tell you –'

She rose suddenly, very pale, and her eyes haggard.

'You will not tell my brother?'

She came towards me – her gold hair flaming in the sunset light.

'Why are you so angry with me?' she said. 'Be reasonable. What else could I do?'

'I don't know.'

'Would it have been right not to tell you?'

'I don't know. I only know that you've put the sun out, and I haven't got used to the dark yet.'

'Believe me,' she said, coming still nearer to me, and laying her hands in the lightest touch on my shoulders, 'believe me, she never loved you.'

There was a softness in her tone that irritated and stimulated me. I moved gently back, and her hands fell by her sides.

'I beg your pardon,' I said. 'I have behaved very badly. You were quite right to come, and I am not ungrateful. Will you post a letter for me?'

I sat down and wrote –

I give you back your freedom. The only gift of mine that can please you now –

ARTHUR

I held the sheet out to Miss Helmont, but she would not look at it. I folded, sealed, stamped, and addressed it.

'Goodbye,' I said then, and gave her the letter. As the door closed behind her, I sank into my chair, and cried like a child, or a fool, over my lost plaything – the little, dark-haired woman who loved someone else with 'body, soul, and spirit'.

I did not hear the door open or any foot on the floor, and therefore I started when a voice behind me said: 'Are you so very unhappy? Oh, Arthur, don't think I am not sorry for you!'

'I don't want anyone to be sorry for me, Miss Helmont,' I said.

She was silent a moment. Then, with a quick, sudden, gentle movement she leaned down and kissed my forehead – and I heard the door softly close. Then I knew that the beautiful Miss Helmont loved me.

At first that thought only fleeted by – a light cloud against a grey sky – but the next day reason woke, and said: 'Was Miss Helmont speaking the truth? Was it possible that –'

I determined to see Elvira, to know from her own lips whether by happy fortune this blow came, not from her, but from a woman in whom love might have killed honesty.

I walked from Hampstead to Gower Street. As I trod its long length, I saw a figure in pink come out of one of the houses. It was Elvira. She walked in front of me to the corner of Store Street. There she met Oscar Helmont. They turned and met me face to face, and I saw all I needed to see. They loved each other. Ida Helmont had spoken the truth. I bowed and passed on. Before six months were gone, they were married, and before a year was over, I had married Ida Helmont.

What did it, I don't know. Whether it was remorse for having, even for half a day, dreamed that she could be so base as to forego a lie to gain a lover, or whether it was her beauty, or the sweet flattery of the preference of a woman who had half her acquaintance at her feet, I don't know; anyhow, my thoughts turned to her as to their natural home. My heart, too, took that road, and before very long I loved her as I never loved Elvira. Let no-one doubt that I loved her – as I shall never love again – please God!

There never was anyone like her. She was brave and beautiful, witty and wise, and beyond all measure adorable. She was the only woman in the world. There was a frankness – a largeness of heart – about her that made all other women seem small and contemptible.

She loved me and I worshipped her. I married her, I stayed with her for three golden weeks, and then I left her. Why?

Because she told me the truth. It was one night – late – we had sat all the evening in the verandah of our seaside lodging, watching the moonlight on the water, and listening to the soft sound of the sea on the sand. I have never been so happy; I shall never be happy any more, I hope.

'My dear, my dear,' she said, leaning her gold head against my shoulder, 'how much do you love me?'

'How much?'

'Yes – how much? I want to know what place I hold in your heart. Am I more to you than anyone else?'

'My love!'

'More than yourself?'

'More than my life.'

'I believe you,' she said. Then she drew a long breath, and took my hands in hers. 'It can make no difference. Nothing in heaven or earth can come between us now.'

'Nothing,' I said. 'But, my dear one, what is it?'

For she was trembling, pale.

'I must tell you,' she said; 'I cannot hide anything now from you, because I am yours – body, soul and spirit.'

The phrase was an echo that stung.

The moonlight shone on her gold hair, her soft, warm, gold hair, and on her pale face.

'Arthur,' she said, 'you remember my coming to Hampstead with that letter.'

'Yes, my sweet, and I remember how you –'

'Arthur!' she spoke fast and low – 'Arthur, that letter was a forgery. She never wrote it. I –'

She stopped, for I had risen and flung her hands from me, and stood looking at her. God help me! I thought it was anger at the lie I felt. I know now it was only wounded vanity that smarted in me. That *I* should have been tricked, that *I* should have been deceived, that *I* should have been led on to make a fool of myself. That *I* should have married the woman who had befooled me. At that moment she was no longer the wife I adored – she was only a woman who had forged a letter and tricked me into marrying her.

I spoke: I denounced her; I said I would never speak to her again. I felt it was rather creditable in me to be so angry. I said I would have no more to do with a liar and a forger.

I don't know whether I expected her to creep to my knees and implore forgiveness. I think I had some vague idea that I could by-and-by consent with dignity to forgive and forget. I did not mean what I said. No, oh no, no; I did not mean a word of it. While I was saying it, I was longing for her to weep and fall at my feet, that I might raise her and hold her in my arms again.

But she did not fall at my feet; she stood quietly looking at me.

'Arthur,' she said, as I paused for breath, 'let me explain – she – I –'

'There is nothing to explain,' I said hotly, still with that foolish sense of there being something rather noble in my indignation, the kind of thing one feels when one calls one's self a miserable sinner. 'You are a liar and a forger, that is enough for me. I will never speak to you again. You have wrecked my life –'

'Do you mean that?' she said, interrupting me, and leaning forward to look at me. Tears lay on her cheeks, but she was not crying now.

I hesitated. I longed to take her in my arms and say – 'What does all that old tale matter now? Lay your head here, my darling, and cry here, and know how I love you.'

But instead I said nothing.

'*Do* you mean it?' She persisted.

Then she put her hand on my arm. I longed to clasp it and draw her to me.

Instead, I shook it off, and said – 'Mean it? Yes – of course I mean it. Don't touch me, please. You have ruined my life.'

She turned away without a word, went into our room, and shut the door.

I longed to follow her, to tell her that if there was anything to forgive, I forgave it.

Instead, I went out on the beach, and walked away under the cliffs.

The moonlight and the solitude, however, presently brought me to a better mind. Whatever she had done, had been done for love of me – I knew that. I would go home and tell her so – tell her that whatever she had done, she was my dear life, my heart's one treasure. True, my ideal of her was shattered, at least I felt I ought to think that it was shattered, but, even as she was, what was the whole world of women compared to her? And to be loved like that . . . was that not sweet food for vanity? To be loved more than faith and fair dealing, and all the traditions of honesty and honour? I hurried back, but in my resentment and evil temper I had walked far, and the way back was very long. I had been parted from her for three hours by the time I opened the door of the little house where we lodged. The house was dark and very still. I slipped off my shoes and crept up the narrow stairs, and opened the door of our room quite softly. Perhaps she would have cried herself to sleep, and I would lean over her and waken her with my kisses, and beg her to forgive me. Yes, it had come to that now.

I went into the room – I went towards the bed. She was not there. She was not in the room, as one glance showed me. She was not in the house, as I knew in two minutes. When I had wasted a precious hour in searching the town for her, I found a note on my pillow –

'Goodbye! Make the best of what is left of your life. I will spoil it no more.'

She was gone, utterly gone. I rushed to town by the earliest morning train, only to find that her people knew nothing of her. Advertisement failed. Only a tramp said he had seen a white lady on the cliff, and a fisherman brought me a handkerchief, marked with her name, which he had found on the beach.

I searched the country far and wide, but I had to go back to London at last, and the months went by. I won't say much about those months, because even the memory of that suffering turns me faint and sick at heart. The police and detectives and the Press railed wildly indignant with me, especially her brother, now living very happily with my first love.

I don't know how I got through those long weeks and months. I tried to write; I tried to read; I tried to live the life of a reasonable human being. But it was impossible. I could not endure the companionship of my kind. Day and night I almost saw her face – almost heard her voice. I took long walks in the country, and her figure was always just round the next turn of the road – in the next glade of the wood. But I never quite saw her, never quite heard her. I believe I was not all together sane at that time. At last, one morning, as I was setting out for one of those long walks that had no goal but weariness, I met a telegraph boy, and took the red envelope from his hand.

On the pink paper inside was written –

Come to me at once I am dying you must come. Ida.
                                    Apinshaw Farm, Mellor, Derbyshire

There was a train at twelve to Marple, the nearest station. I took it. I tell you there are some things that cannot be written about. My life for those long months was one of them, that journey was another. What had her life been for those months? That question troubled me, as one is troubled in every nerve by the sight of a surgical operation, or a wound inflicted on a being dear to one. But the overmastering sensation was joy – intense, unspeakable joy. She was alive. I should see her again. I took out the telegram and looked at it: 'I am dying.' I simply did not believe it. She could not die till she had seen me. And if she had lived all these months without me, she could live now, when I was with her again, when she knew of the hell I had endured apart from her, and the heaven of our meeting. She must live; I could not let her die.

There was a long drive over bleak hills. Dark, jolting, infinitely wearisome. At last we stopped before a long, low building, where one or two lights gleamed faintly. I sprang out.

The door opened. A blaze of light made me blink and draw back. A woman was standing in the doorway.

'Art thee Arthur Marsh?' she said.

'Yes.'

'Then th'art ower late. She's dead.'

## 2

I went into the house, walked to the fire, and held out my hands to it mechanically, for though the night was May, I was cold to the bone. There were some folks standing round the fire, and lights flickering. Then an old woman came forward, with the northern instinct of hospitality.

'Thou'rt tired,' she said, 'and mazed-like. Have a sup o' tea.'

I burst out laughing. I had travelled two hundred miles to see *her*. And she was dead, and they offered me tea. They drew back from me as if I had been a wild beast, but I could not stop laughing. Then a hand was laid on my shoulder and someone led me into a dark room, lighted a lamp, set me in a chair, and sat down opposite me. It was a bare parlour, coldly furnished with rush chairs and much-polished tables and presses. I caught my breath, and grew suddenly grave, and looked at the woman who sat opposite me.

'I was Miss Ida's nurse,' said she, 'and she told me to send for you. Who are you?'

'Her husband –'

The woman looked at me with hard eyes, where intense surprise struggled with resentment.

'Then may God forgive you!' she said. 'What you've done I don't know, but it'll be hard work forgivin' *you*, even for *Him*!'

'Tell me,' I said, 'my wife –'

'Tell you!' The bitter contempt in the woman's tone did not hurt me. What was it to the self-contempt that had gnawed my heart all these months. 'Tell you! Yes, I'll tell you. Your wife was that ashamed of you she never so much as told me she was married. She let me think anything I pleased sooner than that. She just come 'ere, an' she said, "Nurse, take care of me, for I am in mortal trouble. And don't let them know where I am," says she. An' me being well married to an honest man, and well-to-do here, I was able to do it, by the blessing.'

'Why didn't you send for me before?' It was a cry of anguish wrung from me.

'I'd *never* 'a sent for you. It was *her* doin'. Oh, to think as God A'mighty's made men able to measure out such-like pecks o' trouble for us womenfolk! Young man, I don't know what you did to 'er to make 'er leave you; but it muster bin something cruel, for she loved the ground you walked on. She useter sit day after day a-lookin' at your picture, an' talkin' to it, an' kissin' of it, when she thought I wasn't takin' no notice, and cryin' till she made me cry too. She useter cry all night 'most. An' one day, when I tells 'er to pray to God to 'elp 'er through 'er trouble, she outs with *your* putty face on a card, she does, an', says she, with her poor little smile, "That's my god, Nursey," she says.'

'Don't!' I said feebly, putting out my hands to keep off the torture; 'not any more. Not now.'

'*Don't*,' she repeated. She had risen, and was walking up and down the room with clasped hands. 'Don't, indeed! No, I won't; but I shan't forget you! I tell you, I've had you in my prayers time and again, when I thought you'd made a light-o'-love of my darling. I shan't drop you outer them now, when I know she was your own wedded wife, as you chucked away when you tired of her, and left 'er to eat 'er 'art out with longin' for you. Oh! I pray to God above us to pay you scot and lot for all you done to 'er. You killed my pretty. The price will be required of you, young man, even to the uttermost farthing. Oh God in Heaven, make him suffer! Make him feel it!'

She stamped her foot as she passed me. I stood quite still. I bit my lip till I tasted the blood hot and salt on my tongue.

'She was nothing to you,' cried the woman, walking faster up and down between the rush chairs and the table; 'any fool can see that with half an eye. You didn't love her, so you don't feel nothin' now; but some day you'll care for someone, and then you shall know what she felt – if there's any justice in Heaven.'

I, too, rose, walked across the room, and leaned against the wall. I heard her words without understanding them.

'Can't you feel *nothin*'? Are you mader stone? Come an' look at 'er lyin' there so quiet. She don't fret arter the likes o' you no more now. She won't sit no more a-lookin' outer winder an' sayin' nothin' – only droppin' 'er tears one by one, slow, slow on her lap. Come an' see 'er; come an' see what you done to my pretty – an' then you can go. Nobody wants you 'ere. *She* don't want you now. But p'raps you'd like to see 'er safe under ground afore yer go? I'll be bound you'll put a big stone slab on 'er – to make sure she don't rise again.'

I turned on her. Her thin face was white with grief and rage. Her claw-like hands were clenched.

'Woman,' I said, 'have mercy.'

She paused and looked at me.

'Eh?' she said.

'Have mercy!' I said again.

'Mercy! You should 'a thought o' that before. You 'adn't no mercy on 'er. She loved you – she died loving you. An' if I wasn't a Christian woman, I'd kill you for it – like the rat you are! That I would, though I 'ad to swing for it afterwards.'

I caught the woman's hands and held them fast, though she writhed and resisted.

'Don't you understand?' I said savagely. 'We loved each other. She died loving me. I have to live loving her. And it's *her* you pity. I tell you it was all a mistake – a stupid, stupid mistake. Take me to her, and for pity's sake, let me be left alone with her.'

She hesitated; then said, in a voice only a shade less hard: 'Well, come along, then.'

We moved towards the door. As she opened it, a faint, weak cry fell on my ear. My heart stood still.

'What's that?' I asked, stopping on the threshold.

'Your child,' she said shortly.

That too! Oh, my love! oh, my poor love! All these long months!

'She allus said she'd send for you when she'd got over her trouble,' the woman said, as we climbed the stairs. "I'd like him to see his little baby, nurse," she says; "our little baby. It'll be all right when the baby's born," she says. "I know he'll come to me then. You'll see." And I never said nothin', not thinkin' you'd come if she was your leavin's and not dreamin' you could be 'er 'usband an' could stay away from 'er a hour –'er bein' as she was. Hush!'

She drew a key from her pocket and fitted it to a lock. She opened the door, and I followed her in. It was a large, dark room, full of old-fashioned furniture and a smell of lavender, camphor, and narcissus.

The big four-post bed was covered with white.

'My lamb – my poor, pretty lamb!' said the woman, beginning to cry for the first time as she drew back the sheet. 'Don't she look beautiful?'

I stood by the bedstead. I looked down on my wife's face. Just so I had seen it lie on the pillow beside me in the early morning, when the wind and the dawn came up from beyond the sea. She did not look like one dead. Her lips were still red, and it seemed to me that a tinge of colour lay on her cheek. It seemed to me, too, that if I kissed her she would awaken, and put her slight hand on my neck, and lay her cheek against mine – and that we should tell each other everything, and weep together, and understand, and be comforted.

So I stooped and laid my lips to hers as the old nurse stole from the room.

But the red lips were like marble, and she did not waken. She will not waken now ever any more.

I tell you again there are some things that cannot be written.

## 3

I lay that night in a big room, filled with heavy dark furniture, in a great four-poster hung with heavy, dark curtains – a bed, the counterpart of that other bed from whose side they had dragged me at last.

They fed me, I believe, and the old nurse was kind to me. I think she saw now that it is not the dead who are to be pitied most.

I lay at last in the big, roomy bed, and heard the household noises grow fewer and die out, the little wail of my child sounding latest. They had brought the child to me, and I had held it in my arms, and bowed my head over its tiny face and frail fingers. I did not love it then. I told myself it had cost me her life. But my heart told me it was I who had done that. The tall clock at the stair-head sounded the hours – eleven, twelve, one, and still I could not sleep. The room was dark and very still.

I had not yet been able to look at my life quietly. I had been full of the intoxication of grief – a real drunkenness, more merciful than the sober calm that comes afterwards.

Now I lay still as the dead woman in the next room, and looked at what was left of my life. I lay still, and thought, and thought, and thought. And in those hours I tasted the bitterness of death. It must have been about three when I first became aware of a slight sound that was not the ticking of a clock. I say I first became aware, and yet I knew perfectly that I had heard that sound more than once before, and had yet determined not to hear it, *because it came from the next room* – the room where the corpse lay.

And I did not wish to hear that sound, because I knew it meant that I was nervous – miserably nervous – a coward, and a brute. It meant that I, having killed my wife as surely as though I had put a knife in her breast, had now sunk so low as to be afraid of her dead body – the dead body that lay in the next room to mine. The heads of the beds were placed against the same wall: and from that wall I had fancied that I heard slight, slight, almost inaudible sounds.

So that when I say I became aware of them, I mean that I, at last, heard a sound so definite as to leave no room for doubt or question. It brought me to a sitting position in the bed, and the drops of sweat gathered heavily on my forehead and fell on my cold hands, as I held my breath and listened.

I don't know how long I sat there – there was no further sound – and at last my tense muscles relaxed, and I fell back on the pillow.

'You fool!' I said to myself; 'dead or alive, is she not your darling, your heart's heart? Would you not go near to die of joy, if she came back to you? Pray God to let her spirit come back and tell you she forgives you!'

'I wish she would come,' myself answered in words, while every fibre of my body and mind shrank and quivered in denial.

I struck a match, lighted a candle, and breathed more freely as I looked at the polished furniture – the commonplace details of an ordinary room. Then I thought of her, lying alone so near me, so quiet under the white sheet. She was dead; she would not wake or move. But suppose she did move? Suppose she turned back the sheet and got up and walked across the floor, and turned the door-handle?

As I thought it, I heard – plainly, unmistakably heard – the door of the chamber of death open slowly. I heard slow steps in the passage, slow, heavy steps. I heard the touch of hands on my door outside, uncertain hands that felt for the latch.

Sick with terror, I lay clenching the sheet in my hands.

I knew well enough what would come in when that door opened – that door on which my eyes were fixed. I dreaded to look, yet dared not turn away my eyes. The door opened slowly, slowly, slowly, and the figure of my dead wife came in. It came straight towards the bed, and stood at the bed foot in its white grave-clothes, with the white bandage under its chin. There was a scent of lavender and camphor and white narcissus. Its eyes were wide open, and looked at me with love unspeakable.

I could have shrieked aloud.

My wife spoke. It was the same dear voice that I had loved so to hear, but it was very weak and faint now; and now I trembled as I listened.

'You aren't afraid of me, darling, are you, though I am dead? I heard all you said to me when you came, but I couldn't answer. But now I've come back from the dead to tell you. I wasn't really so bad as you thought me. Elvira had told me she loved Oscar. I only wrote the letter to make it easier for you. I was too proud to tell you when you were so angry, but I am not proud any more now. You'll love again now, won't you, now I am dead. One always forgives dead people.'

The poor ghost's voice was hollow and faint. Abject terror paralysed me. I could answer nothing.

'Say you forgive me,' the thin, monotonous voice went on; 'say you love me again.'

I had to speak. Coward as I was, I did manage to stammer – 'Yes; I love you. I have always loved you, God help me.'

The sound of my own voice reassured me, and I ended more firmly than I began. The figure by the bed swayed a little, unsteadily.

'I suppose,' she said wearily, 'you would be afraid, now I am dead, if I came round to you and kissed you?'

She made a movement as though she would have come to me.

Then I did shriek aloud, again and again, and covered my face with the sheet and wound it round my head and body, and held it with all my force. There was a moment's silence. Then I heard my door close, and then a sound of feet and of voices, and I heard something heavy fall. I disentangled my head from the sheet. My room was empty. Then reason came back to me. I leaped from the bed.

'Ida, my darling, come back! I am not afraid! I love you. Come back! Come back!'

I sprang to my door and flung it open. Someone was bringing a light along the passage. On the floor, outside the door of the death chamber, was a huddled heap – the corpse, in its grave-clothes. Dead, dead, dead.

She is buried in Mellor churchyard, and there is no stone over her.

Now, whether it was catalepsy, as the doctor said, or whether my love came back, even from the dead, to me who loved her, I shall never know; but this I know, that if I had held out my arms to her as she stood at my bed-foot – if I had said, 'Yes, even from the grave, my darling – from hell itself, come back, come back to me!' – if I had had room in my coward's heart for anything but the unreasoning terror that killed love in that hour, I should not now be here alone. I shrank from her – I feared her – I would not take her to my heart. And now she will not come to me any more.

Why do I go on living?

You see, there is the child. It is four years old now, and it has never spoken and never smiled.

# The Three Drugs

Roger Wroxham looked round his studio before he blew out the candle, and wondered whether, perhaps, he looked for the last time. It was large and empty, yet his trouble had filled it, and, pressing against him in the prison of those four walls, forced him out into the world, where lights and voices and the presence of other men should give him room to draw back, to set a space between it and him, to decide whether he would ever face it again – he and it alone together. The nature of his trouble is not germane to this story. There was a woman in it, of course, and money, and a friend, and regrets and embarrassments – and all of these reached out tendrils that wove and interwove till they made a puzzle-problem of which heart and brain were now weary. It was as though his life depended on his deciphering the straggling characters traced by some spider who, having fallen into the ink-well, had dragged clogged legs in a black zigzag across his map of the world.

He blew out the candle and went quietly downstairs. It was nine at night, a soft night of May in Paris. Where should he go? He thought of the Seine, and took – an omnibus. The chestnut trees of the Boulevards brushed against the sides of the one that he boarded blindly in the first light street. He did not know where the omnibus was going. It did not matter. When at last it stopped he got off, and so strange was the place to him that for an instant it almost seemed as though the trouble itself had been left behind. He did not feel it in the length of three or four streets that he traversed slowly. But in the open space, very light and lively, where he recognised the Taverne de Paris and knew himself in Montmartre, the trouble set its teeth in his heart again, and he broke away from the lamps and the talk to struggle with it in the dark quiet streets beyond.

A man braced for such a fight has little thought to spare for the detail of his surroundings. The next thing that Wroxham knew of the outside world was the fact that he had known for some time that he was not alone in the street. There was someone on the other side of the road keeping pace with him – yes, certainly keeping pace, for, as he slackened his own, the feet on the other pavement also went more slowly. And now they were four feet, not two. Where had the other man sprung from? He had not been there a moment ago. And now, from an archway a little ahead of him, a third man came.

Wroxham stopped. Then three men converged upon him, and, like a sudden magic-lantern picture on a sheet prepared, there came to him all that he had heard and read of Montmartre – dark archways, knives, Apaches, and men who went away from homes where they were beloved and never again returned. He, too – well, if he never returned again, it would be quicker than the Seine, and, in the event of ultra-mundane possibilities, safer.

He stood still and laughed in the face of the man who first reached him.

'Well, my friend?' said he, and at that the other two drew close.

'Monsieur walks late,' said the first, a little confused, as it seemed, by that laugh.

'And will walk still later, if it pleases him,' said Roger. 'Good-night, my friends.'

'Ah!' said the second, 'friends do not say adieu so quickly. Monsieur will tell us the hour.'

'I have not a watch,' said Roger, quite truthfully.

'I will assist you to search for it,' said the third man, and laid a hand on his arm.

Roger threw it off. That was instinctive. One may be resigned to a man's knife between one's ribs, but not to his hands pawing one's shoulders. The man with the hand staggered back.

'The knife searches more surely,' said the second.

'No, no,' said the third quickly, 'he is too heavy. I for one will not carry him afterwards.'

They closed round him, hustling him between them. Their pale, degenerate faces spun and swung round him in the struggle. For there was a struggle. He had not meant that there should be a struggle. Someone would hear – someone would come.

But if any heard, none came. The street retained its empty silence, the houses, masked in close shutters, kept their reserve. The four were wrestling, all pressed close together in a writhing bunch, drawing breath hardly through set teeth, their feet slipping, and not slipping, on the rounded cobble-stones.

The contact with these creatures, the smell of them, the warm, greasy texture of their flesh as, in the conflict, his face or neck met neck or face of theirs – Roger felt a cold rage possess him. He wrung two clammy hands apart and threw something off – something that staggered back clattering, fell in the gutter, and lay there.

It was then that Roger felt the knife. Its point glanced off the cigarette-case in his breast pocket and bit sharply at his inner arm. And at the sting of it Roger knew that he did not desire to die. He feigned a reeling weakness, relaxed his grip, swayed sideways, and then suddenly caught the other two in a new grip, crushed their faces together, flung them off, and ran. It was but for an instant that his feet were the only ones that echoed in the steep. Then he knew that the others too were running.

It was like one of those nightmares wherein one runs for ever, leaden-footed, through a city of the dead. Roger turned sharply to the right. The sound of the other footsteps told that the pursuers also had turned that corner. Here was another street – a steep ascent. He ran more swiftly – he was running now for his life – the life that he held so cheap three minutes before. And all the streets were empty – empty like dream-streets, with all their windows dark and unhelpful, their doors fast closed against his need.

Far away down the street and across steep roofs lay Paris, poured out like a pool of light in the mist of the valley. But Roger was running with his head down – he saw nothing but the round heads of the cobble-stones. Only now and again he glanced to right or left, if perchance some window might show light to justify a cry for help, some door advance the welcome of an open inch.

There was at last such a door. He did not see it till it was almost behind him. Then there was the drag of the sudden stop – the eternal instant of indecision. Was there time? There must be. He dashed his fingers through the inch-crack, grazing the backs of them, leapt within, drew the door after him, felt madly for a lock or bolt, found a key, and, hanging his whole weight on it, strove to get the door home. The key turned. His left hand, by which he braced himself against the door-jamb, found a hook and pulled on it. Door and door-post met – the latch clicked – with a spring as it seemed. He turned the key, leaning against the door, which shook to the deep sobbing breaths that shook him, and to the panting bodies that pressed a moment without. Then someone cursed breathlessly outside; there was the sound of feet that went away.

Roger was alone in the strange darkness of an arched carriageway, through the far end of which showed the fainter darkness of a courtyard, with black shapes of little formal tubbed orange trees. There was no sound at all there but the sound of his own desperate breathing; and, as he stood, the slow, warm blood crept down his wrist, to make a little pool in the hollow of his hanging, half-clenched hand. Suddenly he felt sick.

This house, of which he knew nothing, held for him no terrors. To him at that moment there were but three murderers in all the world, and where they were not, there safety was. But the spacious silence that soothed at first, presently clawed at the set, vibrating nerves already overstrained. He found himself listening, listening, and there was nothing to hear but the silence, and once, before he thought to twist his handkerchief round it, the drip of blood from his hand.

By and by, he knew that he was not alone in this house, for from far away there came the faint sound of a footstep, and, quite near, the faint answering echo of it. And at a window, high up on the other side of the courtyard, a light showed. Light and sound and echo intensified, the light passing window after window, till at last it moved across the courtyard, and the little trees threw back shifting shadows as it came towards him – a lamp in the hand of a man.

It was a short, bald man, with pointed beard and bright, friendly eyes. He held the lamp high as he came, and when he saw Roger, he drew his breath in an inspiration that spoke of surprise, sympathy, and pity.

'Hold! hold!' he said, in a singularly pleasant voice, 'there has been a misfortune? You are wounded, monsieur?'

'Apaches,' said Roger, and was surprised at the weakness of his own voice.

'Your hand?'

'My arm,' said Roger.

'Fortunately,' said the other, 'I am a surgeon. Allow me.'

He set the lamp on the step of a closed door, took off Roger's coat, and quickly tied his own handkerchief round the wounded arm.

'Now,' he said, 'courage! I am alone in the house. No-one comes here but me. If you can walk up to my rooms, you will save us both much trouble. If you cannot, sit here and I will fetch you a cordial. But I advise you to try and walk. That *porte cochère* is, unfortunately, not very strong, and the lock is a common spring lock, and your friends may return with *their* friends; whereas the door across the courtyard is heavy and the bolts are new.'

Roger moved towards the heavy door whose bolts were new. The stairs seemed to go on for ever. The doctor lent his arm, but the carved banisters and their lively shadows whirled before Roger's eyes. Also, he seemed to be shod with lead, and to have in his legs bones that were red-hot. Then the stairs ceased, and there was light, and a cessation of the dragging of those leaden feet. He was on a couch, and his eyes might close. There was no need to move any more, nor to look, nor to listen.

When next he saw and heard, he was lying at ease, the close intimacy of a bandage clasping his arm, and in his mouth the vivid taste of some cordial.

The doctor was sitting in an armchair near a table, looking benevolent through gold-rimmed pince-nez.

'Better?' he said. 'No, lie still, you'll be a new man soon.'

'I am desolated,' said Roger, 'to have occasioned you all this trouble.'

'Not at all,' said the doctor. 'We live to heal, and it is a nasty cut, that in your arm. If you are wise, you will rest at present. I shall be honoured if you will be my guest for the night.'

Roger again murmured something about trouble.

'In a big house like this,' said the doctor, as it seemed a little sadly, 'there are many empty rooms, and some rooms which are not empty. There is a bed altogether at your service, monsieur, and I counsel you not to delay in seeking it. You can walk?'

Wroxham stood up. 'Why, yes,' he said, stretching himself. 'I feel, as you say, a new man.'

A narrow bed and rush-bottomed chair showed like doll's-house furniture in the large, high, gaunt room to which the doctor led him.

'You are too tired to undress yourself,' said the doctor, 'rest – only rest,' and covered him with a rug, roundly tucked him up, and left him.

'I leave the door open,' he said, 'in case you have any fever. Good night. Do not torment yourself. All goes well.'

Then he took away the lamp, and Wroxham lay on his back and saw the shadows of the window-frames cast on the wall by the moon now risen. His eyes, growing accustomed to the darkness, perceived the carving of the white panelled walls and mantel-piece. There was a door in the room, another door from the one which the doctor had left open. Roger did not like open doors. The other door, however, was closed. He wondered where it led, and whether it were locked. Presently he got up to see. It was locked. He lay down again.

His arm gave him no pain, and the night's adventure did not seem to have overset his nerves. He felt, on the contrary, calm, confident, extraordinarily at ease, and master of himself. The trouble – how could that ever have seemed important? This calmness – it felt like the calmness that precedes sleep. Yet sleep was far from him. What was it that kept sleep away? The bed was comfortable – the pillows soft. What was it? It came to him presently that it was the scent which distracted him, worrying him with a memory that he could not define. A faint scent of – what was it? Perfumery? Yes – and camphor – and something else – something vaguely disquieting. He had not noticed it before he had risen and tried the handle of that other door. But now – He covered his face with the sheet, but through the sheet he smelt it still. He rose and threw back one of the long French windows. It opened with a click and a jar, and he looked across the dark well of the courtyard. He leaned out, breathing the chill, pure air of the May night, but when he withdrew his head, the scent was there again. Camphor – perfume – and something else. What was it that it reminded him of? He had his knee on the bed-edge when the answer came to that question. It was the scent that had struck at him from a darkened room when, a child, clutching at a grown-up hand, he had been led to the bed where, amid flowers, something white lay under a sheet – his mother they had told him. It was the scent of death, disguised with drugs and perfumes.

He stood up and went, with carefully controlled swiftness, towards the open door. He wanted light and a human voice. The doctor was in the room upstairs; he –

The doctor was face to face with him on the landing, not a yard away, moving towards him quietly in shoeless feet.

'I can't sleep,' said Wroxham, a little wildly, 'it's too dark –'

'Come upstairs,' said the doctor, and Wroxham went.

There was comfort in the large, lighted room, with its shelves and shelves full of well-bound books, its tables heaped with papers and pamphlets – its air of natural everyday work. There was a warmth of red curtain at the windows. On the window ledge a plant in a pot, its leaves like red misshapen hearts. A green-shaded lamp stood on the table. A peaceful, pleasant interior.

'What's behind that door,' said Wroxham, abruptly – 'that door downstairs?'

'Specimens,' the doctor answered, 'preserved specimens. My line is physiological research. You understand?'

So that was it.

'I feel quite well, you know,' said Wroxham, laboriously explaining – 'fit as any man – only I can't sleep.'

'I see,' said the doctor.

'It's the scent from your specimens, I think,' Wroxham went on; 'there's something about that scent –'

'Yes,' said the doctor.

'It's very odd.' Wroxham was leaning his elbow on his knee and his chin on his hand. 'I feel so frightfully well – and yet – there's a strange feeling –'

'Yes,' said the doctor. 'Yes, tell me exactly what you feel.'

'I feel,' said Wroxham, slowly, 'like a man on the crest of a wave.'

The doctor stood up.

'You feel well, happy, full of life and energy – as though you could walk to the world's end, and yet –'

'And yet,' said Roger, 'as though my next step might be my last – as though I might step into my grave.'

He shuddered.

'Do you,' asked the doctor, anxiously – 'do you feel thrills of pleasure – something like the first waves of chloroform – thrills running from your hair to your feet?'

'I felt all that,' said Roger, slowly, 'downstairs before I opened the window.'

The doctor looked at his watch, frowned and got up quickly. 'There is very little time,' he said.

Suddenly Roger felt an unexplained opposition stiffen his mind.

The doctor went to a long laboratory bench with bottle-filled shelves above it, and on it crucibles and retorts, test tubes, beakers – all a chemist's apparatus – reached a bottle from a shelf, and measured out certain drops into a graduated glass, added water, and stirred it with a glass rod.

'Drink that,' he said.

'No,' said Roger, and as he spoke a thrill like the first thrill of the first chloroform wave swept through him, and it was a thrill, not of pleasure, but of pain. 'No,' he said, and 'Ah!' for the pain was sharp.

'If you don't drink,' said the doctor, carefully, 'you are a dead man.'

'You may be giving me poison,' Roger gasped, his hands at his heart.

'I may,' said the doctor. 'What do you suppose poison makes you feel like? What do you feel like now?'

'I feel,' said Roger, 'like death.'

Every nerve, every muscle thrilled to a pain not too intense to be underlined by a shuddering nausea.

'Then drink,' cried the doctor, in tones of such cordial entreaty, such evident anxiety, that Wroxham half held his hand out for the glass. 'Drink! Believe me, it is your only chance.'

Again the pain swept through him like an electric current. The beads of sweat sprang out on his forehead.

'That wound,' the doctor pleaded, standing over him with the glass held out. 'For God's sake, drink! Don't you understand, man? You *are* poisoned. Your wound –'

'The knife?' Wroxham murmured, and as he spoke, his eyes seemed to swell in his head, and his head itself to grow enormous. 'Do you know the poison – and its antidote?'

'I know all.' The doctor soothed him. 'Drink, then, my friend.'

As the pain caught him again in a clasp more close than any lover's he clutched at the glass and drank. The drug met the pain and mastered it. Roger, in the ecstasy of pain's cessation, saw the world fade and go out in a haze of vivid violet.

*2*

Faint films of lassitude, shot with contentment, wrapped him round. He lay passive, as a man lies in the convalescence that follows a long fight with Death. Fold on fold of white peace lay all about him.

'I'm better now,' he said, in a voice that was a whisper – tried to raise his hand from where it lay helpless in his sight, failed, and lay looking at it in confident repose – 'much better.'

'Yes,' said the doctor, and his pleasant, soft voice had grown softer, pleasanter. 'You are now in the second stage. An interval is necessary before you can pass to the third. I will enliven the interval by conversation. Is there anything you would like to know?'

'Nothing,' said Roger; 'I am quite contented.'

'This is very interesting,' said the doctor. 'Tell me exactly how you feel.'

Roger faintly and slowly told him.

'Ah!' the doctor said, 'I have not before heard this. You are the only one of them all who ever passed the first stage. The others –'

'The others?' said Roger, but he did not care much about the others.

'The others,' said the doctor frowning, 'were unsound. Decadent students, degenerate Apaches. You are highly trained – in fine physical condition. And your brain! God be good to the Apaches, who so delicately excited it to just the degree of activity needed for my purpose.'

'The others?' Wroxham insisted.

'The others? They are in the room whose door was locked. Look – you should be able to see them. The second drug should lay your consciousness before me, like a sheet of white paper on which I can write what I choose. If I choose that you should see my specimens – *Allons donc.* I have no secrets from you now.

Look – look – strain your eyes. In theory, I know all that you can do and feel and see in this second stage. But practically – enlighten me – look – shut your eyes and look!'

Roger closed his eyes and looked. He saw the gaunt, uncarpeted staircase, the open doors of the big rooms, passed to the locked door, and it opened at his touch. The room inside was like the others, spacious and panelled. A lighted lamp with a blue shade hung from the ceiling, and below it an effect of spread whiteness. Roger looked. There *were* things to be seen.

With a shudder he opened his eyes on the doctor's delightful room, the doctor's intent face.

'What did you see?' the doctor asked. 'Tell me!'

'Did you kill them all?' Roger asked back.

'They died – of their own inherent weakness,' the doctor said. 'And you saw them?'

'I saw,' said Roger, 'the quiet people lying all along the floor in their death clothes – the people who have come in at that door of yours that is a trap – for robbery, or curiosity, or shelter, and never gone out any more.'

'Right,' said the doctor. 'Right. My theory is proved at every point. You can see what I choose you to see. Yes, decadents all. It was in embalming that I was a specialist before I began these other investigations.'

'What,' Roger whispered – 'what is it all for?'

'To make the superman,' said the doctor. 'I will tell you.'

He told. It was a long story – the story of a man's life, a man's work, a man's dreams, hopes, ambitions.

'The secret of life,' the doctor ended. 'That is what all the alchemists sought. They sought it where Fate pleased. I sought it where I have found it – in death.'

Roger thought of the room behind the locked door.

'And the secret is?' he asked.

'I have told you,' said the doctor impatiently; 'it is in the third drug that life – splendid, superhuman life – is found. I have tried it on animals. Always they became perfect, all that an animal should be. And more, too – much more. They were too perfect, too near humanity. They looked at me with human eyes. I could not let them live. Such animals it is not necessary to embalm. I had a laboratory in those days – and assistants. They called me the Prince of Vivisectors.'

The man on the sofa shuddered.

'I am naturally,' the doctor went on, 'a tender-hearted man. You see it in my face; my voice proclaims it. Think what I have suffered in the sufferings of these poor beasts who never injured me. My God! Bear witness that I have not buried my talent. I have been faithful. I have laid down all – love, and joy, and pity, and the little beautiful things of life – all, all, on the altar of science, and seen them consume away. I deserve my heaven, if ever man did. And now by all the saints in heaven I am near it!'

'What is the third drug?' Roger asked, lying limp and flat on his couch.

'It is the Elixir of Life,' said the doctor. 'I am not its discoverer; the old alchemists knew it well, but they failed because they sought to apply the elixir to a normal – that is, a diseased and faulty – body. I knew better. One must have first a body abnormally healthy, abnormally strong. Then, not the elixir, but the two drugs that prepare. The first excites prematurely the natural conflict between the principles of life and death, and then, just at the point where Death is about to win his victory, the second drug intensifies life so that it conquers – intensifies, and yet chastens. Then the whole life of the subject, risen to an ecstasy, falls prone in an almost voluntary submission to the coming super-life. Submission – submission! The garrison must surrender before the splendid conqueror can enter and make the citadel his own. Do you understand? Do you submit?'

'I submit,' said Roger, for, indeed, he did. 'But – soon – quite soon – I will not submit.'

He was too weak to be wise, or those words had remained unspoken.

The doctor sprang to his feet.

'It works too quickly!' he cried. 'Everything works too quickly with you. Your condition is too perfect. So now I bind you.'

From a drawer beneath the bench where the bottles gleamed, the doctor drew rolls of bandages – violet, like the haze that had drowned, at the urgence of the second drug, the consciousness of Roger. He moved, faintly resistant, on his couch. The doctor's hands, most gently, most irresistibly, controlled his movement.

'Lie still,' said the gentle, charming voice. 'Lie still; all is well.' The clever, soft hands were unrolling the bandages – passing them round arms and throat – under and over the soft narrow couch. 'I cannot risk your life, my poor boy. The least movement of yours might ruin everything. The third drug, like the first, must be offered directly to the blood which absorbs it. I bound the first drug as an unguent upon your knife-wound.'

The swift hands, the soft bandages, passed back and forth, over and under – flashes of violet passed to and fro in the air, like the shuttle of a weaver through his warp. As the bandage clasped his knees, Roger moved.

'For God's sake, no!' the doctor cried; 'the time is so near. If you cease to submit it is death.'

With an incredible, accelerated swiftness he swept the bandages round and round knees and ankles, drew a deep breath – stood upright.

'I must make an incision,' he said – 'in the head this time. It will not hurt. See! I spray it with the Constantia Nepenthe; that also I discovered. My boy, in a moment you know all things – you are as God. For God's sake, be patient. Preserve your submission.'

And Roger, with life and will resurgent hammering at his heart, preserved it.

He did not feel the knife that made the cross-cut on his temple, but he felt the hot spurt of blood that followed the cut; he felt the cool flap of a plaster, spread with some sweet, clean-smelling unguent that met the blood and stanched it. There was a moment – or was it hours? – of nothingness. Then from that cut on his forehead there seemed to radiate threads of infinite length, and of a strength that one could trust to – threads that linked one to all knowledge past and present. He felt that he controlled all wisdom, as a driver controls his four-in-hand. Knowledge, he perceived, belonged to him, as the air belongs to the eagle. He swam in it, as a great fish in a limitless ocean.

He opened his eyes and met those of the doctor, who sighed as one to whom breath has grown difficult.

'Ah, all goes well. Oh, my boy, was it not worth it? What do you feel?'

'I. Know. Everything,' said Roger, with full stops between the words.

'Everything? The future?'

'No. I know all that man has ever known.'

'Look back – into the past. See someone. See Pharaoh. You see him – on his throne?'

'Not on his throne. He is whispering in a corner of his great gardens to a girl, who is the daughter of a water-carrier.'

'Bah! Any poet of my dozen decadents, who lie so still, could have told me that. Tell me secrets – the *Masque de Fer*.'

The other told a tale, wild and incredible, but it satisfied the teller.

'That too – it might be imagination. Tell me the name of the woman I loved and –'

The echo of the name of the anaesthetic came to Roger; 'Constantia,' said he, in an even voice.

'Ah,' the doctor cried, 'now I see you know all things. It was not murder. I hoped to dower her with all the splendours of the super-life.'

'Her bones lie under the lilacs, where you used to kiss her in the spring,' said Roger, quite without knowing what it was that he was going to say.

'It is enough,' the doctor cried. He sprang up, ranged certain bottles and glasses on a table convenient to his chair. 'You know all things. It was not a dream, this, the dream of my life. It is true. It is a fact accomplished. Now I, too, will know all things. I will be as the gods.'

He sought among leather cases on a far table, and came back swiftly into the circle of light that lay below the green-shaded lamp.

Roger, floating contentedly on the new sea of knowledge that seemed to support him, turned eyes on the trouble that had driven him out of that large, empty studio so long ago, so far away. His newfound wisdom laughed at that problem, laughed and solved it. 'To end that trouble I must do so-and-so, say such-and-such,' Roger told himself again and again.

And now the doctor, standing by the table, laid on it his pale, plump hand outspread. He drew a knife from a case – a long, shiny knife – and scored his hand across and across its back, as a cook scores pork for cooking. The slow blood followed the cuts in beads and lines.

Into the cuts he dropped a green liquid from a little bottle, replaced its stopper, bound up his hand and sat down.

'The beginning of the first stage,' he said; 'almost at once I shall begin to be a new man. It will work quickly. My body, like yours, is sane and healthy.'

There was a long silence.

'Oh, but this is good,' the doctor broke it to say. 'I feel the hand of Life sweeping my nerves like harp-strings.'

Roger had been thinking, the old common sense that guides an ordinary man breaking through this consciousness of illimitable wisdom. 'You had better,' he said, 'unbind me; when the hand of Death sweeps your nerves, you may need help.'

'No,' the doctor said, 'and no, and no, and no many times. I am afraid of you. You know all things, and even in your body you are stronger than I. When I, too, am a god, and filled with the wine of knowledge, I will loose you, and together we will drink of the fourth drug – the mordant that shall fix the others and set us eternally on a level with the immortals.'

'Just as you like, of course,' said Roger, with a conscious effort after commonplace. Then suddenly, not commonplace any more – 'Loose me!' he cried; 'loose me, I tell you! I am wiser than you.'

'You are also stronger,' said the doctor, and then suddenly and irresistibly the pain caught him. Roger saw his face contorted with agony, his hands clench on the arm of his chair; and it seemed that, either this man was less able to bear pain than he, or that the pain was much more violent than had been his own. Between the grippings of the anguish the doctor dragged on his watch-chain; the watch leapt from his pocket, and rattled as his trembling hand laid it on the table.

'Not yet,' he said, when he had looked at its face, 'not yet, not yet, not yet.' It seemed to Roger, lying there bound, that the other man repeated those words for long days and weeks. And the plump, pale hand, writhing and distorted by anguish, again and again drew near to take the glass that stood ready on the table, and with convulsive self-restraint again and again drew back without it.

The short May night was waning – the shiver of dawn rustled the leaves of the plant whose leaves were like red misshaped hearts.

'Now!' The doctor screamed the word, grasped the glass, drained it and sank back in his chair. His hand struck the table beside him. Looking at his limp body and head thrown back, one could almost see the cessation of pain, the coming of kind oblivion.

### 3

The dawn had grown to daylight, a poor, grey, rain-stained daylight, not strong enough to pierce the curtains and persiennes; and yet not so weak but that it could mock the lamp, now burnt low and smelling vilely.

Roger lay very still on his couch, a man wounded, anxious, and extravagantly tired. In those hours of long, slow dawning, face to face with the unconscious figure in the chair, he had felt, slowly and little by little, the recession of that sea of knowledge on which he had felt himself float in such content. The sea had withdrawn itself, leaving him high and dry on the shore of the normal. The only relic that he had clung to and that he still grasped was the answer to the problem of the trouble – the only wisdom that he had put into words. These words remained to him, and he knew that they held wisdom – very simple wisdom, too.

'To end the trouble, I must do so-and-so and say such-and-such.'

But of all that had seemed to set him on a pinnacle, had evened him with the immortals, nothing else was left. He was just Roger Wroxham – wounded, and bound, in a locked house, one of whose rooms was full of very quiet people, and in another room himself and a dead man. For now it was so long since the doctor had moved that it seemed he must be dead. He had got to know every line of that room, every fold of drapery, every flower on the wall-paper, the number of the books, the shapes and sizes of things. Now he could no longer look at these. He looked at the other man.

Slowly a dampness spread itself over Wroxham's forehead and tingled among the roots of his hair. He writhed in his bonds. They held fast. He could not move hand or foot. Only his head could turn a little, so that he could at will see the doctor or not see him. A shaft of desolate light pierced the persienne at its hinge and rested on the table, where an overturned glass lay.

Wroxham thrilled from head to foot. The body in the chair stirred – hardly stirred – shivered rather – and a very faint, far-away voice said: 'Now the third – give me the third.'

'What?' said Roger, stupidly; and he had to clear his throat twice before he could say even that.

'The moment is now,' said the doctor. 'I remember all. I made you a god. Give me the third drug.'

'Where is it?' Roger asked.

'It is at my elbow,' the doctor murmured. 'I submit – I submit. Give me the third drug, and let me be as you are.'

'As *I* am?' said Roger. 'You forget. *I* am bound.'

'Break your bonds,' the doctor urged, in a quick, small voice. 'I trust you now. You are stronger than all men, as you are wiser. Stretch your muscles, and the bandages will fall asunder like snow-wreaths.'

'It is too late,' Wroxham said, and laughed; 'all that is over. I am not wise any more, and I have only the strength of a man. I am tired and wounded. I cannot break your bonds – I cannot help you!'

'But if you cannot help me – it is death,' said the doctor.

'It is death,' said Roger. 'Do you feel it coming on you?'

'I feel life returning,' said the doctor; 'it is now the moment – the one possible moment. And I cannot reach it. Oh, give it me – give it me!'

Then Roger cried out suddenly, in a loud voice: 'Now, by God in heaven, you damned decadent, I am *glad* that I cannot give it. Yes if it costs me my life, it's worth it, you madman, so that your life ends too. Now be silent, and die like a man, if you have it in you.'

Only one word seemed to reach the man in the chair.

'A decadent!' he repeated. 'I? But no, I am like you – I see what I will. I close my eyes, and I see – no – not that – ah! – not that!' He writhed faintly in his chair, and to Roger it seemed that for that writhing figure there would be no return of power and life and will.

'Not that,' he moaned. 'Not that,' and writhed in a gasping anguish that bore no more words.

Roger lay and watched him, and presently he writhed from the chair to the floor, tearing feebly at it with his fingers, moaned, shuddered, and lay very still.

Of all that befell Roger in that house, the worst was now. For now he knew that he was alone with the dead, and between him and death stretched certain hours and days. For the *porte cochère* was locked; the doors of the house itself were locked – heavy doors and the locks new.

'I am alone in the house,' the doctor had said. 'No-one comes here but me.'

No-one would come. He would die there – he, Roger Wroxham – 'poor old Roger Wroxham, who was no one's enemy but his own.' Tears pricked his eyes. He shook his head impatiently and they fell from his lashes.

'You fool,' he said, 'can't *you* die like a man either?'

Then he set his teeth and made himself lie still. It seemed to him that now Despair laid her hand on his heart. But, to speak truth, it was Hope whose hand lay there. This was so much more than a man should be called on to bear – it could not be true. It was an evil dream. He would wake presently. Or if it were, indeed, real – then someone would come, someone must come. God could not let nobody come to save him.

And late at night, when heart and brain had been stretched to the point where both break and let in the sea of madness, someone came.

The interminable day had worn itself out. Roger had screamed, yelled, shouted till his throat was dried up, his lips baked and cracked. No-one heard. How should they? The twilight had thickened and thickened, till at last it made a shroud for the dead man on the floor by the chair. And there were other dead men in that house; and as Roger ceased to see the one he saw the others – the quiet, awful faces, the lean hands, the straight, stiff limbs laid out one beyond another in the room of death. They at least were not bound. If they should rise in their white wrappings and, crossing that empty sleeping chamber very softly, come slowly up the stairs –

A stair creaked.

His ears, strained with hours of listening, thought themselves befooled. But his cowering heart knew better.

Again a stair creaked. There was a hand on the door.

'Then it is all over,' said Roger in the darkness, 'and I *am* mad.'

The door opened very slowly, very cautiously. There was no light. Only the sound of soft feet and draperies that rustled.

Then suddenly a match spurted – light struck at his eyes; a flicker of lit candle-wick steadying to flame. And the things that had come were not those quiet people creeping up to match their death with his death in life, but human creatures, alive, breathing, with eyes that moved and glittered, lips that breathed and spoke.

'He must be here,' one said. 'Lisette watched all day; he never came out. He must be here – there is nowhere else.'

Then they set up the candle-end on the table, and he saw their faces. They were the Apaches who had set on him in that lonely street, and who had sought him here – to set on him again.

He sucked his dry tongue, licked his dry lips, and cried aloud: – 'Here I am! Oh, kill me! For the love of God, brothers, kill me *now*!'

And even before he spoke, they had seen him, and seen what lay on the floor.

'He died this morning. I am bound. Kill me, brothers; I cannot die slowly here alone. Oh, kill me, for Christ's sake!'

But already the three were pressing on each other at a doorway suddenly grown too narrow. They could kill a living man, but they could not face death, quiet, enthroned.

'For the love of Christ,' Roger screamed, 'have pity! Kill me outright! Come back – come back!'

And then, since even Apaches are human, one of them did come back. It was the one he had flung into the gutter. The feet of the others sounded on the stairs as he caught up the candle and bent over Roger, knife in hand.

'Make sure,' said Roger, through set teeth.

'*Nom d'un nom*,' said the Apache, with worse words, and cut the bandages here, and here, and here again, and there, and lower, to the very feet.

Then this good Samaritan helped Roger to rise, and when he could not stand, the Samaritan half pulled, half carried him down those many steps, till they came upon the others putting on their boots at the stair-foot.

Then between them the three men who could walk carried the other out and slammed the outer door, and presently set him against a gate-post in another street, and went their wicked ways.

And after a time, a girl with furtive eyes brought brandy and hoarse, muttered kindnesses, and slid away in the shadows.

Against that gate-post the police came upon him. They took him to the address they found on him. When they came to question him he said, 'Apaches', and his late variations on that theme were deemed sufficient, though not one of them touched truth or spoke of the third drug.

There has never been anything in the papers about that house. I think it is still closed, and inside it still lie in the locked room the very quiet people; and above, there is the room with the narrow couch and the scattered, cut, violet bandages, and the thing on the floor by the chair, under the lamp that burned itself out in that May dawning.

# The Pavilion

There was never a moment's doubt in her own mind. So she said afterwards. And everyone agreed that she had concealed her feelings with true womanly discretion. Her friend and confidante, Amelia Davenant, was at any rate completely deceived. Amelia was one of those featureless blondes who seem born to be overlooked. She adored her beautiful friend, and never, from first to last, could see any fault in her, except, perhaps, on the evening when the real things of the story happened. And even in that matter she owned at the time that it was only that her darling Ernestine did not understand.

Ernestine was a prettyish girl with the airs, so irresistible and misleading, of a beauty; most people said that she was beautiful, and she certainly managed, with extraordinary success, to produce the illusion of beauty. Quite a number of plainish girls achieve that effect nowadays. The freedom of modern dress and coiffure and the increasing confidence in herself which the modern girl experiences, aid her in fostering the illusion; but in the sixties, when everyone wore much the same sort of bonnet, when your choice in coiffure was limited to bandeaux or ringlets, and the crinoline was your only wear, something very like genius was needed to deceive the world in the matter of your personal charms. Ernestine had that genius; hers was the smiling, ringleted, dark-haired, dark-eyed, sparkling type.

Amelia had blonde bandeaux and kind, appealing blue eyes, rather too small and rather too dull; her hands and ears were beautiful, and she kept them out of sight as much as possible. In our times the blonde hair would have been puffed out to make a frame for the forehead, a little too high; a certain shade of blue and a certain shade of boldness would have made her eyes effective. And the beautiful hands would have learned that flowerlike droop of the wrist so justly and so universally admired. But as it was, Amelia was very nearly plain, and in her secret emotional self-communings told herself that she was ugly. It was she who, at the age of fourteen, composed the remarkable poem beginning:

> I know that I am ugly: did I make
> The face that is the laugh and jest of all?

and goes on, after disclaiming any personal responsibility for the face, to entreat the kind earth to 'cover it away from mocking eyes', and to 'let the daisies blossom where it lies'.

Amelia did not want to die, and her face was not the laugh and jest, or indeed the special interest, of anyone. All that was poetic licence. Amelia had read perhaps a little too much poetry of the type of '*Quand je suis morte, mes amies, plantez un saule au cimetière*'; but really life was a very good thing to Amelia, especially when she had a new dress and someone paid her a compliment. But she went on writing verses extolling the advantages of The Tomb, and grovelling metrically at the feet of One who was Another's until that summer, when she was nineteen, and went to stay with Ernestine at Doricourt. Then her Muse took flight, scared, perhaps, by the possibility, suddenly and threateningly presented, of being asked to inspire verse about the real things of life.

At any rate, Amelia ceased to write poetry about the time when she and Ernestine and Ernestine's aunt went on a visit to Doricourt, where Frederick Powell lived with his aunt. It was not one of those hurried motor-fed excursions which we have now, and call weekends, but a long leisurely visit, when all the friends of the static aunt called on the dynamic aunt, and both returned the calls with much state, a big barouche and a pair of fat horses. There were croquet parties and archery parties and little dances, all pleasant informal little gaieties arranged without ceremony among people who lived within driving distance of each other and knew each other's tastes and incomes and family history as well as they knew their own. The habit of importing huge droves of strangers from distant countries for brief harrying raids did not then obtain. There was instead a wide and constant circle of pleasant people with an unflagging stream of gaiety, mild indeed, but delightful to unjaded palates.

And at Doricourt life was delightful even on the days when there was no party. It was perhaps more delightful to Ernestine than to her friend, but even so, the one least pleased was Ernestine's aunt.

'I do think,' she said to the other aunt whose name was Julia – 'I daresay it is not so to you, being accustomed to Mr W. Frederick, of course, from his childhood, but I always find gentlemen in the house so unsettling, especially young gentlemen, and when there are young ladies also. One is always on the *qui vive* for excitement.'

'Of course,' said Aunt Julia, with the air of a woman of the world, 'living as you and dear Ernestine do, with only females in the house . . .'

'We hang up an old coat and hat of my brother's on the hat stand in the hall,' Aunt Emmeline protested.

' . . . The presence of gentlemen in the house must be a little unsettling. For myself, I am inured to it. Frederick has so many friends. Mr Thesiger, perhaps, the greatest. I believe him to be a most worthy young man, but peculiar.' She leaned forward across her bright-tinted Berlin woolwork and spoke impressively, the needle with its trailing red poised in air. 'You know, I hope you will not think it indelicate of me to mention such a thing, but dear Frederick . . . your dear Ernestine would have been in every way so suitable.'

'Would have been?' Aunt Emmeline's tortoise-shell shuttle ceased its swift movement among the white loops and knots of her tatting.

'Well, my dear,' said the other aunt, a little shortly, 'you must surely have noticed . . .'

'You don't mean to suggest that Amelia . . . I thought Mr Thesiger and Amelia . . .'

'Amelia! I really must say! No, I was alluding to Mr Thesiger's attentions to dear Ernestine. Most marked. In dear Frederick's place I should have found some excuse for shortening Mr Thesiger's visit. But, of course, I cannot interfere. Gentlemen must manage these things for themselves. I only hope that there will be none of that trifling with the most holy affections of others which . . .'

The less voluble aunt cut in hotly with: 'Ernestine's incapable of anything so unladylike.'

'Just what I was saying,' the other rejoined blandly, got up and drew the blind a little lower, for the afternoon sun was glowing on the rosy wreaths of the drawing-room carpet.

Outside in the sunshine Frederick was doing his best to arrange his own affairs. He had managed to place himself beside Miss Ernestine Meutys on the stone steps of the pavilion; but then, Mr Thesiger lay along the lower step at her feet, a very good position for looking up into her eyes. Amelia was beside him, but then it never seemed to matter whom Amelia sat beside.

They were talking about the pavilion on whose steps they sat, and Amelia who often asked uninteresting questions had wondered how old it was. It was Frederick's pavilion after all, and he felt this when his friend took the words out of his mouth and used them on his own account, even though he did give the answer in the form of an appeal.

'The foundations are Tudor, aren't they?' he said. 'Wasn't it an observatory or laboratory or something of that sort in Fat Henry's time?'

'Yes,' said Frederick, 'there was some story about a wizard or an alchemist or something, and it was burned down, and then they rebuilt it in its present style.'

'The Italian style, isn't it?' said Thesiger; 'but you can hardly see what it is now, for the creeper.'

'Virginia creeper, isn't it?' Amelia asked, and Frederick said: 'Yes, Virginia creeper.' Thesiger said it looked more like a South American plant, and Ernestine said Virginia was in South America and that was why. 'I know, because of the war,' she said modestly, and nobody smiled or answered. There were manners in those days.

'There's a ghost story about it surely,' Thesiger began again, looking up at the dark closed doors of the pavilion.

'Not that I ever heard of,' said the pavilion's owner. 'I think the country people invented the tale because there have always been so many rabbits and weasels and things found dead near it. And once a dog, my uncle's favourite spaniel. But of course that's simply because they get entangled in the Virginia creeper – you see how fine and big it is – and can't get out, and die as they do in traps. But the villagers prefer to think it's ghosts.'

'I thought there was a real ghost story,' Thesiger persisted.

Ernestine said: 'A ghost story. How delicious! Do tell it, Mr Doricourt. This is just the place for a ghost story. Out of doors and the sun shining, so that we can't *really* be frightened.'

Doricourt protested again that he knew no story.

'That's because you never read, dear boy,' said Eugene Thesiger. 'That library of yours. There's a delightful book – did you never notice it? – brown tree calf with your arms on it; the head of the house writes the history of the house as far as he knows it. There's a lot in that book. It began in Tudor times – 1515 to be exact.'

'Queen Elizabeth's time,' Ernestine thought that made it so much more interesting. 'And was the ghost story in that?'

'It isn't exactly a ghost story,' said Thesiger. 'It's only that the pavilion seems to be an unlucky place to sleep in.'

'Haunted?' Frederick asked, and added that he must look up that book.

'Not haunted exactly. Only several people who have slept the night there went on sleeping.'

'Dead, he means,' said Ernestine, and it was left for Amelia to ask: 'Does the book tell anything particular about how the people died? What killed them, or anything?'

'There are suggestions,' said Thesiger; 'but there, it *is* a gloomy subject. I don't know why I started it. Should we have time for a game of croquet before tea, Doricourt?'

'I *wish you'd* read the book and tell me the stories,' Ernestine said to Frederick, apart, over the croquet balls.

'I will,' he answered fervently, 'you've only to tell me what you want.'

'Or perhaps Mr Thesiger will tell us another time – in the twilight. Since people like twilight for ghosts. Will you, Mr Thesiger?' She spoke over her blue muslin shoulder.

Frederick certainly meant to look up the book, but he delayed till after supper; the half-hour before bed when he and Thesiger put on their braided smoking-jackets and their braided smoking-caps with the long yellow tassels, and smoked the cigars which were, in those days still, more of a luxury than a necessity. Ordinarily, of course, these were smoked out of doors, or in the smoking-room, a stuffy little den littered with boots and guns and yellow-backed railway novels. But tonight Frederick left his friend in that dingy hutch, and went alone to the library, found the book and took it to the circle of light made by the colza lamp.

'I can skim through it in half an hour,' he said, and wound up the lamp and lighted his second cigar. Then he opened the shutters and windows, so that the room should not smell of smoke in the morning. Those were the days of consideration for the ladies who had not yet learned that a cigarette is not exclusively a male accessory like a beard or a bass voice.

But when, his preparations completed, he opened the book, he was compelled to say 'Pshaw!' Nothing short of this could relieve his feelings. (You know the expression I mean, though of course it isn't pronounced as it's spelt, any more than Featherstonehaugh or St Maur are.)

'Pshaw!' said Frederick, fluttering the pages. His remark was justified. The earlier part of the book was written in the beautiful script of the early sixteenth century, that looks so plain and is so impossible to read, and the later pages, though the handwriting was clear and Italian enough, left Frederick helpless, for the language was Latin, and Frederick's Latin was limited to the particular passages he had 'been through' at his private school. He recognised a word here and there, *mors*, for instance, and *pallidus* and *pavor* and *arcanum*, just as you or I might; but to read the complicated stuff and make sense of it . . . ! Frederick said something just a shade stronger than 'Pshaw!' – 'Botheration!' I think it was; replaced the book on the shelf, closed the shutters and turned out the lamp. He thought he would ask Thesiger to translate the thing, but then again he thought he wouldn't. So he went to bed wishing that he had happened to remember more of the Latin so painfully beaten into the best years of his boyhood.

And the story of the pavilion was, after all, told by Thesiger.

There was a little dance at Doricourt next evening, a carpet dance, they called it. The furniture was pushed back against the walls, and the tightly stretched Axminster carpet was not so bad to dance on as you might suppose. That, you see, was before the days of polished floors and large rugs with loose edges that you can catch your feet in. A carpet was a carpet in those days, well and truly laid, conscientiously exact to the last recess and fitting the floor like a skin. And on this quite tolerable surface the young people danced very happily, some ten or twelve couples. The old people did not dance in those days, except sometimes a quadrille of state to 'open the ball'. They played cards in a room provided for the purpose, and in the dancing-room three or four kindly middle-aged ladies were considered to provide ample chaperon-age. You were not even expected to report yourself to your chaperone at the conclusion of a dance. It was not like a real ball. And even in those far-off days there were conservatories.

It was on the steps of the conservatory, not the steps leading from the dancing-room, but the steps leading to the garden, that the story was told. The four young people were sitting together, the girls' crinolined flounces spreading round them like huge pale roses, the young men correct in their high-shouldered coats and white cravats. Ernestine had been very kind to both the men – a little too kind, perhaps, who can tell? At any rate, there was in their eyes exactly that light which you may imagine in the eyes of rival stags in the mating season. It was Ernestine who asked

Frederick for the story, and Thesiger who, at Amelia's suggestion, told it.

'It's quite a number of stories,' he said, 'and yet it's really all the same story. The first man to sleep in the pavilion slept there ten years after it was built. He was a friend of the alchemist or astrologer who built it. He was found dead in the morning. There seemed to have been a struggle. His arms bore the marks of cords. No; they never found any cords. He died from loss of blood. There were curious wounds. That was all the rude leeches of the day could report to the bereaved survivors of the deceased.'

'How sunny you are, Mr Thesiger,' said Ernestine with that celebrated soft low laugh of hers. When Ernestine was elderly, many people thought her stupid. When she was young, no-one seems to have been of this opinion.

'And the next?' asked Amelia.

'The next was sixty years later. It was a visitor that time, too. And he was found dead with just the same marks, and the doctors said the same thing. And so it went on. There have been eight deaths altogether – unexplained deaths. Nobody has slept in it now for over a hundred years. People seem to have a prejudice against the place as a sleeping apartment. I can't think why.'

'Isn't he simply killing?' Ernestine asked Amelia, who said: 'And doesn't anyone know how it happened?' No-one answered till Ernestine repeated the question in the form of: 'I suppose it was just an accident?'

'It was a curiously recurrent accident,' said Thesiger, and Frederick, who throughout the conversation had said the right things at the right moment, remarked that it did not do to believe all these old legends. Most old families had them, he believed. Frederick had inherited Doricourt from an unknown great-uncle of whom in life he had not so much as heard, but he was very strong on the family tradition. 'I don't attach any importance to these tales myself.'

'Of course not. All the same,' said Thesiger deliberately, 'you wouldn't care to pass a night in that pavilion.'

'No more would you,' was all Frederick found on his lips.

'I admit that I shouldn't enjoy it,' said Eugene, 'but I'll bet you a hundred you don't *do* it.'

'Done,' said Frederick.

'Oh, Mr Doricourt,' breathed Ernestine, a little shocked at betting 'before ladies'.

'Don't!' said Amelia, to whom, of course, no-one paid any attention, 'don't do it.'

You know how, in the midst of flower and leafage, a snake will suddenly, surprisingly rear a head that threatens? So, amid friendly talk and laughter, a sudden fierce antagonism sometimes looks out and vanishes again, surprising most of all the antagonists. This antagonism spoke in the tones of both men, and after Amelia had said, 'Don't,' there was a curiously breathless little silence. Ernestine broke it. 'Oh,' she said, 'I do wonder which of you will win. I should like them both to win, wouldn't you, Amelia? Only I suppose that's not always possible, is it?'

Both gentlemen assured her that in the case of bets it was very rarely possible.

'Then I wish you wouldn't,' said Ernestine. 'You could *both* pass the night there, couldn't you, and be company for each other? I don't think betting for such large sums is quite the thing, do you, Amelia?'

Amelia said No, she didn't, but Eugene had already begun to say: 'Let the bet be off then, if Miss Meutys doesn't like it. That suggestion was invaluable. But the thing itself needn't be off. Look here, Doricourt. I'll stay in the pavilion from one to three and you from three to five. Then honour will be satisfied. How will that do?'

The snake had disappeared.

'Agreed,' said Frederick, 'and we can compare impressions afterwards. That will be quite interesting.'

Then someone came and asked where they had all got to, and they went in and danced some more dances. Ernestine danced twice with Frederick and drank iced sherry and water and they said good-night and lighted their bedroom candles at the table in the hall.

'I do hope they won't,' Amelia said as the girls sat brushing their hair at the two large white muslin frilled dressing-tables in the room they shared.

'Won't what?' said Ernestine, vigorous with the brush.

'Sleep in that hateful pavilion. I wish you'd ask them not to, Ernestine. They'd mind, if *you* asked them.'

'Of course I will if you like, dear,' said Ernestine cordially. She was always the soul of good nature. 'But I don't think you ought to believe in ghost stories, not really.'

'Why not?'

'Oh, because of the Bible and going to church and all that,' said Ernestine. 'Do you really think Rowland's Macassar has made any difference to my hair?'

'It is just as beautiful as it always was,' said Amelia, twisting up her own little ashen-blonde handful. 'What was that?'

That was a sound coming from the little dressing-room. There was no light in that room. Amelia went into the little room though Ernestine said: 'Oh, don't! How can you? It might be a ghost or a rat or something,' and as she went she whispered: 'Hush!'

The window of the little room was open and she leaned out of it. The stone sill was cold to her elbows through her print dressing-jacket.

Ernestine went on brushing her hair. Amelia heard a movement below the window and listened. 'Tonight will do,' someone said.

'It's too late,' said someone else.

'If you're afraid, it will always be too late or too early,' said someone. And it was Thesiger.

'You know I'm not afraid,' the other one, who was Doricourt, answered hotly.

'An hour for each of us will satisfy honour,' said Thesiger carelessly. 'The girls will expect it. I couldn't sleep. Let's do it now and get it over. Let's see. Oh, damn it!'

A faint click had sounded.

'Dropped my watch. I forgot the chain was loose. It's all right though; glass not broken even. Well, are you game?'

'Oh, yes, if you insist. Shall I go first, or you?'

'I will,' said Thesiger. 'That's only fair, because I suggested it. I'll stay till half-past one or a quarter to two, and then you come on. See?'

'Oh, all right. I think it's silly, though,' said Frederick.

Then the voices ceased. Amelia went back to the other girl.

'They're going to do it tonight.'

'Are they, dear?' Ernestine was placid as ever. 'Do what?'

'Sleep in that horrible pavilion.'

'How do you know?'

Amelia explained how she knew.

'Whatever can we do?' she added.

'Well, dear, suppose we go to bed,' suggested Ernestine helpfully. 'We shall hear all about it in the morning.'

'But suppose anything happens?'

'What could happen?'

'Oh, *anything*,' said Amelia. 'Oh, I do wish they wouldn't! I shall go down and ask them not to.'

'*Amelia!*' the other girl was at last aroused. 'You *couldn't*. I shouldn't *let* you dream of doing anything so unladylike. What would the gentlemen think of you?'

The question silenced Amelia, but she began to put on her so lately discarded bodice.

'I won't go if you think I oughtn't,' she said.

'Forward and fast, auntie would call it,' said the other. 'I am almost sure she would.'

'But I'll keep dressed. I shan't disturb you. I'll sit in the dressing-room. I *can't* go to sleep while he's running into this awful danger.'

'Which he?' Ernestine's voice was very sharp. 'And there isn't any danger.'

'Yes, there is,' said Amelia sullenly, 'and I mean *them*. Both of them.'

Ernestine said her prayers and got into bed. She had put her hair in curl-papers which became her like a wreath of white roses.

'I don't think auntie will be pleased,' she said, 'when she hears that you sat up all night watching young gentlemen. Goodnight, dear!'

'Goodnight, darling,' said Amelia. 'I know you don't understand. It's all right.'

She sat in the dark by the dressing-room window. There was no moon, but the starlight lay on the dew of the park, and the trees massed themselves in bunches of a darker grey, deepening to black at the roots of them. There was no sound to break the stillness, except the little cracklings of twigs and rustlings of leaves as birds or little night wandering beasts moved in the shadows of the garden, and the sudden creakings that furniture makes if you sit alone with it and listen in the night's silence.

Amelia sat on and listened, listened. The pavilion showed in broken streaks of pale grey against the wood, that seemed to be clinging to it in dark patches. But that, she reminded herself, was only the creeper. She sat there for a very long time, not knowing how long a time it was. For anxiety is a poor chronometer, and the first ten minutes had seemed an hour. She had no watch. Ernestine had – and slept with it under her pillow. The stable clock was out of order; the man had been sent for to see to it. There was nothing to measure time's flight by, and she sat there rigid, straining her ears for a footfall on the grass, straining her eyes to see a figure come out of the dark pavilion and across the dew-grey grass towards the house. And she heard nothing, saw nothing.

Slowly, imperceptibly, the grey of the sleeping trees took on faint dreams of colour. The sky turned faint above the trees, the moon perhaps was coming out. The pavilion grew more clearly visible. It seemed to Amelia that something moved along the leaves that surrounded it, and she looked to see him come out. But he did not come.

'I wish the moon would really shine,' she told herself. And

suddenly she knew that the sky was clear and that this growing light was not the moon's cold shiver, but the growing light of dawn.

She went quickly into the other room, put her hand under the pillow of Ernestine, and drew out the little watch with the diamond 'E' on it.

'A quarter to three,' she said aloud. Ernestine moved and grunted.

There was no hesitation about Amelia now. Without another thought for the ladylike and the really suitable, she lighted her candle and went quickly down the stairs, paused a moment in the hall, and so out through the front door. She passed along the terrace. The feet of Frederick protruded from the open French window of the smoking-room. She set down her candle on the terrace – it burned clearly enough in that clear air – went up to Frederick as he slept, his head between his shoulders and his hands loosely hanging, and shook him.

'Wake up,' she said – 'Wake up! Something's happened! It's a quarter to three and he's not come back.'

'Who's not what?' Frederick asked sleepily.

'Mr Thesiger. The pavilion.'

'Thesiger! – the ... You, Miss Davenant? I beg your pardon. I must have dropped off.'

He got up unsteadily, gazing dully at this white apparition still in evening dress with pale hair now no longer wreathed.

'What is it?' he said. 'Is anybody ill?'

Briefly and very urgently Amelia told him what it was, implored him to go at once and see what had happened. If he had been fully awake, her voice and her eyes would have told him many things.

'He said he'd come back,' he said. 'Hadn't I better wait? You go back to bed, Miss Davenant. If he doesn't come in half an hour ...'

'If you don't go this minute,' said Amelia tensely, 'I shall.'

'Oh, well, if you insist,' Frederick said. 'He has simply fallen asleep as I did. Dear Miss Davenant, return to your room, I beg.

In the morning when we are all laughing at this false alarm, you will be glad to remember that Mr Thesiger does not know of your anxiety.'

'I hate you,' said Amelia gently, 'and I am going to see what has happened. Come or not, as you like.'

She caught up the silver candlestick and he followed its wavering gleam down the terrace steps and across the grey dewy grass.

Halfway she paused, lifted the hand that had been hidden among her muslin flounces and held it out to him with a big Indian dagger in it.

'I got it out of the hall,' she said. 'If there's any *real* danger. Anything living. I mean. I thought . . . But I know I couldn't use it. Will you take it?'

He took it, laughing kindly.

'How romantic you are,' he said admiringly and looked at her standing there in the mingled gold and grey of dawn and candlelight. It was as though he had never seen her before.

They reached the steps of the pavilion and stumbled up them. The door was closed but not locked. And Amelia noticed that the trails of creeper had not been disturbed, they grew across the doorway, as thick as a man's finger, some of them.

'He must have got in by one of the windows,' Frederick said. 'Your dagger comes in handy, Miss Davenant.'

He slashed at the wet sticky green stuff and put his shoulder to the door. It yielded at a touch and they went in.

The one candle lighted the pavilion hardly at all, and the dusky light that oozed in through the door and windows helped very little. And the silence was thick and heavy.

'Thesiger!' said Frederick, clearing his throat. 'Thesiger! Hullo! Where are you?'

Thesiger did not say where he was. And then they saw.

There were low seats to the windows, and between the windows low stone benches ran. On one of these something dark, something dark and in places white, confused the outline of the carved stone.

'Thesiger,' said Frederick again in the tone a man uses to a room that he is almost sure is empty. 'Thesiger!'

But Amelia was bending over the bench. She was holding the candle crookedly so that it flared and guttered.

'Is he there?' Frederick asked, following her; 'is that him? Is he asleep?'

'Take the candle,' said Amelia, and he took it obediently. Amelia was touching what lay on the bench. Suddenly she screamed. Just one scream, not very loud. But Frederick remembers just how it sounded. Sometimes he hears it in dreams and wakes moaning, though he is an old man now and his old wife says: 'What is it, dear?' and he says: 'Nothing, my Ernestine, nothing.'

Directly she had screamed she said: 'He's dead,' and fell on her knees by the bench. Frederick saw that she held something in her arms.

'Perhaps he isn't,' she said. 'Fetch someone from the house, brandy – send for a doctor. Oh, go, go, go!'

'I can't leave you here,' said Frederick with thoughtful propriety; 'suppose he revives?'

'He will not revive,' said Amelia dully, 'go, go, go! Do as I tell you. Go! If you don't go,' she added suddenly and amazingly, 'I believe I shall kill you. It's all your doing.'

The astounding sharp injustice of this stung Frederick into action. 'I believe he's only fainted or something,' he said. 'When I've roused the house and everyone has witnessed your emotion you will regret . . .'

She sprang to her feet and caught the knife from him and raised it, awkwardly, clumsily, but with keen threatening, not to be mistaken or disregarded. Frederick went.

When Frederick came back, with the groom and the gardener (he hadn't thought it well to disturb the ladies), the pavilion was filled full of white revealing daylight. On the bench lay a dead man and kneeling by him a living woman on whose warm breast his cold and heavy head lay pillowed. The dead man's hands were full of the green crushed leaves, and thick twining tendrils were about his wrists and throat. A wave of green seemed to have swept from the open window to the bench where he lay.

The groom and the gardener and the dead man's friend looked and looked.

'Looks like as if he'd got himself entangled in the creeper and lost 'is 'ead,' said the groom, scratching his own.

'How'd the creeper get in, though? That's what I says,' it was the gardener who said it.

'Through the window,' said Doricourt, moistening his lips with his tongue.

'The window was shut, though, when I come by at five yesterday,' said the gardener stubbornly. ''Ow did it get all that way since five?'

They looked at each other, voicing, silently, impossible things.

The woman never spoke. She sat there in the white ring of her crinolined dress like a broken white rose. But her arms were round Thesiger and she would not move them.

When the doctor came, he sent for Ernestine who came, flushed and sleepy-eyed and very frightened, and shocked.

'You're upset, dear,' she said to her friend, 'and no wonder. How brave of you to come out with Mr Doricourt to see what happened. But you can't do anything now, dear. Come in and I'll tell them to get you some tea.'

Amelia laughed, looked down at the face on her shoulder, laid the head back on the bench among the drooping green of the creeper, stooped over it, kissed it and said quite quietly and gently: 'Goodbye, dear, goodbye!' – took Ernestine's arm and went away with her.

The doctor made an examination and gave a death-certificate. 'Heart failure', was his original and brilliant diagnosis. The certificate said nothing, and Frederick said nothing, of the creeper that was wound about the dead man's neck, nor of the little white wounds, like little bloodless lips half-open, that they found about the dead man's neck.

'An imaginative or uneducated person,' said the doctor, 'might suppose that the creeper had something to do with his death. But we mustn't encourage superstition. I will assist my man to prepare the body for its last sleep. Then we need not have any chattering woman.'

'Can you read Latin?' Frederick asked. The doctor could, and, later, did.

It was the Latin of that brown book with the Doricourt arms on it that Frederick wanted read. And when he and the doctor had been together with the book between them for three hours, they closed it, and looked at each other with shy and doubtful eyes.

'It can't be true,' said Frederick.

'If it is,' said the more cautious doctor, 'you don't want it talked about. I should destroy that book if I were you. And I should root up that creeper and burn it. It is quite evident, from what you tell me, that your friend believed that this creeper was a man-eater, that it fed, just before its flowering time, as the book tells us, at dawn; and that he fully meant that the thing when it crawled into the pavilion seeking its prey should find you and not him. It would have been so, I understand, if his watch had not stopped at one o'clock.'

'He dropped it, you know,' said Doricourt like a man in a dream.

'All the cases in this book are the same,' said the doctor, 'the strangling, the white wounds. I have heard of such plants; I never believed.' He shuddered. 'Had your friend any spite against you? Any reason for wanting to get you out of the way?'

Frederick thought of Ernestine, of Thesiger's eyes on Ernestine, of her smile at him over her blue muslin shoulder.

'No,' he said, 'none. None whatever. It must have been an accident. I am sure he did not know. He could not read Latin.' He lied, being, after all, a gentleman, and Ernestine's name being sacred.

'The creeper seems to have been brought here and planted in Henry the Eighth's time. And then the thing began. It seems to have been at its flowering season that it needed the . . . that, in short, it was dangerous. The little animals and birds found dead near the pavilion ... But to move itself all that way, across the floor! The thing must have been almost conscient,' he said with a sincere shudder. 'One would think,' he corrected himself at once, 'that it knew what it was doing, if such a thing were not plainly contrary to the laws of nature.'

'Yes,' said Frederick, 'one would. I think if I can't do anything more I'll go and rest. Somehow all this has given me a turn. Poor Thesiger!'

His last thought before he went to sleep was one of pity.

'Poor Thesiger,' he said, 'how violent and wicked! And what an escape for me! I must never tell Ernestine. And all the time there was Amelia ... Ernestine would never have done *that* for *me*.' And on a little pang of regret for the impossible he fell asleep.

Amelia went on living. She was not the sort that dies even of such a thing as happened to her on that night, when for the first and last time she held her love in her arms and knew him for the murderer he was. It was only the other day that she died, a very old woman. Ernestine who, beloved and surrounded by children and grandchildren, survived her, spoke her epitaph: 'Poor Amelia,' she said, 'nobody ever looked the same side of the road where she was. There was an indiscretion when she was young. Oh, nothing disgraceful, of course. She was a lady. But people talked. It was the sort of thing that stamps a girl, you know.'

# The Judgment: A Broadmoor Biography

Yes, a villainous-looking brute, as you say, sir; and I thank the Lord he's got all he earned, and more. Sometimes the beggars has grit and more pluck than some folk like to see in such vermin, but some of them ain't no more spunk nor a mouse. I love pluck myself, though; if a man's good he's the better for it, and if he's bad he ain't none the worse. Most of them as come here commit crimes through their madness; but it wasn't that way quite with him, and yet here he is at Broadmoor.

Do you know, he's almost the only one here I never felt a bit of pity for – and you'll feel the same, see if you don't when you've heard all about him.

Now don't you be interrupting me by asking me how I know this and that and the other. I got it all out of the evidence only I pieced it together, so as to tell myself how it all happened.

He'd always been a regular bad one, he had – and the Lord only knows what he hadn't done in his time – but he'd never been lagged for anything more than thieving, till he met with a cleverer chap than him, and together they did more than one bad night's work, I know. Well, this other chap, he found out somehow that there was something about a certain house in a certain village that made it worth while for him to hang around there above a bit.

'It's a first-class job,' says he to our man here. 'If we pull it off, it's idleness and the fat of the land for the rest of our born days. Are you on?'

'I'm on,' says our man, like the brute he is, never so much as asking what it is he's on in.

This house was called Chudleigh Abbey, and it seems it was an old house, all over ivy and creepers; and an old lady lived there with a young nephew and a pretty niece. Of course you guess there must be some sort of love-making when a young man and his pretty cousin live under one roof. So there was, so there was. And their sort of love-making was the marrying sort. The question was popped, and the day was named, and then my young sir must needs get the family diamonds out of the bank to see how his sweetheart looked in them! He thought she looked sweetly in them, you may be sure, and he gave them to her to keep, just telling her not to let anyone know she'd got them till he'd got a safe to keep them in. So she takes them up to her room, and she hides them. Now, he thought, and she thought, no one knew about them diamonds; but I don't need to tell *you*, sir, that valuable stones don't change their addresses without its being known somehow to more than one and more than two. And among those that knew were our man and his mate.

Well, they meant to have the diamonds, and they laid their plan. And there was two things made their plan easy to work. First, the young lady slept in a room at the far end of a long passage with no-one near her. It was the oldest part of the house, and she liked it, because it was 'so romantic'. You know what young ladies be, sir! Next, the young gentleman, what always slept at home, was to sleep at the inn the night before the wedding. You know, sir, it's a custom with gentlefolks. So the plan was that on the night before the wedding, when there was only the women in the house, our man was to climb up the ivy and creep into the young lady's room and take the diamonds.

'It'll take me some time to find where she's hid them,' he says to the other chap, 'so I'd better *make the girl safe first.*'

It was decided that our man was to go right away for a week, so that there mightn't be any suspicion, and when he came back his mate would meet him at a certain place and hour and tell him if any change was wanted in the plan. If his mate didn't meet him he was to go to the house at once.

So he climbed up one night and filed the window-bars nearly through, and got all ready, and then he went away.

After a week he came back.

It was a very dark night. He waited a quarter of an hour by the old wall, but no-one came, so he took his knife in his teeth, and climbed up the ivy, going very slow and quiet. The bars were just as he had left them. He took one out very gently, and laid it down and got into the room. It was very, very dark, and smelt of scent and camphor like a chemist's shop. He listened for the girl's breathing to guide him to the bed, but he heard nothing. Presently, feeling about, his hand touched the bed-post. Then he wraps his red cotton handkerchief round his hand, to put over her mouth, and he takes his knife in the other hand, and feels for her face . . . and pulls the sheet off her neck . . . She never moved, and it was done in a minute! Then he lays down his wet knife on the bed, and strikes a match quite at his ease to look for the diamonds.

He lights a candle that stands by the bed-head, and then sees the bed and what's on it, and he gives a yell that fetches every soul in the house awake, and he goes off then and there stark raving, screaming mad. The sight of what he meant all along to do? Not it! Conscience? Not a bit of it! Sheer fright at the sight of what he'd done and *hadn't* meant to do.

The candle showed him the bed – all a mass of white flowers – and what was lying on it under the white sheet had laid there dead long afore *he* came anigh the place. I've heard say as corpses can't bleed . . . Well, all I know is . . . Well, I won't say any more about that part of it, sir, if you don't like it. It ain't pleasant even to hear about and the sight of it sent '*im* clean off 'is head. It was a corpse's throat he'd cut, the blundering, murdering villain, and when the servants ran in with lights they found him lying across the bed-foot, foaming at the mouth and mad as a hatter. If he'd had any sense left for thinking he wouldn't ha' known what to think.

But this is what really happened. The other chap – once our man was out of the way – thinks to have a try for the diamonds off his own bat; but meantime the young lady at the Abbey'd found out the filed window-bars, and, when he tried it on, the young master an' the undergardener was ready for him, and took him with the knife in his hand bending over the empty bed. Thinks he, t'other chap shan't get off then, neither; so off he goes to jail, leaving his mate to be copped when he comes back to try it on according to agreement. And in jail he turned funky, and choked himself with his belt, for there was other things against him, besides their having found out he was the Peckham Mystery.

And no-one in the Abbey expecting any more visitors through the window, they didn't have the bars mended; but a silly maid who's frightened out of her wits sticks 'em up again to look like they did afore.

And how come the young lady to be dead already? Why, bless your soul, sir, didn't I tell you? It wasn't the young lady at all; it was the old housekeeper, as had been ailing this long time, and had gone off sudden with the turn the first chap give her when he screamed as he was took. And they laid her out in that room, being furthest from the other rooms.

And if he'd had an ounce of pluck our man might ha' got away. But it's my belief he wasn't meant to. The judgment takes folk queer ways sometimes.

# To the Adventurous

## 1

His mind was made up. There should be no looking back, no weakening, no foolish relentings. Civilisation had no place for him in her scheme of things; and he in his turn would show the jade that he was capable of a scheme in which she had no place, she and her pinchbeck meretricious substitutions of stones for bread, serpents for eggs. What exactly it was that had gone wrong does not matter. There was a girl in it perhaps; a friend most likely. Almost certainly money and pride and the old detestation of arithmetic played their part. His mother was now dead, and his father was dead long since. There was no one nearer than a great-uncle to care where he went or what he did; whether he throve or went under, whether he lived or died. Also it was springtime.

His thoughts turned longingly to the pleasant green country, the lush meadows, the blossoming orchards, nesting birds and flowering thorn, and to roads that should wind slowly, pleasantly between these. The remembrance came to him of another spring day when he had played truant, had found four thrushes' nests and a moorhen's, and tried to draw a kingfisher on the back of his Latin prose; had paddled in a mill stream between bright twinkling leaves and the bright twinkling counterfeits in the glassy water, had been caned at school next day, and his mother had cried when he told her. He remember how he had said: 'I will be good, oh, mother, I will!' and then added with one of those odd sudden cautions that lined the fluttering garment of his impulsive soul, 'at least, I'll try to be good.'

Well, he had tried. For more than a year he had tried, bearing patiently the heavy yoke of ledger and costs book, the weary life of the office the great-uncle had found for him. There had been a caged bird at the cobbler's in the village at home, that piped sweetly in its prison and laboured to draw up its own drinking water by slow chained thimblefulls. He sometimes thought that he was like that caged bird, straining and straining for ever at the horrible machinery which grudgingly yielded to his efforts the little pittance that kept him alive. And all the while the woods and fields and the long white roads were calling, calling.

And now the chief had been more than usually repulsive, and the young man stood at the top of the stairs, smoothing the silk hat that stood for so much, and remembering in detail the unusual repulsiveness of the chief. An error of two and sevenpence in one column, surely a trivial error, and of two hundred pounds in another, quite an obvious error that, and easily rectified, had been the inspiration of the words that sang discordantly to his revolted soul. He suddenly tossed his hat in the air, kicked it as it fell, black and shining, and sent it spinning down the stairs. The office boy clattered out, thin-necked, red-eared, slack mouth well open.

'My hat!' was his unintentionally appropriate idiom.

'Pardon me, *my* hat,' said the young man suavely. But the junior was genuinely shocked.

'I say, Mr Sellinge,' he said solemnly, 'it'll never be the same again, that tile won't. Ironing it won't do it, no, nor yet blocking.'

'Bates,' the young man retorted with at least equal solemnity, 'I shall never wear that hat again. Remove your subservient carcase. I'm going back to tell the chief.'

'About your hat?' the junior asked, breathless, incredulous.

'About my hat,' Sellinge repeated.

The chief looked up a little blankly. Clerks who had had what he was well aware they called the rough side of his tongue rarely returned to risk a second helping. And now this hopeless young incompetent, this irreverent trifler with the columns of the temple of the gods L. S. and D., was standing before him, and plainly standing there to speak, not merely to be spoken to.

'Well, Sellinge,' he said, frowning a little, but not too much, lest he should scare away an apology more ample than that with which Sellinge had met the rough side. 'Well, what is it?'

Sellinge, briefly, respectfully, but quite plainly told him what it was. And the chief listened, hardly able to believe his respectable ears.

'And so,' the tale ended, 'I should like to leave at once, please, sir.'

'Do you realise, young man,' the head of the firm asked heavily, 'that you are throwing away your career?'

Sellinge explained what he did realise.

'Your *soul*, did you say?' the portly senior looked at him through gold-rimmed glasses. 'I never heard of such a thing in my life.'

Sellinge waited respectfully, and the head of the house looked suddenly older. The unusual is the disconcerting. The chief was not used to hearing souls mentioned except on Sundays. Yet the boy was the grand-nephew of an old friend, a valued and useful business friend, a man whom it would be awkward for him to offend or annoy. This is the real meaning of friendship in the world of business. So he said: 'Come, come, now, Sellinge; think it over. I've had occasion to complain, but I've not complained unjustly – not unjustly, I think. Your opportunities in this office – what did you say?'

The young man had begun to say, quite politely, what he thought of the office.

'But, God bless my soul!' said the older man, quite flustered by this impossible rebellion. 'What is it you want? Come now,' he said, remembering the usefulness of that eminent great-uncle, and unbending as he remembered, 'if this isn't good enough for you, a respectable solicitor's office and every chance of rising – every chance,' he repeated pensively, oblivious now of all that the rough side had said; 'if this isn't good enough for you, what is? What would you like?' he asked, with a pathetic mixture of hopelessness, raillery, and the certitude that his question was unanswerable.

'I should like,' said Sellinge slowly, 'to be a tramp, or a burglar . . .'

('Great Heavens!' said the chief.)

'– or a detective. I want to go about and do things. I want . . .'

'A detective?' said the chief. 'Have you ever . . .'

'No,' said Sellinge, 'but I could.'

'A new Sherlock Holmes, eh?' said the chief, actually smiling.

'Never,' said the clerk firmly, and he frowned. 'May I go now, sir? I've no opening in the burgling or the detective line, so I shall be a tramp, for this summer at least. Perhaps I'll go to Canada. I'm sorry I haven't been a success here. Bates is worth twice my money. He never wavers in his faith. Seven nines are always sixty-three with Bates.'

Again the chief thought of his useful city friend.

'Never mind Bates,' he said. 'Is the door closed? Right. Sit down, if you please, Mr Sellinge. I have something to say to you.'

Sellinge hesitated, looked round at the dusty leather-covered furniture, the worn Turkey carpet, the black, shiny deed-boxes, and the shelves of dull blue and yellow papers. The brown oblong of window framed a strip of blue sky and a strip of the opposite office's dirty brickwork. A small strayed cloud, very white and shining, began to cross the strip of sky.

'It's very kind of you, sir,' said Sellinge, his mind more made up than ever; 'but I wouldn't reconsider my decision for ten times what I've been getting.'

'Sit down,' said the chief again. 'I assure you I do not propose to raise your salary, nor to urge you to reconsider your decision. I merely wish to suggest an alternative – one of your own alternatives,' he added persuasively.

'Oh!' said Sellinge, sitting down abruptly, 'which?'

2

And now behold the dream realised. A young man with bare sun-bleached hair that looks as though it had never known the shiny black symbol of civilisation, boots large and dusty, and on his back the full equipment of an artist in oils; a little too new the outfit, but satisfactory and complete. He goes slowly along through the clean white dust of the roads, and his glance to right and left embraces green field and woodland with the persuasive ardour of a happy lover. The only blot on the fair field of life outspread before him the parting words of the chief.

'It's a very simple job for a would-be detective. Just find out whether the old chap's mad or not. You get on with the lower orders, you tell me. Well, get them to talk to you. And if you find that out, well, there may be a career for you. I've long been dissatisfied with the ordinary enquiry agent. Yes, two pounds a week, and expenses. But in reason. Not first-class, you know.'

This much aloud. To himself he had said: 'A simpleton's useful sometimes, if he's honest. And if he doesn't find out anything we shall be no worse off than we were before, and I shall be able to explain to his uncle that I really gave him exceptional opportunities – exceptional.'

Sellinge also, walking along between the dusty powdered white-flowered hedges, felt that the opportunity was exceptional. All his life people had told him things, and the half-confidences of two people often make up a complete sphere of knowledge, if only the confidant possess the power of joining the broken halves. This power Sellinge had. He knew many things; the little scandals, the parochial intrigues and intricacies of the village where he was born were clearer to him than to the principal performers. He looked forward pleasantly to the lodging in the village ale-house, and to the slow gossip on the benches by the door.

The village (he was nearing it now) was steep and straggling, displaying its oddly assorted roofs amid a flutter of orchard trees, a carpet of green spaces. The Five Bells stood to the left, its tea-gardens beside it, cool and alluring.

Sellinge entered the dark sandy passage where the faint smell of last night's tobacco and this morning's beer contended with the fresh vigour of a bunch of wallflowers in a blue jug on the ring-marked bar.

Within ten minutes he had engaged his room, a little hot white attic under the roof, and had learned that it was Squire who lived in the big house, and that there was a lot of tales, so there was, but it didn't do to believe all you heard, nor yet more'n half you see, and least said soonest mended, and the house was worth looking at, or so people said as took notice of them old ancient tumble-down places. No, it wasn't likely you could get in. Used to be open of a Thursday, the 'ouse and grounds, but been closed to visitors this many year. Also that, for all it looked so near, the house was a good four and a half miles by the road.

'And Squire's mighty good to the people in the village,' the pleasant-faced old landlady behind the bar went on: 'pays good wages, 'e does, and if anyone's in trouble he's always got his hand in his pocket. I don't believe he spends half on himself to what he gives away. It'll be a poor day for Jevington when anything happens to him, sir, you take that from me. No harm in your trying to see the house, sir, but as for seeing him, he never sees no one. Why, listen,' – there was the sound of hoofs and wheels in the road – 'look out, sir, quick!'

Sellinge looked out to see an old-fashioned carriage and pair sweep past, in the carriage a white-haired old man with a white thin face and pale clouded eyes.

'That's him,' said the landlady beside him, ducking as the carriage passed. 'Yes, four and a half miles by the road, sir.'

Harnessed in his trappings of colour-box and easel, the young detective set out. There was about him none of the furtivity of your stage detective. His disguise was perfect, mainly because it was not a disguise. Such disguise as there was hung over his soul, which was pretending to itself that the errand was one of danger and difficulty. The attraction of the detective's career was to him not so much the idea of hunting down criminals as the dramatic attitude of one who goes about the world with a false beard and a make-up box in one hand and his life in the other. To find out the truth about an old gentleman's eccentricities was quite another pair of sleeves, but of these, as yet, our hero perceived neither the cut nor the colour. He had wanted to be a tramp or a detective, and here he was, both. One has to earn one's bread, and what better way than this?

A smooth worn stile prefaced a path almost hidden in grass up for hay, a blaze of red sorrel, buttercups, ox-eyed daisies in the feathery foam of flowered grasses. The wood of the stile was warm to his hand, and the grasses that met over the path powdered his boots with their little seeds.

Then there was a copse, and a rabbit warren, and short crisp grass dry on the chalk it thinly covered. The sun shone hardly in a sky of brass. The wayfarer panted for shade. It showed far ahead like a mirage in a desert, a group of pines, a flat whiteness of pond-water, a little house. One might ask the way at that house, and get – talk.

He fixed his eyes on it and walked on, the leather straps hot on his shoulders, his oak stick-handle hot in his hand. Then suddenly he saw on the hill, pale beyond the pines, someone coming down the path. He knew the magnet that a planted easel is to rustic minds. This might perhaps be, after all, the better way. Never did artist prepare so rapidly the scene that should attract the eye of the rustic gazer, the lingering but inevitable approach of the rustic foot.

In three minutes he was seated on his camp-stool, a canvas before him, his palette half-set. Four minutes saw a good deal of blue on the canvas. Purple, too, at the fifth minute, because the sky had turned that colour in the west, purple and, moreover, a strange threatening tint that called for burnt sienna and mid chrome and a dash of madder. The white advancing figure had disappeared among the pines. He madly squeezed green paint on to the foreground; one must at least have a picture begun. And the sun searched intolerably every bit of him as he sat in the shadeless warren awaiting the passing of the other.

And then, more sudden than an earthquake or the birth of love, a mighty rushing wind fell on him, caught up canvas and easel, even colour-box and oak staff, and whirled them away like leaves in an autumn equinox. His hat went too, not that that mattered, and the virgin sketch book whirled white before a wind that, the papers said next day, travelled at the rate of five-and-fifty miles an hour. The wonderful purple and copper of the west rushed up across the sky, a fierce spatter of rain stung face and hands. He pursued the colour-box, which had lodged in the front entry of a rabbit's house, caught at the canvas, whose face lay closely pressed to a sloe-bush, and ran for the nearest shelter, the house among the pines. In a rain like that one has to run head down or be blinded, and so he did not see till he drew breath in the mouldering rotten porch of it that his shelter was not of those from which hospitality can be asked.

A little lodge it was, long since deserted; walls and ceiling bulging and discoloured with damp, its latticed windows curtained only by the tapestry of the spider, its floors carpeted with old dust and drift of dry pine needles, and on its hearth the nests of long-fledged birds had fallen on the ashes of a fire gone out a very long time ago. A blazing lightning-flash dazzled him as he tried the handle of the door, and the door, hanging by one rusty hinge, yielded to his push as the first shattering peal of thunder clattered and cracked over-head. So a shelter it was, though the wind drove the rain almost horizontally through the broken window and across the room. He reached through the casement, and at the cost of a soaked coat-sleeve pulled to a faded green shutter, and made this fast. Then he explored the upper rooms. Holes in the thatch had let through the weather, and the drop, drop of the water that wears away stone had worn away the boards of the floor, so that they bent dangerously to his tread. The half-way landing of the little crooked staircase seemed the dryest place. He sat down there with his back against the wall and listened to the cracking and blundering of the thunder, watched through the skylight the lightning shoot out of the clouds, rapid and menacing as the tongue from the mouth of a snake.

No man who is not a dreamer chooses as a symbolic rite the kicking of a tall black hat down the stairs of the office he has elected to desert. Sellinge, audience at first to the glorious orchestra, fell from hearing to a waking dream, and the waking dream merged in a dreamless sleep.

When he awoke he knew at once that he was not alone in the little forgotten house. A tramp perhaps, a trespasser almost certainly. He had not had time to move under this thought before the other overpowered it. It was *he* who was the tramp, the trespasser. The other might be the local police. Have you ever tried to explain anything to the police in a rural district? It would be better to lie quietly, holding one's breath, and so, perhaps, escape an interview that could not be to his advantage, and might, in view of the end he pursued, be absolutely the deuce-and-all.

So he lay quietly, listening. To almost nothing. The other person, whoever it was, moved hardly at all; or perhaps the movements were drowned in the mutter of the thunder and the lashing of the rain, for Sellinge had not slept out the storm. But its violence had lessened while he slept, and presently the great thunders died away in slow sulky mutterings, and the fierce rain settled to a steady patter on the thatch and a slow drip, drip from the holes in the roof to the rotting boards below. And the dusk was falling; shadows were setting up their tents in the corners of the stairs and of the attic whose floor was on a level with his eyes. And below, through the patter of the rain, he could hear soft movements. How soft, his strained ears hardly knew till the abrupt contrast of a step on the earth without reminded him of the values of the ordinary noises that human beings make when they move.

The step on the hearth outside was heavy and plashy in the wet mould; the touch on the broken door was harsh, and harshly the creaking one hinge responded. The footsteps on the boarded floor of the lower room were loud and echoing. Those other sounds had been as the half-heard murmur of summer woods in the ears of one half asleep. This was definite, undeniable as the sound of London traffic.

Suddenly all sounds ceased for a moment, and in that moment Sellinge found time to wish that he had never found this shelter. The wildest, wettest, stormiest weather out under the sky seemed better than this little darkening house which he shared with these two others. For there were two. He knew it even before the man began to speak. But he had not known till then that the other, the softly moving first-comer, was a woman, and when he knew it, he felt, in a thrill of impotent resentment, the shame of his situation and the impossibility of escaping from it. He was an eaves-dropper. He had not, somehow, thought of eavesdropping as incidental to the detective career. And there was nothing he could do to make things better which would not, inevitably, make them worse. To declare himself now would be to multiply a thousandfold everything which he desired to minimise. Because the first words that came to him from the two below were love-words, low, passionate, and tender, in the voice of a man. He could not hear the answer of the woman, but there are ways of answering which cannot be overheard.

'Stay just as you are,' he heard the man's voice again, 'and let me stay here at your feet and worship you.'

And again: 'Oh, my love, my love, even to see you like this! It's all so different from what we used to think it would be; but it's heaven compared with everything else in the world.'

Sellinge supposed that the woman answered, though he caught no words, for the man went on:

'Yes, I know it's hard for you to come, and you come so seldom. And even when you're not here, I know you understand. But life's very long and cold, dear. They talk about death being cold. It's life that's the cold thing, Anna.'

Then the voice sank to a murmur, cherishing, caressing, hardly articulate, and the shadows deepened, deepened inside the house. But outside it grew lighter because the moon had risen and the clouds and the rain had swept away, and sunset and moonrise were mingling in the clear sky.

'Not yet; you will not send me away yet?' he heard. 'Oh, my love, such a little time, and all the rest of life without you! Ah! let me stay beside you a little while!'

The passion and the longing of the voice thrilled the listener to an answering passion of pity. He himself had read of love, thought of it, dreamed of it; but he had never heard it speak; he had not known that its voice could be like this.

A faint whispering sound came to him; the woman's answer, he thought, but so low was it that it was lost even as it reached him in the whisper of a wet ivy-branch at the window. He raised himself gently and crept on hands and knees to the window of the upper room. His movements made no sound that could have been heard below. He felt happier there, looking out on the clear, cold, wedded lights, and also he was as far as he could be, in the limits of that house, from those two poor lovers.

Yet still he heard the last words of the man, vibrant with the agony of a death-parting.

'Yes, yes, I will go.' Then, 'Oh, my dear, dear love; good-bye, good-bye!'

The sound of footsteps on the floor below, the broken hinged door was opened and closed again from without; he heard its iron latch click into place. He looked from the window. The last indiscretion of sight was nothing to the indiscretions of hearing that had gone before, and he wanted to see this man to whom all his soul had gone out in sympathy and pity. He had not supposed that he could ever be so sorry for anyone.

He looked to see a young man bowed under a weight of sorrow, and he saw an old man bowed with the weight of years. Silver-white was the hair in the moonlight, thin and stooping the shoulders, feeble the footsteps, and tremulous the hand that closed the gate of the little enclosure that had been a garden. The figure of a sad old man went away alone through the shadows of the pine-trees.

And it was the figure of the old man who had driven by the Five Bells in the old-fashioned carriage, the figure of the man he had come down to watch, to spy upon. Well, he had spied, and he had found out – what?

He did not wait for anyone else to unlatch that closed door and come out into the moonlight below the window. He thinks now that he knew even then that no-one else would come out. He went down the stairs in the darkness, careless of the sound of his feet on the creaking boards. He lighted a match and held it up and looked round the little bare room with its one shuttered window and its one door, close latched. And there was no-one there, no-one at all. The room was as empty and cold as any last year's nest.

He got out very quickly and got away, not stopping to shut door or gate nor to pick up the colour-box and canvas from the foot of the stairs where he had left them. He went very quickly back to the Five Bells, and he was very glad of the lights and the talk and the smell and sight and sound of living men and women.

It was next day that he asked his questions; this time of the round-faced daughter of the house.

'No,' she told him, 'Squire wasn't married,' and 'Yes, there was a sort of story.'

He pressed for the story, and presently got it.

'It ain't nothing much. Only they say when Squire was a young man there was some carryings on with the gamekeeper's daughter up at the lodge. Happen you noticed it, sir, an old tumble-down place in the pine woods.'

Yes, he had happened to notice it.

'Nobody knows the rights of it now,' the girl told him; 'all them as was in it's under the daisies this long time, except Squire. But he went away and there was some mishap; he got thrown from his horse and didn't come home when expected, and the girl she was found drownded in the pond nigh where she used to live. And Squire he waren't never the same man. They say he hangs about round the old lodge to this day when it's full moon. And they do say . . . But there, I dunno, it's all silly talk, and I hope you won't take no notice of anything I've said. One gets talking.'

Caution, late born, was now strong in her, and he could not get any more.

'Do you remember the girl's name?' he asked at last, finding all assaults vain against the young woman's caution.

'Why, I wasn't born nor yet thought of,' she told him, and

laughed and called along the fresh sanded passage: 'Mother, what was that girl's name, you know, the one up at the lodge that . . .'

'Ssh!' came back the mother's voice; 'you keep a still tongue, Lily; it's all silly talk.'

'All right, mother, but what *was* her name?'

'Anna,' came the voice along the fresh sanded passage.

'Dear sir,' ran Sellinge's report, written the next day, 'I have made enquiries and find no ground for supposing the gentleman in question to be otherwise than of sound mind. He is much respected in the village and very kind to the poor. I remain here awaiting your instructions.'

While he remained there awaiting the instructions he explored the neighbourhood, but he found nothing of much interest except the grave on the north side of the churchyard, a grave marked by no stone, but covered anew every day with fresh flowers. It had been so covered every day, the sexton told him, for fifty years.

'A long time, fifty years,' said the man, 'a long time, sir. A lawyer in London, he pays for the flowers, but they do say . . .'

'Yes,' said Sellinge quickly, 'but then people say all sorts of things, don't they?'

'Some on 'em's true though,' said the sexton.

# PENGUIN WORLDS

**Classic science fiction introduced by brilliant contemporary novelists**

Science fiction is a genre that gives us gripping plots and fantastical creations. It is also a genre that challenges us with fresh ideas about all kinds of things – politics, philosophy, technology – how the world works and what it means to be human. The Penguin Worlds project celebrates this incredible range, richness and invention, taking the very best from the twentieth century science fiction canon.

This series includes prescient environmental dystopia, a pioneering example of early cyberpunk, classic urban fantasy, chilling short fiction, and one of the most influential voices in feminist science fiction. Each one is a ground-breaking classic of its day; Penguin is proud to bring these classics to a whole new generation of readers.

Penguin Worlds is curated by Hari Kunzru and Naomi Alderman.

Hari Kunzru is the bestselling author of *The Impressionist* and *Transmission*. His new novel, *White Tears*, is published by Penguin in 2017.

Naomi Alderman is the acclaimed author *Disobedience, The Lessons* and *The Liars' Gospel*. Her latest novel, *The Power*, is published by Penguin in 2016.

# PENGUIN WORLDS

## WE WHO ARE ABOUT TO... BY JOANNA RUSS

*'In the event of mechanical dysfunction, the ship's computer goes for the nearest "tagged" planet, ie where human life is supposed to be possible, then ejects the passenger compartment separately. Lays an egg you might say . . .'*

After an accident destroys their starship and leaves them stranded on an uncharted but apparently hospitable planet - crewless, with few supplies and without tools - the five female and three male passengers debate how to survive. When it is decided that it is their human duty to colonize and populate their new home, one woman resists. But on an alien world where survival dictates conformity, her rebellion is seen as the worst kind of betrayal. . .

'*We Who Are About To*. . . does what the best SF ought to do, using speculation to unsettle and challenge, to strip away tired preconceptions and ask us to see our own world anew' Hari Kunzru, from the introduction

# PENGUIN WORLDS

**TRUE NAMES BY VERNOR VINGE**

*'The first hint that Mr Slippery had that his own True Name might be known came with the appearance of two black Lincolns humming up the long dirt driveway. . .'*

Roger Pollack is Mr Slippery, a computer hacker who inhabits the 'other plane' - where like-minded individuals penetrate the world's computers for profit or kicks. Unfortunately, the US government has discovered Mr Slippery's identity, his True Name. They force Roger to track down the Mailman, a new hacker wreaking havoc in the real world. But the closer Mr Slippery gets to the Mailman, the more frightening he appears. Who is the Mailman? Is he even human? And how on earth can Roger stop him?

'Stands beside William Gibson's *Neuromancer* as one of the primary shapers of what might be called the internet imaginary, the thought of what the net could become' Hari Kunzru, from the introduction

# PENGUIN WORLDS

### THE WORLD IN WINTER BY JOHN CHRISTOPHER

*'January and February were savagely cold. The Thames froze almost up to Tower Bridge; beyond that the Pool and the estuary were thick with floating ice...'*

The sun wanes and a new ice age descends on the world. Swiftly, the old industrial nations die. Their populations flock to Africa or South America - wherever crops will grow and life is sustainable. But what will become of the millions of refugees, swelling already strained equatorial cities? For Andrew Leedon, a documentary maker recording Britain's collapse, the future holds but one cold certainty - survival depends not on what you know, but who you know...

'A novel that still has the power to thrill and disturb, performing one of the signal services of fiction, forcing the reader to inhabit other realities, other possibilities and perspectives' Hari Kunzru, from the introduction

# PENGUIN WORLDS

### WAR FOR THE OAKS BY EMMA BULL

'When I heard you, I was drawn, forgive the coarse and common simile, like a moth to flame, and when I saw you, you glowed like the moon's own face and blinded me . . .'

Eddi McCandry lives in Minneapolis and plays guitar in a rock'n'roll band. Or at least she did until they split after a disastrous gig. Her night doesn't improve any when she's followed home by a fierce black dog. A talking dog, it turns out, who says that he's now her bodyguard. Why? Because Eddi's just been drafted into a war between the courts of the Seelie and the Unseelie. A faerie war that needs a mortal at its heart to make it true, real and deadly. But Eddi's a musician not a soldier. She's not one for following orders . . .

'Fantasy speaks the language of the subconscious, which is the language of dreams' – Naomi Alderman, from the introduction